THE RIDDLE OF THE ROSES

SILVER AND GREY
BOOK 8

MARY LANCASTER

ARE YOU SIGNED UP FOR DRAGONBLADE'S BLOG?

You'll get the latest news and information on exclusive giveaways, exclusive excerpts, coming releases, sales, free books, cover reveals and more.

Check out our complete list of authors, too!

No spam, no junk. That's a promise!

Sign Up Here

www.dragonbladepublishing.com

Dearest Reader;

Thank you for your support of a small press. At Dragonblade Publishing, we strive to bring you the highest quality Historical Romance from some of the best authors in the business. Without your support, there is no 'us', so we sincerely hope you adore these stories and find some new favorite authors along the way.

Happy Reading!

CEO, Dragonblade Publishing

ADDITIONAL DRAGONBLADE BOOKS BY AUTHOR MARY LANCASTER

Silver and Grey Series
Murder in Moonlight (Book 1)
Evidence of Evil (Book 2)
Ghost in the Garden (Book 3)
The Trick of the Treasure (Book 4)
Word of the Wicked (Book 5)
Vengeance in Venice (Book 6)
Death on the Doorstep (Book 7)
The Riddle of the Roses (Book 8)

One Night in Blackhaven Series
The Captain's Old Love (Book 1)
The Earl's Promised Bride (Book 2)
The Soldier's Impossible Love (Book 3)
The Gambler's Last Chance (Book 4)
The Poet's Stern Critic (Book 5)
The Rake's Mistake (Book 6)
The Spinster's Last Dance (Book 7)

The Duel Series
Entangled (Book 1)
Captured (Book 2)
Deserted (Book 3)
Beloved (Book 4)
Haunted (Novella)

Last Flame of Alba Series
Rebellion's Fire (Book 1)
A Constant Blaze (Book 2)
Burning Embers (Book 3)

Gentlemen of Pleasure Series
The Devil and the Viscount (Book 1)
Temptation and the Artist (Book 2)
Sin and the Soldier (Book 3)
Debauchery and the Earl (Book 4)
Blue Skies (Novella)

Pleasure Garden Series
Unmasking the Hero (Book 1)
Unmasking Deception (Book 2)
Unmasking Sin (Book 3)
Unmasking the Duke (Book 4)
Unmasking the Thief (Book 5)

Crime & Passion Series
Mysterious Lover (Book 1)
Letters to a Lover (Book 2)
Dangerous Lover (Book 3)
Lost Lover (Book 4)
Merry Lover (Novella)
Ghostly Lover (Novella)

The Husband Dilemma Series
How to Fool a Duke (Book 1)

Season of Scandal Series
Pursued by the Rake (Book 1)
Abandoned to the Prodigal (Book 2)
Married to the Rogue (Book 3)
Unmasked by her Lover (Book 4)
Her Star from the East (Novella)

Imperial Season Series
Vienna Waltz (Book 1)
Vienna Woods (Book 2)
Vienna Dawn (Book 3)

Blackhaven Brides Series
The Wicked Baron (Book 1)

The Wicked Lady (Book 2)
The Wicked Rebel (Book 3)
The Wicked Husband (Book 4)
The Wicked Marquis (Book 5)
The Wicked Governess (Book 6)
The Wicked Spy (Book 7)
The Wicked Gypsy (Book 8)
The Wicked Wife (Book 9)
Wicked Christmas (Book 10)
The Wicked Waif (Book 11)
The Wicked Heir (Book 12)
The Wicked Captain (Book 13)
The Wicked Sister (Book 14)

Unmarriageable Series
The Deserted Heart (Book 1)
The Sinister Heart (Book 2)
The Vulgar Heart (Book 3)
The Broken Heart (Book 4)
The Weary Heart (Book 5)
The Secret Heart (Book 6)
Christmas Heart (Novella)

The Lyon's Den Series
Fed to the Lyon

De Wolfe Pack: The Series
The Wicked Wolfe
Vienna Wolfe

Also from Mary Lancaster
Madeleine (Novella)
The Others of Ochil (Novella)

CHAPTER ONE

S ILVER AND GREY were celebrating.

Constance and Solomon, as owners of the firm, were dispensing a buffet lunch with wine to all three members of their staff, in recognition of their excellent work in finding a missing child before real harm befell her. As a bonus to this triumph, the child's doting parents were fabulously wealthy and had paid liberally for their speedy success.

Janey, the firm's inquiries assistant, and carpenter Lenny Knox, their occasional helper, had done much of the slog of this search, and it was largely down to them that the case had been solved so quickly. Lenny looked slightly bemused to be so feted, Janey was thoroughly delighted, and Hat, the receptionist, was smiling with pleasure to be included.

Chatter and laughter and the sweet satisfaction of success in such a harrowing case surrounded Constance. She would never grow tired of sharing such moments with her husband and partner. So it was a silly time for a quarrel.

"You see?" Solomon murmured. "We are an odd mix of people, and yet we are happy."

"Yes," she said at once, "but can you really imagine your respectable business associates bringing their wives to such a gathering? For longer than half a minute?"

"Yes. Many of them."

"And to the other half, you are forever tainted by association. Turning a blind eye to your unwise marriage is not the same as publicly endorsing it. It's a lovely idea, Solomon, but not a practical one."

They were not, of course, talking about this impromptu staff celebration but about Solomon's wish to hold an evening party at their marital home. Constance was more than happy to entertain his friends, just not alongside her own. For one thing, his friends would not bring their wives.

"Don't you see that it would be turning our home into another establishment?" she said, intensely. "And you want that as little as I do."

In fact, it was strange of him altogether, for he was hardly the most sociable of men.

"The establishment is already more respectable than before," he pointed out.

The establishment, which had begun as Constance's well-run brothel with a charitable sideline, had, largely thanks to Solomon, recently become more of a charity with a disreputable sideline. At least, that was the perception they were aiming at, largely because Constance did not want Solomon's wife to be known as a courtesan, or worse. The civilized evening parties for gentlemen to choose their companions had begun to double as fundraising events, so that no one knew anymore who attended for the girls and who for philanthropic intent. In fact, many came from mere curiosity and still stayed for one reason or the other.

But the *new* house, her and Solomon's home, should be inviolate.

"Then let's not make our home less respectable," she snapped. "It won't do, Solomon. Unless you hold the party while I am out."

"That does not work."

"It is the only way it *will* work," she said. "I cannot change who I am. Can't you be content as we are?"

"*Content?*" he repeated, staring at her. A rare spark of anger flashed in his shrewd, dark eyes, as if the tameness of the word offended him. "Constance…"

He blinked, gazing beyond her to the doorway.

Hat stood there, clearly having answered the front door that the others had been too preoccupied to hear. Behind her stood a distinguished man Constance had never expected to see again.

Sebastian Kellar.

"Oh—oh," she said involuntarily, even while she summoned a delighted smile and hurried to meet him. "Mr. Kellar, what a delightful surprise."

"Mrs. Grey, a pleasure to see you again!" He bowed over her hand and turned to shake hands with Solomon. "How are you, Grey? I'm sorry. I seem to have interrupted—"

"Not at all," Solomon said. "Are you hungry? A glass of wine, perhaps?"

"Actually, no. Happy though I am to see you both again, I'm afraid this is not a social call. It is business."

"Then perhaps we should go through to my office," Constance suggested, relieved. She nodded to Hat, who looked uncertain. "You do have another half-hour for luncheon," she reminded the girl, and led the way out of Solomon's office, and along the hallway to her own.

Kellar gazed about him. "Charming offices," he said mildly. "I should not be surprised. Is it someone's birthday next door?"

"No," Constance replied, going at once to her desk—Kellar had clearly stated business, after all. "Do sit down. How long have you been back in England?"

They had last seen him in Venice during their honeymoon in March. A British diplomat with a roaming brief and unclear duties, he had been on his way to Rome when he took his leave of them, mentioning a subsequent intention to return to England. That had been four months ago, in March.

"Just a few weeks," Kellar replied vaguely. "You?"

"Since May," Solomon replied, placing a third chair at the side of the desk, at a right angle to both the others, and sitting down. "What can we do to help you?"

Don't mention my mother. Don't mention my mother... In Venice

Constance had been stunned to discover that Kellar, obviously a gentleman, had once wanted to marry her mother Juliet, who, he seemed to imagine, was equally respectable. She may have been thirty years ago—though Constance had trouble picturing it—but she certainly wasn't now, with careers of whoring and fencing behind her. Currently, she was running a shop trading in curiosities and antiques. Although Constance owed Kellar for a timely saving of the day in Venice, that debt did not supersede loyalty to the maddening Juliet.

Kellar did not answer for a few moments—which itself was odd. Constance remembered him as the consummate diplomat, a man who thought on his feet and always said the right thing, never by accident. His hesitation implied thoughts were taking a little longer than usual. And now that she focused on him, there was a new tension in the set of his face, in his very posture.

"Over the years," he said at last, "I have developed an instinct for trouble, for the wrongness of a situation. I imagine," he added politely, "that you both have similar kinds of instincts."

"And what is yours telling you?" Solomon asked.

"About you two?" Kellar beamed. "I no longer need instinct. I have made my own inquiries. Honesty and success are a heady combination in any business."

"You forgot discretion," Solomon said. "If that is why you hesitate, our discretion with clients is absolute, unless they have committed a crime."

"*Have* any of them?"

"Not yet, although it's come close. Shall we return to your instincts?"

"By all means." Kellar's smile faded. "A young friend of mine died last night."

"I'm sorry to hear that," Constance said sincerely. "How did it happen?"

"According to the doctor, it was heart failure. She had been troubled by irregularities of the heart over the last year."

"And according to your instincts?"

"They tell me something is wrong. She controlled her heart problem with digitalis prescribed by her doctor, and appeared as healthy as ever. The whole household is astounded as well as devastated."

"And who is the whole household?"

"Her husband, their servants."

"Does the husband accept the doctor's findings? Will there be an autopsy?"

"Yes, Montague accepts it, and no, there will be no autopsy."

"Then have you cause for suspicion?"

"Nothing I can lay my finger on, except she looked exceedingly well when I saw her at the theatre the previous evening. That and the fact that Montague—her husband—inherits all her money."

Constance raised her eyebrows. "You believe he killed her somehow?"

"I will believe *you*," Kellar said, "if and when you tell me he did not."

"You don't like him."

Kellar shrugged. "Not hugely, though I know nothing to his discredit, except that a run of bad luck in business has left him a little short of funds. I always thought him a trifle...dull for someone as bright and vital as Caterina."

"Caterina is the dead lady? Was she very wealthy?"

"She commanded considerable fees for her appearances, plus she had shares in several theatres across the country. And, of course, the money she inherited from her parents."

"Is that a great deal?" Constance asked him.

"It is."

Solomon pounced. "How do you know?"

"Because I arranged to have it removed to England for her."

"From where?"

"Italy." Kellar looked from one to the other. "The deceased is Caterina di Ripoli. You may have heard of her."

Solomon's brows flew up. "The opera singer?"

Kellar inclined his head.

"We saw her only last week at Covent Garden," Constance said, awed and appalled. "In Rigoletto. She didn't *sound* as if she had heart difficulties then."

"No," Kellar agreed. "She didn't last night, either." He stared beyond them, looking indescribably sad. "She would have been wonderful in *La Traviata*."

It was at the opening night of that opera in Venice that Constance had first seen Kellar.

Solomon stirred on his chair. "You call her a friend. How did you know her?"

"We met in Rome several years ago. I knew her parents. They were singers too, famous all over Europe, but they died in 1848. I helped her escape to England."

"With her money," Solomon said.

"That took a little longer, but yes."

"So when exactly did Caterina die?" Constance asked.

"At some point during last night," Kellar said. "Her maid left her at around midnight, and by half past seven, when the maid returned, Caterina was dead."

"Peacefully? Were there signs she had died in distress?"

"None," Kellar said. "Her eyes were closed, her face in repose. The bedding looked quite undisturbed."

"Then you saw the body yourself?" Solomon asked.

Kellar nodded. It troubled him, Constance saw.

"What about the husband?" she asked.

"Montague? He saw her when she came home from the theatre at about eleven last night."

"Then they do not share a bedroom?"

"Apparently not."

"How is he?" Constance asked.

"Shocked. Devastated. If you can trust in outward appearances."

"Which you don't," Solomon said. "Have you involved the police?"

Kellar lifted his shoulders. "With what? Neither her doctor nor her husband believe there was a crime."

"But you do," Constance said, "with no evidence except your instinct."

"Precisely."

Constance cast a quick glance at Solomon. She knew he was thinking much the same as she was. That Kellar's grief—which in itself was vaguely troubling—had induced this denial of a natural death. She did not want to know any more about his relationship with the dead woman. And yet they owed him something.

She said, "We can ask a few questions amongst her neighbors, perhaps speak to servants and her colleagues at the theatre, but we have no authority and no reason to intrude on Mr. Montague's mourning."

"That will not be a problem," Kellar said briskly. "I propose to take you there myself—now, if you are free."

Annoyingly, they *were* free. They had not yet begun the next case on their list, having pushed everything aside for the missing child. This time, Constance was careful not to look at Solomon. They should not let Kellar jump their waiting list for a non-case. And yet if by any chance he was right about foul play, speed was of the essence. The body would not remain on view for long.

"We will come," Solomon said. "Though it is only fair to tell you we doubt there is a case. We are agreeing only to a preliminary visit."

"There speaks the careful merchant," Kellar murmured. He rose to his feet. "Shall we go? I have my carriage waiting."

THE HOUSE WHERE the much lauded soprano Caterina di Ripoli had lived and died was in one of those almost-hidden, easily forgotten parts of London, a square close to Fleet Street, on the edges of the City itself. Some of the buildings looked old enough to have escaped the Great Fire, although in reality they had probably been built in the century after. Eagle Square was surprisingly quiet for its situation, mostly residential, with a few quaint, half-timbered houses built around a small, square garden that was a riot of bright yellow, white, and red roses.

Kellar handed Constance down from the carriage and led the way up the short path to a front door. A mourning wreath, veiled in black net, hung there. The curtains had been drawn across all the front-facing windows.

A young maidservant with watery eyes, wearing a starched cap and apron, opened the door. She seemed surprised to see Kellar—presumably because she had shown him out not so long ago—but admitted him and his companions at once.

"Is Mr. Montague still at home?" Kellar asked her.

"Yes, sir. I'll tell him you're here, if you'd care to wait in the morning room."

The girl hurried silently up the hall, leaving Kellar to show the other guests the way. Obviously, he was a frequent visitor.

Despite its low ceilings with exposed beams, Constance rather liked the house. Or, at least, she would when the yards of black crepe draped over everything were taken down. As a home, it had character, though she noticed Solomon had to duck his head as he passed through the morning room doorway. At least they were at the back of the house, and the curtains had been left open.

They had barely sat down on comfortable sofas before the maid returned and led them across the wainscoted hall to a larger room, where the master of the house stood with his back to the empty fireplace, dressed all in somber black. He wore the dazed expression Constance had recently grown used to among the bereaved, although he seemed genuinely pleased to welcome them. She had the impression he didn't know what else to do with himself.

He was a little older than she had expected, well into his forties. A scattering of gray flecked his neat brown hair. Even in the first stage of grief he bore an air of slightly battered distinction.

"These are old friends of mine, Mr. and Mrs. Grey," Kellar said easily. "Also admirers of Caterina's talent. Mr. Digby Montague."

Constance offered her hand. "I'm so sorry, Mr. Montague," she murmured. "Such a terrible loss."

"She was only twenty-eight years old," Montague said. "It seems…monstrous. Please, sit down. Sarah will bring tea…"

They sat in comfortable, well-upholstered chairs. A good-quality carpet lay in the middle of the floor, and long velvet curtains in harmonizing shades framed the windows. Mirrors and pictures, which included a portrait of the dramatically beautiful singer, were draped in black crepe. A rather fine piano stood in one corner, and a violin was propped up against one of its legs. In all, it must have been a rather lovely room before the tragedy and the mourning black.

"I brought Mr. and Mrs. Grey to meet you, Montague," Kellar began, "not just because they are saddened by Caterina's death, but because they are very useful people in puzzling things out."

Montague looked slightly irritated. "There is nothing to puzzle, Kellar. Her heart stopped and she is dead."

"I know," Kellar said soothingly. "And nothing can change that. But would it not mean something to know all the circumstances?"

"Such as what, for heaven's sake?"

"We won't know until they look," Kellar said reasonably.

Montague appeared unimpressed, but he was clearly in no state to argue the matter. He didn't really care, or so Constance gathered. He merely shrugged and flapped one hand as though to say, *Do as you like.*

"Then you don't mind if they ask a few questions, perhaps look around Caterina's room while they pay their respects?"

Montague looked at Solomon. "Ask me anything you like,

but I am no physician."

"May we speak to her physician, too?" Solomon asked. "And to your servants?"

"If you must," Montague said, "though I don't see what good it will do."

Neither did Constance. Montague did not behave much like a husband who had just killed his wife.

"Thank you," Solomon said gravely. "I apologize in advance if our questions cause you pain."

"The cause will not be your questions."

Solomon inclined his head. "When was the last time you saw your wife alive?"

"Last night," Montague said dully. "She came home from the theatre around eleven. We had a glass of sherry together, and then I escorted her upstairs to her room, where Webb, her maid, was waiting for her."

"Did she seem well?"

"A little tired, but yes, very well. She was delighted with how she had sung, and the audience's appreciation always lifts her." His eyelids drooped. "Lifted her."

"And over the past few weeks, did she complain of any symptoms of her heart problem?" Solomon asked. "Did you notice any?"

Montague shook his head. "None. It was more than a year ago that she first noticed it—it interfered with her singing, as you might imagine, and that frightened her more than anything. She could not imagine life without singing. She consulted our doctor, and his prescription worked almost like magic. It was as if she had never been ill."

"Digitalis," Solomon said. "Was Mrs. Montague aware of the dangers of varying her dose?"

"Of course. It was the first thing Dr. Sorenson impressed upon us. Each dose was carefully measured out in powdered form."

"So she would not have taken an extra dose, even secretly?

Perhaps to deal with a return of her symptoms?"

Montague frowned. "No. She was not so foolish. And in any case, Webb—her personal maid—is very careful and observant."

Solomon nodded, as though this was what he had expected to hear.

Constance leaned forward. "Mr. Montague, you said your wife was well and happy last night when she came home. Was this happy state normal for her?"

"Well…yes. Like everyone, she had her moments of gloom or irritability, and certainly she was very cast down when she was ill. But in general, she was contented."

"No recent worries or concerns that troubled her spirit?" Constance pressed.

Montague's eyes flickered. "Nothing that was lasting. Such troubles were quickly solved."

They generally were between compatible married couples, as Constance had discovered over recent months. She knew exactly what Montague meant, and yet that flickering gaze bothered her. He was hiding something. But then, he was a bereaved husband and they were strangers. There was a limit to how far they could pry without cruelty.

So she gave an understanding nod and asked gently, "How long were you married, sir?"

"Almost three years," he said, a catch in his voice.

A pitifully short time that made her want to physically hold on to Solomon. "How did you meet?"

In the chair opposite, Kellar's brow twitched in impatience, but Montague did not mind the question.

"At a private concert. She had not long arrived in this country from Italy, and she was not yet well known. But as soon as I saw her, I knew…" His lips twisted. "You will think me foolish."

Constance, who had felt that sudden blaze on her first contact with Solomon—although she'd denied it for a long time—merely shook her head.

"Everything about her," Montague said, "overwhelmed me—

her beauty, her laughter, her voice… The whole woman. Of course, she had that effect on everyone. I didn't really expect her to notice me."

From Kellar's expression, which he didn't trouble to hide, neither had anyone else.

"But she did," Montague said. "She felt it too, you see."

Again, Constance flicked a glance at Kellar. Was that pity she glimpsed before his usual veils came down? Again, she realized how shaken the man was. Normally, his emotions would have been kept so much better hidden.

"Would you mind if we paid our respects now?" Solomon asked. Which was, of course, a polite way of asking to examine the dead woman and her surroundings.

"I can take them up," Kellar said, rising to his feet, "if you like."

Montague nodded. "Thank you, Kellar."

CHAPTER TWO

As he followed Constance and Kellar upstairs, Solomon's unease stemmed partly from a sort of fellow feeling for Montague, another man who had married out of his worldly class. No matter how successful and admired Caterina di Ripoli had been, she performed on the stage for money, and that made her an unsuitable wife for a respectable man. For some reason, this made Solomon feel just a little grubby for poking around the man's grief.

And Kellar, taking advantage of the widower's shock, was managing the business. Solomon did not like that either.

The doors in this house were all of the old-fashioned variety, with latches. Kellar walked straight to the second of these off the landing and opened it with familiarity.

The room smelled of roses.

It was quickly clear why. Although the curtains were drawn, there was easily enough light to see the large glass vase full of glorious red blooms that stood on the table at the center of the room. But Solomon's eyes were quickly drawn to the four-poster, curtained bed opposite the window.

Caterina di Ripoli lay as though sleeping, her eyes closed, the quilt drawn up over her shoulders. Kellar turned up the lamp by the bed. Solomon recognized her at once from the Covent Garden stage as well as from her portrait downstairs. Her clear skin was of the slightly darker complexion seen more in the south of Italy and the Mediterranean in general, her features delicate and even. The tragedy hit him afresh. That anyone so young and vital and talented should be struck down seemed utterly wrong. And yet it happened every day, and to those much younger, too.

"May I see her hands?" Constance asked, reaching for the quilt.

Kellar was before her, drawing the covers down far enough to show the dead woman's slender hands lying against her chest, palms down. A gold wedding ring adorned her left hand.

Constance lifted her right hand. The stiffness of death, rigor mortis, was already fading from her muscles, for it came easily. Solomon knew she was looking for any signs of a struggle, but the palms and fingertips appeared as smooth as the backs of Caterina's hands, and the nails were clean and shapely.

"Has the body been moved at all?" Solomon asked. "Or is this just how she was found? Were her hands in this position?"

"More or less," Kellar said, "but the doctor examined her, so she may have been laid out like that later. You should speak to the maid who found her."

Constance, no doubt remembering a previous case, drew up Caterina's eyelid, looking for the tiny red dots that could be a sign of asphyxiation. There were certainly no marks on the slender throat revealed by the fine lawn nightgown.

She looked up at Kellar. "Do you want us to look at the rest of her?" she asked bluntly.

Something very like a spasm passed across Kellar's face and vanished, though he stepped away from the bed and turned his back, walking quickly toward the roses. Taking that as assent, Solomon raised the body in his arms, letting Constance look first beneath and between the two pillows on which Caterina's head had lain, and then under the nightgown at the skin of her back. Solomon laid her back on the pillows and drew back the covers.

Despite his usual dispassion in their investigations, Solomon looked away, relying on Constance to do the observing. It felt like a violation, and he wasn't at all sure the widower downstairs had agreed to this in his unspecified permission.

At last, Constance spread the nightgown carefully back down and rearranged Caterina's hands exactly where they had been. Solomon drew the covers back up.

Constance smoothed the lace-trimmed pillowcases on either side of the dead woman's head. "I can't see any marks on her at all, let alone any of violence."

The bed was smooth, too, quite without the tangle that would have been created by a struggle for life.

"Will you look around?" Kellar asked, although it sounded more of a curt order than a request. At the same time, the plea in his eyes overcame Solomon's reluctance.

Kellar cared.

While Solomon went toward the little bureau in the window embrasure, Constance began by looking under the spare two pillows on the bed.

He dealt quickly with Caterina's correspondence, largely because there wasn't a great deal. Most of it was to do with singing engagements at theatres and private concerts. She appeared to have been a shrewd businesswoman, and her English was fluent. There was one unfinished letter in Italian, to an old friend in Rome, mentioning people he had never heard of, telling amusing stories of her life. Her husband's name was scattered across the page, and Solomon found no expression of discontent, let alone fear or concern.

"Do you really suspect Montague?" Solomon asked, tucking the letters away and moving to the lower drawers.

"You don't?" Kellar returned. "Please don't be misled by his maudlin talk of love at first sight and the perfect marriage. It was not."

"In what way?" Solomon asked, rifling through the contents of the last drawer without much expectation. "He does not give the impression of a straying husband, and he is only three years married."

"I did not say he strayed. But she did so."

Both Solomon and Constance straightened and looked at Kellar.

"With whom?" Solomon asked.

He would not have been surprised if Kellar had answered, *Me.* It would have explained his almost proprietary attitude toward the dead woman.

"To my knowledge," Kellar said, "a violinist. And I suspect there was someone before him, but I was not in the country then to observe. Either way, does a woman take a lover when she is happily married?"

"You are sure this went on *after* her marriage?" Solomon asked, while Constance went back to looking under drawers and rummaging in cupboards.

"Until her death, as far as I know," Kellar replied.

"And you made it your business to know?" Solomon said.

"I felt responsible for her. I brought her here."

"Then you were not," Solomon said with deliberation, "one of her lovers?"

Kellar blinked. "Good God, no, she could be my daughter!"

"Is she?" Constance asked, straightening once more from the wardrobe.

"No."

It might have been the truth. It might not. With Kellar, it was hard to tell.

Solomon wandered to the fireplace. In the middle of summer, it was empty and had clearly not been used for some weeks. However, a charred flake caught in the grate made him crouch down to look beneath. There were no coal ashes, just a little pile of what he was sure was burned paper.

"What is it?" Constance asked.

"Something was burned here recently. Letters, perhaps."

Kellar strode toward him. "Perhaps Montague had found out about Darrow."

"And perhaps she was just tidying her desk," Solomon said. "She was clearly a tidy person. Did you find anything out of place, Constance?"

She shook her head. "I'll ring for the maid."

The maid appeared with unexpected speed, as though she had bolted upstairs. She was a statuesque woman with a stern, pale face and fierce eyes that were red-rimmed. Throwing open the door, she halted in her tracks to find so many people in the room.

Kellar addressed her kindly. "Webb, this is Mr. and Mrs. Grey, who are paying their last respects to your mistress. They have a few questions for you, since you were the last person to see her."

"She never said she was ill," Webb said. "She never looked ill. Even now, you'd think she were only sleeping."

"She is at peace," Constance said as the maid tore her eyes from Caterina's dead face. "What is your name?"

"Mary Webb, ma'am."

"And how long were you Mrs. Montague's maid?"

"Since before she was married. Four years? Almost since she came to England."

"Was she happy when you last saw her?" Constance asked.

"Oh yes, ma'am." A frown marred Mary's brow. "At least, she *was* happy, ebullient, like, when she came into the room. More thoughtful while we got her ready for bed. Expect she was tired. She is, after a performance."

"I can imagine. Did she confide her thoughts to you?"

"No. And I didn't ask. I knew she would tell me if she wanted me to do anything for her. But she just lay down and went to sleep."

"Like that?" Solomon asked, indicating the bed. Mary looked, frowned again, and shook her head emphatically.

"Not quite like that. She never slept with her pillows like that."

Constance took a step nearer her. "Didn't she? You know that because you arranged them for her?"

"Every night," Mary said.

"Including last night?" Solomon said, and the maid nodded. "How were they usually arranged?

"Well, she often liked to read for a little before she went to sleep. And then, in the morning, to pull herself easy into a comfortable sitting position for a cup of tea in bed. So she had two pillows propped up and crossed behind her like this..." Reaching over the body, Mary all but snatched up the spare pillows to demonstrate how they were stood up on their ends and crossed. "Then she slept flat with her head on one pillow."

"When you found her this morning," Constance said, "were her pillows arranged in the usual way? Or as they are now?"

"As they are now," the maid replied promptly. "She was lying like that, too, with the bed barely disturbed."

Which was surely interesting...

"Her preferred arrangement only uses up three pillows," Solomon pointed out. "What did she do with the fourth?"

Mary blushed. "That was in case the master visited," she said primly.

"Did he visit her last night?" Constance asked.

Mary's nostrils flared with distaste. "I could not say, ma'am." Then, almost immediately correcting herself, she said, "No, he didn't, for her door were locked this morning when I brought her tea."

Solomon's breath caught. His gaze found Constance's. "Then how did *you* get into the room?"

Mary produced a key from her apron pocket.

"Was it usual for her to lock her door?" Kellar asked.

"Not *unusual*," the maid replied. "Sometimes she did, sometimes she didn't. Either way, I had my key to make her mornings comfortable."

Solomon decided to leave the matter there for now. But if the door had been locked, then it was a lot less likely that someone else had harmed Caterina, whatever the arrangement of the pillows.

"You are very observant," he said. "Besides the arrangement of the pillows, did you notice anything else unusual about the room when you first came in this morning?"

"Not apart from the roses."

Everyone looked at the roses.

"What's odd about them?" Constance asked.

"Nothing," the maid replied, "except they weren't there last night when I left her."

"WELL?" KELLAR DEMANDED, as soon as his carriage, bearing the three of them, began to move away from Montague's house. "Am I right to have doubts about Caterina's death?"

Opposite Solomon, who sat on the back-facing bench, Constance shifted with the tiny wriggle she gave when she was uncomfortable.

Solomon said carefully, "There are one or two things that don't make sense without further explanation. But there is no sign of physical attack, and even an overdose of digitalis is unlikely. The maid is clearly keeping close track of every dose, and she was happy enough to show the powders to us. She has marked a date on each. And by everyone's account—including yours—Mrs. Montague was not suicidally inclined."

"The doctor could have given her an extra dose," Kellar said mulishly.

"Why would he do that?" Solomon asked.

"You said you would speak to him," Kellar countered.

Constance turned her head to look at him. Then she met Solomon's gaze.

Solomon sighed. "Are you asking us to take this matter on as a formal investigation?"

"Yes," Kellar said.

"Even though we have advised you there is likely nothing to investigate?"

"Find the answer to the matter of the roses. Look into the household, the doctor, the violinist and any other lover you come across, and if you find nothing suspicious and no other inquiries to follow, then so be it. I am happy to pay for your time."

"Good," Constance said. "Because that is how we avoid—for the most part—frivolous cases. People prepared to pay have genuine concerns."

That formula didn't work so well with the poorest in society, but even there, the proffered mite made a point.

"I have," Kellar said, "genuine concerns."

"What we discover may tarnish Mrs. Montague's reputation," Solomon warned. "You may not like what we uncover."

"I believe I already know her flaws. They do not change my affection for her. Do you have some kind of contract for me to sign?"

"Yes," Constance said. "And we are not cheap."

⊱✦⊰

"I WONDER," CONSTANCE murmured, as they finally waved off Sebastian Kellar in his carriage and closed Silver and Grey's black-painted door, "if we will regret this."

"We never have before," Solomon pointed out.

"We never worked for anyone who knows my mother before. He didn't mention her once."

Solomon raised his eyebrows. "Are you outraged on her behalf?"

"No," she said crossly. "Well, yes, perhaps. I'm not sure he's telling the truth about his relationship with Caterina. It would explain why he helped her come to England, and why he's so antagonistic toward her husband. But in fact, I'm relieved—or I should be—that he didn't ask about Juliet."

Her relationship with her mother was always complicated and often seemed contradictory. In this case, mostly, she was probably thinking of her mother's pride. The no doubt beautiful and pure young woman of Kellar's memory had been badly ravaged by life. What Juliet's happiness depended on was anyone's guess, though Constance seemed to think it was staying away from men altogether.

"You've never had that conversation with her?" he asked.

"She's never brought him up, so neither did I after the first time. But I suppose having him as a client is no reason why they should ever meet. Unless she chooses to. Are we wasting our time and his money, Solomon?"

"Probably," he said, strolling into his office. "But with luck, we can quickly put his mind to rest. I'll write the report about the child, and then, I think, we can go home for the day."

"Excellent plan," she agreed.

She followed him across to his desk and picked up the piece of paper on which Kellar had written down the name and address of the violinist he believed to have been Caterina's lover.

"Carl Darrow," she read aloud, slowly raising her eyes to Solomon's. "We know him. He played at one of our charity evenings at the establishment."

"And I thought we could invite him to play at our soiree," Solomon said ruefully.

Her eyes narrowed. "What soiree?"

"The one you are considering."

"The one I have considered and rejected," she said.

He reached across the desk to kiss her full on the mouth. "Keep considering for a little while longer."

MARY WEBB HAD nothing to do, nothing to prepare for her mistress. In fact, she no longer had a position. Tomorrow she would have to begin looking for another. For now, late in the afternoon, when she often helped Mrs. Montague to dress for the theatre, there was no reason why she should not sit in the bedchamber with the body of her beautiful, turbulent, flawed mistress.

She opened the bedchamber door, and the instant scent of roses immediately reminded her of the people asking questions. A lot of questions, which she had been too stunned not to answer—though looking back, they were insolent and not anyone's business but hers. She was the keeper of Mrs. Montague's secrets.

She would pray beside her, pray for peace for them both.

Something moved on the bed, and she gasped, falling back and clutching at her heart. Wild hope mingled with startled fear, just for an instant, until she realized it was not Mrs. Montague who had risen from the bed, but the master.

The lamp was not lit. In the gloom caused by the closed curtains, he was a stranger. And yet he had been lying on the bed beside his dead wife. She pitied him. But still, at this moment, she felt a thrill of something close to fear. She should apologize for disturbing his privacy, and yet she froze, unable to find the words.

He said, "They will take her away tomorrow."

He had always been a gently spoken man. At this moment, half visible by the body of his wife, he sounded positively…sepulchral.

She shivered, but at least her tongue loosened. "I know. I came to pray, but I'll come back…"

She had already turned away when he spoke again. "They asked you questions. Here."

How does he know that? Did they tell him? "Yes." What else could she say? "He was fond of her, Mr. Kellar," she blurted. "I never saw that couple before, but they seemed very concerned…"

"What did you tell them?"

Mary turned back to face him. "The truth, sir."

"They will be back," he said, his quiet voice curiously expressionless. "It might be best if you were gone by then."

CHAPTER THREE

SINCE THEY HAD left the office a little early and were able to enjoy the special pleasure of dining together in their own home, Constance was surprised by her urge to call in at the establishment.

Since returning from Venice, she had often forced herself to go out of duty rather than the powerful need to protect that had consumed her when she lived there. In truth, like Solomon with his many businesses, she had delegated to the right people, and the establishment more or less ran itself. She had thought this would pique her, but her life was now so interwoven with Solomon's that she was glad.

Inevitably, as they took their wine to the comfortable drawing room, conversation turned to the latest case.

"Even if it is no case at all," Constance said, "we should prove it as quickly as we can. I could call in at the establishment this evening and speak to Edith, who has spent some time with Darrow."

"Who may or may not have been Caterina's lover," Solomon said thoughtfully. "Did you like him?"

"Yes. He was reserved but polite, and after he spoke to Edith at the establishment, he gave her at least one more lesson. I suppose he might have revealed something of his private life."

"Did you want to stay there for long?" he asked.

"Probably not, unless they need me. Why?"

"I thought we might drop in on the Tizsas," Solomon said.

"Lady Griz knows many musicians. And Dragan may well have heard of Caterina's physician, Dr. Sorenson."

"True." Lady Grizelda Tizsa was the eccentric daughter of a duke who had married a multi-talented Hungarian refugee, a physician by profession. The couple, who were primarily responsible for Constance and Solomon's meeting in the first place, were equally addicted to mysteries, although in an amateur capacity as far as Constance knew. Besides which, they were good company. "Let's do that, then. If they're not at home, we can try again in the morning."

That decided, Constance remembered to summon her new lady's maid before they went up to change. By the time they entered their bedroom, the girl was already there, selecting a choice of gowns for Constance's approval.

Solomon strolled off into his dressing room.

"The pink," Constance decided, and the maid bobbed her head.

Anne Morris was a friend of Janey's, encountered a couple of months ago when they were trying to find who was responsible for leaving a body on the establishment's back doorstep. In many ways, she was the complete opposite of Janey—shy, well spoken, and submissive. She had been the assistant of a fashionable dressmaker whom Silver and Grey were responsible for closing down—and arresting—so Janey had considered they owed Anne a job. At least to teach her to stand up for herself.

"When you worked for Veronique," Constance asked suddenly, "did she ever have a customer called Caterina di Ripoli? Or Caterina Montague? An Italian opera singer."

Anne thought about it while she helped Constance out of her day gown and left her to the washing bowl. "I don't think so," she said at last, clearly disappointed not to be useful.

"Just thought I'd ask."

As Constance sat at her dressing table, having the final pins inserted in her hair, Solomon appeared at his dressing room door, handsome and elegant in evening dress. One of those intense darts of desire took her by surprise, as they often did, and she wondered about leaving Edith until tomorrow and just staying home for the evening. Here. In the bed that loomed suddenly large in her mirror.

"Will that do, ma'am?" Anne asked anxiously.

Constance had to admit that Anne could create rather lovely styles that she would never be able to achieve for herself. And if she stayed at home now, Anne would imagine it was her fault.

In the doorway, Solomon's eyes kindled with amusement, as though he knew exactly what she was thinking. *Drat him.*

"Wonderfully," Constance said briskly, rising to her feet. *I shall be the belle of the brothel.* And she didn't care as long as he looked at her like that. "Thank you, Anne. You needn't wait up for me. I'm not sure when we'll be home."

THEY WERE IN good time for Constance to welcome the early guests to her establishment. The usual evening party had just opened to the delicate strains of a violin recital by Edith. Constance was delighted to see her growing in skill and confidence to this stage. She did not interrupt. Instead, she played hostess, flitting among her guests and making sure all was well with her girls—not just those flirting with the gentlemen in the salon, but the others who, like Edith, were set on other careers, the maids and cooks and bookkeepers. And, of course, the burly footmen who kept them safe.

She was glad to see that Sarah, her more-than-capable lieutenant, made her way to Edith as soon as she stopped playing. Though Edith was not for sale, she played so enchantingly that several of the male guests were clearly interested.

Sarah intercepted them. "Edith will be back to play more in a little," she assured them. "Come, Edith, I think Mrs. Silver wants you…"

Constance was still Mrs. Silver here, though all the staff and most of their customers knew she was Solomon's wife.

Constance took Edith's arm and swept her across the hall to one of the more private rooms, where she complimented Edith sincerely on her playing. "You could start considering private engagements," she said. "Solomon and I both think you are ready."

Edith was shocked. "Oh, no, ma'am, I'm not nearly good enough. I might never be!"

"You held this lot spellbound for twenty minutes," Constance said dryly, "and believe me, they had other things on their minds to distract them. Think about it. But actually, I wanted to ask you about something else. Carl Darrow."

Edith's eyes lit up. "I would love to be half as good as him. Though he taught me a great deal."

"Then he was generous with his advice and guidance?"

"Oh yes. He even let me play along with him."

"Do you still see him? Are you friends?"

"Not friends," she said a little ruefully. "But he was kind."

"He didn't try to take advantage, did he?"

"Oh, no, nothing like that," Edith said at once. "He's not interested in me in that way." Her mouth quirked. "Or at all, really. It's the music that interests him. That made me proud, because I must have some talent to get his attention at all."

"Is he married?" Constance asked.

"No, but I think there is someone. Someone who's more than the music."

"A singer?" Constance suggested.

Edith's eyes widened. "Now that you mention it, I think so, yes. His friend told me he was in love with her. He—the friend—thought I would mind, but I don't."

"Is he a gentle man?" Constance asked. "Did he ever lose his temper around you?"

"Oh, no, though he could be impatient. He was kind, but only up to a point, if you see what I mean."

"Not really."

Edith spread her hands in a helpless little gesture. "Almost as if he was going through the motions, teaching me things that would make the music better, without really noticing *me*."

"Was he like that with everyone?" Constance asked.

"Mostly, I think. Very focused on his own career but not above helping others when he could."

"And this friend who warned you about his affections for the singer—who is he?"

"A pianist. Geoffrey Reid. They play together sometimes. He has lodgings in the same house as Mr. Darrow."

How useful…

It was after ten o'clock before Constance and Solomon left the carriage in Half Moon Street and walked up the dark little lane to the Tizsa house. At least there were lights on, though Constance worried about waking the baby by knocking too loudly.

However, almost as soon as Solomon lifted the knocker the door was opened by a tall, dark, almost impossibly handsome young man.

"Tizsa," Solomon said. "You're going out."

"Actually, no, we just saw you coming," Dragan said in his perfect, only slightly accented English. "From the window. Come in."

He took their hats and Constance's evening cloak before ushering them into the drawing room that doubled as the couple's much-used study.

"Goodness, how lovely you look," Lady Griz said, hurrying to greet them. "Have you been to the opera?"

"Nothing so respectable," Constance said brazenly. "And you're looking rather fine yourself."

"Am I?" Griz said in surprise, her eyebrows rising over the

frames of her spectacles. She was always surprised by compliments, which was odd because she was in fact extremely pretty, in her own careless, eccentric style.

"Although one of the things we wished to ask you does concern opera," Solomon said, as Constance and Griz sat side by side on the large sofa. He took a winged chair opposite them and Dragan slouched into the other. "Do you by chance know the singer Caterina di Ripoli? Otherwise Mrs. Digby Montague."

"We've heard her," Griz said. "At Covent Garden last week, and at some charity concert of Azalea's last year, I think. Or was it two years ago? But I've never met her."

"Does that mean you don't know any gossip?" Constance asked.

"I've never heard any," Griz said apologetically, "but then, I went for the music. If there is any to know, Azalea probably does."

Azalea was Grizelda's sister, Lady Trench, a philanthropic hostess much in the manner of their mother, the Duchess of Kelburn.

"What about the violinist Carl Darrow?" Constance asked.

"We did meet him at one of Azalea's soirees," Griz said, apparently pleased. "Plays divinely."

"But not with you?" Solomon asked.

Griz smiled. "Lord, no, he has no time to waste on amateurs. He is ambitious."

"Driven," Dragan said. "And good enough to fill the largest halls, which I'm sure he will before he is much older."

"Have you ever heard his name coupled with that of Caterina di Ripoli?" Constance asked.

"No," Griz said, though she was frowning. "At least, I don't think so. But perhaps I have, for I don't seem to be surprised. Why do you ask?"

"Caterina is dead," Solomon said, to the clear shock of their hosts. "She died suddenly last night, of a longstanding heart problem. I expect it will be in the morning's newspapers."

"But you are investigating her death?" Griz said shrewdly.

"What sort of heart problem?" Dragan asked.

"Irregular heartbeat. Her physician was treating her with digitalis."

Dragan nodded.

"I don't suppose you know the physician in question?" Solomon asked. "A Dr. Sorenson?"

"No, but I know the name. His patients are largely among the rich of Mayfair and Belgravia. He has a sound reputation." Dragan rose, as though just remembering his manners, and poured four glasses of brandy from a fine crystal decanter. Constance suspected it had been a wedding present. Probably, so was the brandy.

She turned the subject to their hosts' lives, which were generally fascinating. They were enjoying a lively and most amusing conversation when Solomon chose to spoil it.

The conversation had broadened from the personal to the more general, to the apparent blindness of the powerful to the plights of those beneath them, and from there to inequalities in general, and the difficulties of changing that. After her experience in Venice, Constance was looking forward to Dragan's insights into radicalism and revolution, when Solomon suddenly leaned forward.

"A case in point. Theoretically, would you accept Constance's invitation to our house?"

"Of course," Griz said at once.

Constance, who rarely blushed, felt her face flame. How dare Solomon put her or Griz in this position? Though amongst the furious churnings, there might have been a gratitude she hated almost as much.

"And would you allow that?" Solomon threw at Dragan.

Dragan smiled. "There is so much wrong with that question. Firstly, I have never been able to stop Griz doing as she wished. Secondly, I would never try, unless she was putting herself in danger. She would do the same for me, and I trust her. But thirdly, I don't believe I have the right. And fourthly—what kind of egalitarian would I be if I turned up my nose at the birth of another?"

"He's not talking about birth," Constance snapped, "but about *me*. He has the thoroughly ridiculous idea of inviting respectable people to our house, with me as hostess. His question to *you*—and he already guessed what your courteous answer would be—is all about persuading *me* to agree. To an event that would be disastrous for all of us." She grasped her hands tightly together in her lap to hide their shaking. She had never been so angry with Solomon. "You two are the exception, not the rule. And I know you are kind enough to come to my house."

"I would have already, only I know you are always out," Griz said.

"And you would be welcome," Constance said. "But would your sister and her husband come? Would your parents, the duke and duchess? I don't think so."

"You were at the Trenches' house," Dragan said.

"For a particular purpose. I don't need to remind you who else was there." Constance felt as if she were speaking through her teeth and strove to lighten her face and her tone. How dare Solomon do this to her? To the Tizsas? "Forgive us for bringing our silly disagreements to *your* house. How is young Master Tizsa?"

Fortunately, the blatant change of subject to their young son Alexander worked. Although Constance's anger did not subside, she was able to hide it beneath the social manners she had taught herself from an early age. But for the first time ever, she could not bring herself to speak to Solomon.

She felt betrayed by his dragging the Tizsas into the matter, as though he had put all her secret insecurities and vulnerabilities on display to strangers. Just to achieve his own ends, which, to her, were foolish in themselves. Worse, she had never been disappointed in him before, and now she was. *God*, she was. And so enraged she wanted to walk home.

By the time they reached their house, she wished she had stayed at the establishment. She even thought about instructing the coachman to turn back to Mayfair. Instead, tight-lipped, she stepped down from the carriage without help, walked silently into the house, and climbed the stairs to her bedchamber.

There, she lit the lamp, threw her hat and cloak onto a chair, and strode back and forth across the room, too wrapped up in anger even to hear him enter the room. She only saw him when she spun around from the window and pulled up short.

He stood in the middle of the room, watching her, looking his usual calm, elegant, damnably handsome self. He had always been adept at hiding his feelings. But he had to know she was more furious with him than she had ever been. She wanted to lash out, to *hurt*.

Tearing her gaze free, she stalked past him to the door.

Or, at least, she tried to, but at the last moment, he caught her hand and pulled her back to face him.

"Don't," he said softly.

That soft, deep voice had always turned her insides to liquid.

"Don't what?" she demanded. "Go where I like in my own home? Choose whom to have in my house? Dare to disagree with the people you line up to fight your battles for you? Unworthy, Solomon. Unforgivable."

She tugged her hand sharply to free it, but he held on.

"No," he said.

"Again, we differ." Her voice shook. She wanted to cry. "Let me go."

"Where? To storm around the house? To sleep in another room to stoke your anger?"

It was an effort not to give another futile wrench of her hand. Instead, she glared at him. "Dragan would say it is my right. Since you value his opinion so much—"

"Stop," he said. "I asked a theoretical question because I wanted us to hear other opinions. If you think I'm wrong, then let us talk about it. Now."

Her throat tightened. "I can't talk now, Solomon. I am too furious, too *betrayed*..."

Again she pulled away, and again he would not allow it. Instead, he took her in his arms, drawing her rigid body against him from breast to thigh.

"There is no betrayal," he said. "Only love."

She wouldn't, *wouldn't* be softened by that word. She thrust her hand against his chest. "Oh, no. You were pushing your point, quite the ruthless businessman."

"No." He bent his head until his forehead leaned lightly on hers. His touch, his scent, seeped into her anger, threatening it, threatening *her*. "I don't want you to look down on yourself, Constance."

"I don't. But other people do."

"Some people look down on me because my blood is mixed. Some people will never change. But I believe we have enough friends to lead the life we choose."

"That *you* choose," she corrected him at once. But her traitorous body was remembering pleasure. Desire was relaxing the stiffness of her shoulders. Her trembling was no longer due to anger alone.

His lips brushed the corner of her eye, her cheek, her ear. "I would never push anything or anyone onto you. We can choose our guests, agree on them. Or agree to none. But we have to talk and listen to agree."

He stroked her nape, and her breath caught. If she was to resist, she had to break free. Only, his mouth hovered over hers, and...

"You're not *talking*," she said desperately.

"I am," he whispered. "And so are you."

His mouth took hers, and with it, emotion surged in a massive, chaotic tangle. He seduced her, blatantly, with kisses and increasingly intimate caresses, with every movement of his lean, ravishing body. With a gasp that was half sob, she seized him and fought back in a fierce, sensual duel where losing was impossible and the eventual, blinding satisfaction overwhelming.

Afterward, they lay in each other's arms, and she listened to the slowing beat of his heart against her ear.

He said, "I didn't mean it to hurt you."

"I react badly when I'm afraid."

It was an admission she hadn't intended to make. It might have surprised him too, for his arm tightened around her.

"It was you who taught me not to be afraid to grow. But whatever we do—or don't do—it has to be together. We can agree on that much."

"We can." She kissed his chest.

He moved, looming over her. "It is not a condition of love, Constance. That is forever."

This time she let the tears come. "We agree on that, too," she whispered, and pressed her damp cheek to his.

CHAPTER FOUR

THANKS TO THEIR late and strenuous night, they woke too late in the morning to indulge Solomon's desire for a repeat. He was only too aware of the danger he had managed to avert last night, largely through his own desperation, though he hadn't expected the crisis to leave him feeling so vulnerable, so in need of the reassurance of her passion.

Although he truly hadn't meant to hurt Constance by what he had said to the Tizsas, he had been a little too crass in making his point. And no point in the world was worth losing her for.

The making-up of their quarrel had brought a wild new intensity to their lovemaking, of course. The pleasure still made him want to purr. But it had not solved the problem, which, perhaps, they were both making too much of.

Constance, wrapped loosely in her dressing gown, padded toward him with a tray of delicious-smelling coffee. No doubt she had retrieved it from the dressing room, where Anne had developed the habit of leaving it each morning.

"That smells good," he said, struggling into a sitting position to accept his cup.

Constance sat on the edge of the bed beside him. "Shall we try to see Dr. Sorenson this morning? And then perhaps Darrow and his friend."

Solomon nodded, glad of the normality of discussing cases. And yet she was delectable in her half-tied dressing gown with her red-gold hair wild and loose…

Focus, Grey!

"We should probably try to speak to her colleagues at the theatre, too. And then I'd rather like to talk to Montague without Kellar standing over us."

"I thought that. The servants, too." She set her cup on its saucer and rose. "Then I had better ring for Anne."

Solomon had thoroughly approved of her acquiring a lady's maid, even though he avoided a valet of his own. However, there were times when body servants were inconvenient. Constance met his gaze, with complete understanding and a wicked smile.

"It's half past eight," she reminded him.

He sighed. "So it is."

Giving in, he rose and retreated to the dressing room.

SINCE DR. SORENSON dealt largely with the rich and fashionable, his patients did not keep early hours. Constance and Solomon were shown almost immediately into his consulting room, where he had been catching up with his medical reading, judging by the books and journals scattered across his large desk.

He rose at once to greet them, a man of middle years with kind, attentive eyes and a beaming smile. "Mr. Grey, a pleasure to meet you."

"And you, doctor," Solomon said, shaking hands. "This is my wife."

"Charmed," the doctor said, managing to make his eyes smile at her without leering. He was indeed charmed, but most professionally. "Do sit down. Were you recommended to me?"

"In a way," said Solomon. "By Mr. Digby Montague, although we are not here as patients."

"You are friends of Mr. Montague?" Sorenson asked, a certain wariness entering his expression.

"Acquaintances. He has given us permission to inquire into

the circumstances surrounding his wife's sad demise."

Sorenson blinked. "Inquire? What circumstances? It is beyond tragic, of course, both personally for poor Montague, and more broadly for the loss of her great talent. But I fail to see—" He broke off with a sudden frown. "Does he want a postmortem examination now?"

"Would you mind?" Solomon asked.

"No, though I think it unnecessary. However, he has no need to speak to me through anyone else on the matter."

"Oh, no. He didn't mention it to us, and I don't believe he has changed his mind. Yet. It is really a matter of setting his mind at rest, for his sake and that of Mrs. Montague's friends."

"I mean to call on him later today, when we may talk in person." The doctor's mustache bristled. "Are you a physician, sir?"

"I am not," Solomon said.

The doctor reared up from his chair. "Dear God, you're not a journalist, are you? Digging for dirt on the poor—"

"No, sir," Constance intervened soothingly. "We are not journalists, far from it. We are agents of inquiry, engaged to sort out a few muddles that are worrying Mrs. Montague's friends. We understand you treated her for a heart complaint."

The doctor met her gaze with dignity. "I shall not discuss my patients with you. It would be improper of me to do so."

"We understand your duty of confidentiality," Constance said. "But I'm sure we can talk together without breaking it. We are bound, you know, by our own code of discretion. Is it fair to say that the digitalis you prescribed worked well for her and enabled her to carry on with her life and her singing career?"

There was nothing to object to in that, so he didn't. "Quite fair," he said reluctantly.

"Did you examine her regularly to be sure that was the case?" Solomon asked.

"Every month."

"In recent months, did you see any need to increase that dose?"

"None. She responded well."

"When was the last time you saw her?"

The doctor opened a drawer in his desk, consulting whatever was within. An appointment book, judging by the rustle of pages as he turned them.

"Two weeks ago, on the twenty-third of June," he said, closing the drawer with a brisk snap. "It was a routine consultation. She reported being well, and my examination concurred."

"Both Mr. Montague and the maid, Mary Webb, agree that the correct amount of medicine remains. Did you look for yourself?"

"It was one of the first things I did once I had assured myself of her death. All was as it should have been."

"Then you did not provide her with, say, an emergency dose or two?"

"Of course not!"

"Could she have got it from someone else?" Constance asked.

The doctor frowned at her. "Yes, I suppose so, but why would she?"

"Would you have been able to tell if she had?"

"No," he admitted. "But if you are suggesting suicide, she would never have done such a thing."

"Then, in your professional opinion, she showed no signs of melancholy or unhappiness?"

"No," the doctor said firmly, "and you are hardly helping Montague by suggesting such a thing."

Solomon leaned forward. "Doctor, do you have any doubts at all that she died of anything other than heart failure caused by her existing condition?"

"None," Sorenson said firmly.

"Not even why her heart should suddenly fail after a year of healthy response to the drug you prescribed?"

He lifted his shoulders helplessly. "Such things happen without warning sometimes. I wish we could prevent it, but we can't. In this case, I was surprised but hardly astonished." He pulled out his watch. "I am expecting a patient…"

"One last question, if you don't mind," Solomon said. "In your professional opinion, is Mr. Montague healthy in mind and body?"

Sorenson stared at him coldly. "Good day, Mr. Grey. Mrs. Grey."

⟫⟫⟫✖⟪⟪⟪

Since Constance had engaged Carl Darrow to play at the establishment, she knew his address, just to the east of Bloomsbury. Solomon instructed the coachman and joined her in the carriage.

"What do you think of Dr. Sorenson?" he asked, sitting beside her. "Is he covering up misdeeds?"

"If he is, I don't think they are his own," Constance replied. "But he was very reluctant to speak of Montague."

"Montague is still his patient," Solomon pointed out. "It may have been a flat denial caused by his own ethics, or…"

"It wouldn't have given much away to tell us Montague *was* healthy in mind and body," Constance said. "So perhaps he is not."

"Or perhaps Sorenson is suspicious of Montague, too," Solomon said.

"Then why protect him?"

Solomon shrugged. "Lack of evidence? Reluctance to lose another patient? Or simply that we have no authority to question him and he doesn't like us—or at least me."

"Hmm…"

"How should we approach Darrow? Honestly?"

Constance considered and nodded. "I think so. After all, we might want to engage him again."

Solomon could not prevent his quick glance at her, but she had turned her head to gaze out of the window. He didn't know if she referred to engaging the violinist again for the establishment or for the party he wanted to hold at home. And he didn't like the feeling that he would be stepping on eggshells to ask. He let it go.

Darrow lived in the upper rooms of what seemed to be a respectable house. As soon as Solomon stepped down from the carriage, he could hear the strains of the violin floating from the house, a phrase repeated over and over. At first it seemed like exact reproduction, and certainly the notes were the same. Yet by the time the front door opened to his knock, he had recognized the minute changes of touch and delicacy. The music moved on, flowing seamlessly. He did not recognize the piece.

"Yes?" said the woman at the door impatiently, and he realized he had not spoken.

"Mr. Darrow, if you please," Constance said, presenting their *Inquiries* card. "Our name is Grey."

The woman, a stout being of stern expression, looked as if she had no idea what to do with the card. She sniffed and handed it back before opening the door wide. "Top of the stairs and turn right. He won't thank you for the interruption."

In fact, Darrow didn't seem to notice the interruption, despite repeated knocks. It was the door directly facing the stairs that opened to reveal a tousle-headed young man in a hurry.

"He won't answer," the man said cheerfully, brushing past Solomon to throw open the door. "Just go in. Carl!"

The young man clattered off down the stairs, and Solomon entered the room first, just in case Darrow was playing in his underclothes.

The violin had cut off abruptly. Carl Darrow, a good-looking young man with raven-black hair and eyebrows, stood in the middle of the cluttered floor, glowering, violin and bow dangling at his side. He was in his shirt sleeves, but at least he was dressed.

His frown smoothed in recognition. "Mrs. Silver!"

Constance moved toward him with impeccable grace, stepping over discarded clothes and books as though they weren't there, and offering her hand. "Mr. Darrow. You remember my husband, Mr. Grey?"

"Yes, of course," Darrow said, though he gave Solomon an extra peer as though to be sure. "How do you do? Um…sorry for the mess. There's a sitting room that might be better…if Reid's not in it. He's a pianist."

"I think he might have gone out," Solomon said, as Darrow laid his violin and bow in an open case on his unmade bed, then led the way into a parlor that was a good deal tidier and dominated by a slightly battered grand piano.

Darrow gestured politely for them to sit on the sofa. "How can I help you?"

Constance sat while Solomon kept his gaze on Darrow's face. "It is about the death of Mrs. Digby Montague, otherwise Caterina di Ripoli."

Darrow's expression changed at once. It wasn't that he hadn't known, Solomon thought, or even that he was acting, but that he remembered. There was a definite flash of agony in his eyes, an involuntary, tragic grimace before he swung away from them.

"She is a terrible loss," he said, his voice uneven. "But why do you come to me?" He turned back on the last word, a hint of defiance, even challenge, in his manner.

"Because you knew her," Constance said. "And her death was so sudden."

Darrow's eyes widened and then narrowed. "Are you saying it was *not* her heart?"

"What makes you think it was?" Solomon asked.

The dark, pain-filled eyes turned on him. "It was in the newspaper. And she *did* suffer from an irregularity…"

"Did she tell you that?" Constance asked.

"Yes." The defiance was back. "We were friends. I don't understand—why does this concern you?"

"We have been asked to look into the circumstances of Mrs. Montague's death," Solomon said.

Darrow glanced at Constance, looking confused.

"It is another business of ours," she said, holding out the business card that his landlady had rejected. "Inquiries."

"*He* sent you," Darrow said with loathing.

"Who?" Constance asked.

"Montague."

"He has given us leave to speak to those concerned," Constance said carefully.

"And so you come straight to me when you should be looking closer to home. If anyone caused her death, *he* did."

"What makes you say that?" Solomon asked. "Was theirs not a happy marriage?"

"How could it be?" Darrow all but snapped, ramming his fingers through his hair to drag it back from his forehead.

"Because he is a little older than his wife?" Constance asked with deceptive innocence. "Or because he is a mere merchant and not a musician?"

Darrow paused, blinking at her. "Both," he said at last.

"Or," Solomon suggested, "because she was susceptible to your own charms?"

Darrow looked at him, then at Constance. "You know," he said. "You know we were lovers."

There was pride as well as defiance in his thrown-back head, his flashing eyes.

"Did her husband know?" Solomon asked.

Darrow let out a bitter laugh, full of savage contempt. "That dullard could not see what was under his nose. He hasn't got the imagination."

"Was she taking medicine for her heart trouble?" Constance asked.

Darrow nodded.

"Do you think she forgot to take it that day?"

"It's more likely he gave her too much!"

Then he knew how digitalis worked, the lethal importance of the correct dosage. *Interesting.*

Constance leaned back against the sofa cushions. "How did

you meet Caterina?"

"At a charity concert. I was one of a trio playing Mozart. She noticed me and asked me to accompany her when she sang. We worked wonderfully together. It was more than her beauty, you know. More even than her voice. She was…captivating."

"In what way?"

"In every way! Her laughter, her understanding, her interpretation of the music and the sheer emotion… She was sweet, and funny, and vital…" His voice broke and he dashed the back of his hand across his eyes. Moisture still glistened.

"When was this?" Constance asked. "When you first met?"

Darrow shrugged. "A year ago? Just before she became ill. It was months before we met again. That was when we knew."

"When you became lovers?" Constance asked.

Darrow nodded curtly.

"Where did you meet for your assignations?" Solomon asked.

"At the house of a friend from the theatre. She arranged to be out on the afternoons we met."

Constance rummaged in her bag and passed him a pencil and a piece of paper. "Will you write down her name and address?"

Darrow did not hesitate.

While he wrote, Solomon said, "When did you last see Caterina?"

"To speak to? Just a couple of days ago. Tuesday afternoon."

The day before she died… "At this friend's house?" Solomon asked.

Darrow nodded.

"How did she seem to you?" Constance asked. "Well? Happy?"

"Yes," Darrow said. "Just as she always was."

"Did you send her flowers?" Constance asked.

He smiled as he passed the paper and pencil back to Constance. "I gave them to her often. At our meetings. She took them with her to performances and then took them home, telling her husband they had been left at the stage door for her by admirers in the audience."

"Did you give her flowers on Tuesday?"

"Yes."

"What kind?"

"Roses. Red roses."

Solomon did not look at Constance, though they seemed to have solved that mystery. "Where did she go when she left you on Tuesday afternoon?" he asked.

"To Covent Garden."

"Directly?"

"So far as I know."

"Taking the roses with her?"

"Yes."

He left it to Constance to ask the last question. She would appear less threatening.

"Where were you on Wednesday night, Mr. Darrow?"

"At Covent Garden. Thanks to Caterina, I stand in when any of the violinists are absent."

"So you did see her after Tuesday. Did you speak to her at the theatre?" Solomon asked.

"No. She insisted on discretion. She didn't want Montague to find out about us. I didn't care whether he did or not, but I did as she asked to please her."

"Did she sing well?"

"Gloriously," Darrow said with complete sincerity.

"And when she left the stage, did she seem physically well? No signs of illness that you could see?"

Darrow frowned and shook his head. "None. Perhaps I *should* have noticed something. Perhaps I only saw what I wished to, dazzled like everyone else..."

"And when the performance was over," Solomon said, "where did you go?"

"Home," Darrow said in surprise. "Here."

"Alone or with friends?"

Darrow regarded him thoughtfully. He knew what the question meant, but it did not appear to upset him. "Alone. Mrs. Philpot—the dragon downstairs—saw me, if you're looking for witnesses. Reid, who shares these rooms with me, is another. If you suspect someone killed Caterina, look at Montague. She was afraid of him."

"What makes you say that?" Constance asked quickly.

"I told you, she spoke to me. But if you had seen her morbid fear of Montague finding out, you would not doubt me."

"Did he beat her?" Solomon asked steadily.

Darrow shrugged impatiently. "Not that I could ever prove. There are other ways to frighten people. If you really believe her death was not natural, know that I'll help in any way I can. It has to have been *him*."

His young face was earnest, tortured, difficult to look at.

Constance rose to her feet. "Thank you for your time, Mr. Darrow. You've been most helpful."

Darrow nodded. It did not appear to enter his head to show them out. He just bade them goodbye. As Solomon closed the door of the sitting room behind them, Darrow sank onto the piano stool, watching them as though in a daze. The tragic look was back in his eyes, making him seem both younger and more vulnerable, almost like a lost child.

As they descended the stairs, the woman who had let them in waddled up the hall from the depths of the house—presumably Mrs. Philpot, "the dragon downstairs."

"Well, at least you made him stop for five minutes," she said with some satisfaction. "Goes on for hours most days, you know, all that screeching. And when he stops, the other one starts. Gawd knows how the neighbors put up with it. If I didn't make it a rule that there's to be no noise after ten, they'd make their racket all night too."

"You don't care for music?" Solomon asked.

"Not the same few notes over and over! Drive a person to drink, it would."

"It can't be easy," Constance said sympathetically, "having

two lively young men in your house."

Mrs. Philpot sniffed. "They're not so bad. Leastways, not at night. They don't try to hold parties, or bring people—or women!—round late."

Solomon felt his lip twitch. Covering it, he said, "I gather Mr. Darrow came home about eleven on Wednesday—the night before last."

"That he did. And the other came in shortly after—tripped on the stairs, so I reckon he weren't exactly sober."

"You reckon?" Solomon repeated. "Then you didn't actually see them?"

"They use their own keys, and I can tell each of their steps. They're quite distinctive. Carl's is quieter, more careful. Geoffrey races around, jaunty, always in a hurry. Mind you, I did see Carl—Mr. Darrow—that night. He called goodnight when he heard me in the kitchen and I stuck my head round the door. I put the lights out, and five minutes later, I heard Geoffrey—Mr. Reid—clattering about and falling up the stairs."

"I don't suppose you heard either of them go out again that night?" Constance asked.

"Lord, no," Mrs. Philpot said with unexpected indulgence. "They're good boys really, and very good about getting up early—especially Carl, who practices in the mornings."

"So on Thursday morning, Mr. Darrow was practicing his violin as usual?" Solomon asked.

"Oh yes, every day without fail."

Solomon inclined his head and thanked her, and she opened the door for them. The violin remained silent.

CHAPTER FIVE

From the sitting room window, shaded by the curtain, Carl Darrow watched his visitors depart.

What on earth had that been about? He stared at the card he had been given. Silver and Grey. Inquiries. She was a madam, for God's sake, even if a somewhat refined one. For that reason, he had almost turned down her invitation to play at her house in the spring. Yet a powerful courtesan had the kind of clientele he needed, so he had taken the chance—and discovered she was married to that wealthiest of recluses, Solomon Grey.

Well, he didn't seem to be much of a recluse either. He had been present at Carl's recital at that house of civilized ill repute, along with many other influential gentlemen. And there was no denying that it had led to several more lucrative private engagements with the best people. His reputation was growing...

Though how much did that matter without Caterina?

Her loss both filled and emptied him. He needed music... Where was his damned violin?

He was about to turn away from the window when a jaunty figure caught his eye: Reid loping around the corner from the bakery, a loaf in one hand, a small basket of strawberries in the other.

Carl paused, his gaze shifting to the carriage in front of the house. Grey already had the door open, and Carl *willed* Constance Silver into it.

Too late. She had seen Reid.

Grey closed the door again, and Carl's heart sank. For the first time ever, he wished Geoffrey Reid was less good natured. He would never walk past someone who clearly wanted to talk to him, much less be deliberately rude.

Slowly, Carl eased the bottom sash up, careful not to let it rattle. The three people below did not appear to notice. They were too focused on each other. Annoyingly, he could only hear snatches of their conversation, but it was enough to understand.

The courtesan, who was now Mrs. Grey, was clearly asking Reid about Wednesday night.

"He was home before me," Reid answered cheerfully. "Afraid I had a few at the Pig and Whistle."

"Did you see him when you went in?" Grey asked.

"No. He was too grumpy. I scratched at his door, but he told me in no uncertain terms to—er…go away. So I did."

Thank you, Geoff… The last thing Carl needed was to be under suspicion for murder. That it should be *her* murder was unbearable… *Bloody Montague…*

"Did either of you go out again?" Grey asked.

This time Reid's answer was less satisfactory. "*I* didn't. Out like a light as soon as my head touched the pillow. I'd have slept through a riot in the street."

Damn it, Reid…

Mrs. Grey's next words were lost in the breeze, and the call of a costermonger in the next street. But Reid's reply was clear enough.

"Oh no. Carl doesn't go out when he's grumpy. He plays his violin until he feels better."

"Not after ten o'clock, surely," Grey said, which made Reid laugh.

"No, but certainly well before ten the next morning!"

Carl stepped back from the window. Was it enough? He hoped so. He didn't want to think of Caterina, of his loss, of the blackness. Almost blindly, he stumbled back to his own room and snatched his violin off the bed.

It was the only thing to do with grief.

CONSTANCE HAD BEEN aware of the window lifting above her and wondered if Darrow would somehow try to disrupt their conversation with Reid. But if she hoped for a reaction from Caterina's lover, she was disappointed. There was only silence above, and then she heard the violin.

"Were you with him," Solomon asked, his voice low and confidential, "when he learned of Caterina di Ripoli's death?"

Reid's expression grew troubled. "No. I saw it in the newspaper stand around the corner when I was on my way home last night and immediately went in to see him. He already knew."

"How?" Constance asked.

"From the newspaper open on his bed, I suppose. It is hard on him…" Reid straightened his shoulders suddenly, as though pulling himself together. "He knew her, you see. He accompanied her several times, most recently at Covent Garden when he played with the orchestra."

He was endearingly blatant. Constance held his gaze. "But there was a little more to it than that, was there not?"

"He was devoted to her," Reid admitted. "Beyond that, I cannot and will not go."

"Did you never see them together?" she asked.

Reid hesitated. "I had supper with them once. And coffee one afternoon in Covent Garden."

"Was it your impression that she was as devoted as he?"

Reid dragged his gaze free, shifting his feet uncomfortably. "She liked him, certainly, but she never excluded me to make sheep's eyes at him. She was a very charming lady." He seemed to recognize that this was not a terribly satisfactory answer, for he gave a helpless shrug. A young man trying to describe emotion without the aid of music. Or perhaps without landing his friend or his friend's late lover in trouble.

Constance gave him her hand in an encouraging sort of way. He might, after all, have more to tell. "Thank you, Mr. Reid. Goodbye."

Solomon handed her into the carriage, and they set off for Montague's house. They were both silent for several minutes.

Constance said, "I don't think there is a case. Darrow's explanation of the roses makes sense. She left them at the theatre overnight on Tuesday and then brought them home on Wednesday."

"Most likely, but wouldn't she have asked the maid to put them in water? Wouldn't Mary Webb have seen them, at least? She was waiting in the bedroom for Caterina that last night."

"It's possible Caterina hid them—a guilty wife concealing her lover's token." She shifted impatiently, drawing closer to Solomon. "I don't like this case. I'll be glad to tell Kellar there is nothing in his suspicions. A few interviews with the servants and Montague himself, and then we can stop wasting everyone's time."

"I wonder why this matters so much to Kellar?" Solomon mused.

Constance didn't like to think about that either. She wanted to be finished with the whole business and wave Kellar back off to Italy.

It was the same maid who opened the front door of Montague's house and dropped a brief curtsey.

"Good afternoon, sir, ma'am. I'm afraid Mr. Montague is not at home."

"That's fine," Solomon said easily. "I'm sure you were told that we would be asking a few questions. We'll just get that over with now."

A flash of distinct hostility showed in the girl's eyes before her long lashes swept down to cover them. But she stepped back to allow them entry and closed the door behind them.

"Yes, sir," she said woodenly.

"Let's step into the morning room," Constance said. "Remind us of the way, if you please."

The girl led the way and stood stiffly by the door while Constance sat down. Solomon went to the window and leaned against the wall there.

"What is your name?" Constance asked the maid.

"Nancy, ma'am."

"You are the parlor maid, is that right? You are responsible for opening the door to visitors and showing them out again?"

"Yes, ma'am. Unless Mr. Collins—he's the butler—chooses to do it himself." There may have been a shade of insolence there, a contempt for someone who was not sure of the parlor maid's duties. But Constance was used to dealing with insolent girls. Up to a point, she even allowed it. Respect, after all, had to be earned.

"You are happy with your employment in this house, Nancy?" she asked amiably.

"Yes, ma'am." Color began to seep into the girl's pretty face. "That is, I *was*. Until the mistress died. Who could be happy with that?"

"No one," Constance said. "Which is why we—I include Mr. Montague here—need to make as much sense as possible out of what happened. On Wednesday night, was it you who let Mrs. Montague into the house? Or did she use her key?"

"I heard her carriage while I was setting the breakfast parlor for the morning. So I opened the door as soon as she reached the doorstep."

"Did she seem happy to you? Pleased to be home?"

"Oh, yes, ma'am. All smiles, she were, when she greeted me and then all but ran to the master as soon as he poked his head out of the drawing room. She's like that when she's had a good performance."

Or when she's in love? Constance wondered. "Did she leave her bag in the hall for you to take up to her room?" *A large bag hiding a dozen red roses, perhaps?*

Nancy blinked. "She didn't have a bag. She just swept in with her cloak billowing—so graceful, she always was."

No bag? Damn it!

Without a word, Solomon left the room, no doubt going to see if a bag still lurked unnoticed under a hall table or in some other shadowy corner. Nancy's eyes flickered to him as he passed her, then returned to Constance.

"Did you take her cloak?" Constance asked.

"Didn't get the chance. She went into the drawing room wearing it and told me over her shoulder we could all go to bed. So I did. Easy enough to finish the breakfast table in the morning."

"Are you a light sleeper?"

Nancy frowned in quick suspicion. "What does that mean?"

"I mean, does any noise outside or inside the house tend to wake you? Or do you sleep all night without ever being disturbed?"

"Mostly all night, I suppose. Why?"

"Then you wouldn't have heard any sounds of distress from Mrs. Montague's room? Or anyone entering or leaving the house?"

"I don't know. Sometimes I hear Mr. and Mrs. Montague when they come in late. Other times I don't."

Constance sighed. She drummed her fingers on the arm of her chair, then forced them to stop. "You won't want to answer this, because you are clearly a good and loyal servant, but the truth will help Mr. Montague, and even your late mistress. And please don't tell me it's not your place to say, because I know you have an opinion. Were Mr. and Mrs. Montague happy together? As a couple?"

The girl's mouth opened then pressed tight shut on what was no doubt a furious retort. Instead, she said tightly, "Yes, ma'am."

"Then you never heard them quarrel?"

"No, ma'am."

A loyal servant would never tell, but Constance, concentrating on the maid's wooden face rather than on her words, persevered. "Then you saw no signs that either of them ever—er…strayed?"

"What sort of signs?" Nancy asked with undisguised aggression.

"Well, for example, did either of them ever ask you to carry notes by hand, or verbal messages?"

"No, but then they wouldn't, would they? It ain't my place to run messages. Besides, he's got an office full of clerks for that sort of thing, and she's got Miss Webb."

"Then Miss Webb took messages by hand for her?"

"I didn't say that," Nancy protested at once. "I never saw her do so, and she never told me that she did. Just saying no one asked *me*. It's a respectable house."

Solomon re-entered the room, caught Constance's gaze, and shook his head minutely. So no bag had been left in the hall. Well, it was more likely that Caterina had fetched any such bag from its hiding place after both her husband and her maid had left her alone.

Constance stood up. "Thank you, Nancy. How many other servants live in the house?"

"Just me, Mr. Collins, Cook, and Miss Webb. Oh, and Fred the boot boy. Coachman lives above the coach house in the mews."

The boot boy interested Constance, for he had a legitimate reason for wandering the house at night, leaving polished shoes outside doors and collecting any left there.

As though Nancy had heard her thoughts, she said wryly, "Fred's only ten. He gets sent to bed at nine and does the boots in the morning."

Constance inclined her head, grateful for the information. "Who keeps the keys?"

Nancy's eyes widened. "What keys?"

"To the house. And to the rooms within the house."

"Mrs. Montague had keys to the front and back door. I think

Mr. Montague has a full set, outside and in. So does Mr. Collins. Cook's got a back door key. The room keys are all in the locks on the inside of the rooms. They're not used much, so far as I know."

"What about the bedchambers?"

"Oh, Miss Webb's got a key for Mrs. Montague's. She locks it when she wants to be alone."

"So I gather," Constance murmured, rising to her feet. "Thanks for your help. You can go back to your duties now. Ask Miss Webb to join us in Mrs. Montague's room, if you please."

Nancy quite clearly did *not* please, and left tight-lipped.

Constance and Solomon exchanged a speaking look.

"She wouldn't tell us if there were anything really wrong in this house," Constance said, "but I tend to believe her that there wasn't."

Solomon nodded acknowledgment, holding the door for her. With the growing feeling that they were wasting everyone's time, including their own, Constance again climbed the stairs with Solomon and entered the dead woman's bedchamber.

The body had been removed and the bed stripped, but otherwise, the bedchamber looked exactly the same, even with the curtains open. As before, the vase of roses dominated the room in terms of both beauty and scent.

"They're lasting well," Solomon remarked, moving toward the cupboard where they had seen light traveling bags and a case before.

"They do if you change the water every day. Solomon, I think Nancy would have said if Caterina *had* brought a bag back with her that night. Could she have hidden the flowers beneath her cloak?"

"Thorns and all?" Solomon said dubiously. "While embracing her husband and enjoying a glass of sherry with him? I don't understand why she hid them at all, if she was in the habit of bringing favored posies back with her from the theatre. Besides which, they might not have shared a bed every night, but he was likely to look in on her, surely before he went to work in the morning."

"And so was bound to see the roses," Constance said. "Damn it, if we solved that little puzzle, we'd be free."

In fact, if it hadn't been for *that little puzzle*, she doubted they would still be asking questions.

Mary Webb stalked through the open bedroom door. "Nancy said you were here again, asking impertinent questions while Mr. Montague is out."

"It is for Mr. Montague that we're asking them," Solomon said smoothly. "And we all appreciate your help. Tell me, when Mrs. Montague came upstairs on Wednesday night, was she still wearing her cloak?"

"No," the maid said. "It was over her arm. Why?"

"Could you show us the cloak she was wearing?"

With a long-suffering expression, Mary went to the wardrobe and extracted a silk velvet cloak in midnight blue with a luxuriantly large hood. It fell in such generous folds that its wearer could indeed have hidden a bouquet there. But when Constance passed her fingers over the lining with great thoroughness, she found no pulled threads, no tears or bits of thorn or foliage. No bright-red petals. And Caterina had not been wearing it by the time she entered the room.

Solomon said, "When Mrs. Montague locked her door at night, did she take the key out of the lock?"

"Of course. Otherwise, I wouldn't be able to get in of a morning without disturbing her."

Constance glanced at the door. The key was back in the lock on the inside. "Where did she put the key when she removed it?"

"On her bedside table." Mary took the proffered cloak from Constance's hands and hung it back up in the wardrobe.

Solomon waited until she turned to face them again before he said, "Have you ever carried notes or verbal messages between Mrs. Montague and her friends?"

"No," Mary said, not very convincingly.

Constance sighed. "We know all about Carl Darrow. So you might as well tell us."

To her surprise, Mary committed the solecism of sitting down uninvited in the presence of her supposed betters. She sank onto the bed, covering her face with her hands. "Only the once. I didn't like doing it and told her I wouldn't do it again. I don't know why she had to see him at all, with a husband so devoted to her…"

"Did she confide in you?" Constance asked gently.

Mary flapped one damp hand and groped for her handkerchief. "She didn't need to. She was an open book. She just chattered, and all too often recently it was about this violinist. He fascinated her. But she loved the master, she really did. She was just like a child who has to taste the sweet, even when it's forbidden."

"Did Mr. Montague know about Darrow?"

"God, no. She would never hurt him."

"And what he didn't know couldn't," Constance murmured. It was a flawed philosophy. She had used it herself, cynically enough, to justify the straying husbands who flocked to her establishment.

"I left the theatre to be with her when she married Mr. Montague because I wanted the respectability. Better to be a lady's maid than a theatre dresser. Or that's what I told myself." Mary's eyes were streaming again, her voice muffled in her handkerchief. "But I *miss* her…"

Constance went and placed a gentle hand on the maid's shoulder. "I'm sorry."

The handkerchief fell away, and Mary's swimming eyes pleaded with her. "To her, she wasn't being unfaithful, because she never stopped loving her husband."

Another justification Constance had heard used by some men. *Well, what's sauce for the goose…*

"The world won't understand," Mary said intensely. "Don't tell them. For his sake if no other…"

"Do you mean Mr. Montague's sake?" Solomon asked. "Or Mr. Darrow's?"

The maid flapped her hand again. "Both, I suppose."

And her own, no doubt. Servants tended to be tarred with the same immoral brush as their employers. But there was no doubting that Mary Webb was genuinely upset and grieving for her mistress.

"We only want to be sure how she died," Constance said gently. "Not to judge her, or you. Tell me, apart from the roses, have you ever noticed anything else appearing overnight in this room? Other flowers? Gifts? Ornaments?"

Mary wiped her eyes again and frowned in concentration. She shook her head. "No. I don't remember anything."

"Do you think she might have gone out again on Wednesday night when the household was asleep?"

"She *could* have," the maid said, clearly dubious. "But she hated being tired in the morning. She liked to spend time with Mr. Montague before he went to work, and she was always serious about her voice exercises, even on the days she didn't have formal rehearsals or performances. She said if she wasn't rested, it spoiled the clarity of her voice."

"Is that why she and her husband have separate bedrooms?" Solomon asked.

A flush of outrage showed the maid was recovering from her uncontrolled display of emotion. "I couldn't say, sir."

"Had they quarreled recently?" he pursued.

"Not to my knowledge," Mary replied firmly.

"Had she quarreled with Darrow?"

"Not to my knowledge."

"How often does Mr. Kellar come to the house?" Solomon asked unexpectedly.

Mary blinked. "He was away for a long time. Since he's come home, a few times for dinner, a few morning calls when Mrs. Montague was at home."

"And before he went away the last time? Did he come to the

wedding?"

"He gave her away. He was a friend of her parents and helped her escape the nasty revolutions. He'd pop up occasionally after that, always without warning. She was always glad to see him, hopeful he'd be settling in England for good."

"Did your master and mistress quarrel much?" Constance asked.

The maid's lips tightened once more. "No, ma'am."

"Did she quarrel with anyone that you know of?"

Mary shrugged. "A few disagreements in the theatre, nothing she could not deal with. She was the prima donna, after all."

"Did you ever come across unexplained cuts or bruises on her body?" Constance asked. "As if a quarrel had turned violent?"

Mary stared. "*No*, ma'am," she said in outrage.

And that, at least, was truth.

"Thank you," Solomon said, with clear dismissal.

Constance could hardly wait for her footsteps to fade into the distance. "Kellar?" she said accusingly. "Why ask about him?"

Solomon lifted one apologetic shoulder. "Three reasons, I suppose. First, because I thought you'd want to know, and secondly, why is he so keen for us to investigate a death that everyone else regards as easily explained?"

Constance nodded slowly. "I suspect he always has reasons for what he does, and he's not exactly open by nature, is he? You said three reasons."

"He knew the way to her bedchamber. He seemed just a little too familiar there."

It was as valid as his other points. And yet… "He asked us to investigate in the first place. Why would he do that if he were guilty of any impropriety? Which isn't to say his feelings aren't involved." She paced restlessly toward the window. "No. She was a charming and talented woman with a messy life and a heart condition. There are no marks of foul play on her body, and she does not appear to have taken too much of her medicine. Everyone loved her, flaws and all. There is no case here,

Solomon."

She spun around on the final words, and the roses seemed to glare at her accusingly. She scowled back at them. "Do they even matter?"

"We believe Darrow gave them to her on Tuesday and she took them to the theatre with her. On Wednesday she must have brought them home and somehow smuggled them into the house." He came and stood beside her, and they both gazed out of the window at the pretty garden below. "Nancy heard her carriage in the street, so I doubt Caterina had time to run round to the back of the house and hide her roses. If she had, the kitchen staff would probably have seen her. So she must have hidden them at the front of the house somewhere, then, when the house was asleep, slipped out and brought them in."

"That would explain it," Constance said. "Only, why did she bother? She was always bringing flowers back from the theatre. Montague never needed to know they were from Darrow."

"Red roses are a very obvious love token."

"Then why put them on display at all, let alone sneak about to do so?"

Solomon smiled ruefully. "Who is trying to convince whom here? Do we want there to be a case or not?"

"Not," Constance said emphatically. "I just wish we could explain the roses to Kellar's satisfaction, charge him a modest fee, and move on to the next case."

Solomon tilted his head, listening. "That was a key in the front door. I think the master of the house has returned. With luck, one more interview with him will decide the matter."

Accordingly, they left the dead woman's bedroom and went downstairs. They found Montague in the drawing room once more. This time he had his back to them, gazing up at the large portrait of his wife that hung above the fireplace.

Solomon tapped on the open door. "Mr. Montague?"

The widower turned almost reluctantly to face them. "Nancy said you were here again. I hope you have finished upsetting the servants. It isn't pleasant for them either, you know. Particularly if they start imagining some kind of foul play."

"We have found no sign of that," Constance said truthfully. "May we talk to you for a few moments?"

In answer, he merely gestured to the sofa and, when Constance had sat, took the chair opposite.

"I made the funeral arrangements and went to the office," he said. "It seemed better than sitting alone in this house, and there is always much to do. The difficulty is making myself care about work. What is the point without her?"

Constance nodded sympathetically.

Solomon said, "You trade in tea, I believe?"

Montague nodded. "A profitable business. For the most part."

"You have had some bad luck recently?"

"My last cargo went down with its ship. It entails a few…economies, but we can weather the storm. Fortunately, no lives were lost. Do you deal much in tea, Mr. Grey?"

"We ship it. From China and Ceylon and India."

"Perhaps I should look to you for my transport."

"Feel free."

Montague lapsed into silence, so Constance said, "This is a house of great character and charm. Was it always your home, or did you and your wife choose it together?"

Another spark of animation lit Montague's face. "It has been my family's home for generations. Caterina fell in love with it and made many improvements. All the decoration you see is hers—she had a wonderful eye for color."

"It is beautiful," Constance agreed.

"And yet I can't bear to be in it. Can't bear to be away from it, either, which is why I came home early."

"You need time," Constance said.

He nodded, the brief liveliness of his expression fading into bleakness, as though he saw too much time ahead and had no idea what to do with it.

Making an obvious effort, he said, "Have you made enough

inquiries to satisfy Mr. Kellar's view of circumstances?"

"Almost," Solomon said. "The main thing that puzzles us is the vase of roses in her bedchamber. No one saw them come into the house, and they were not there when Caterina's maid left her. Did you ever give roses to your wife?"

"Yes, but if you are imagining I made the romantic gesture of slipping them into her room in the middle of the night, I'm afraid I didn't. She must have had them lying around in her room somewhere and suddenly remembered them."

"Without Miss Webb's seeing?" Constance asked doubtfully.

"Webb sees Caterina and clothes," Montague said with a hint of impatience. "She is not so very observant of anyone or anything else."

Oddly, that possibility had not struck Constance before. It made sense, too. "According to Miss Webb, Mrs. Montague had locked her door on the night she died. Was that significant in any way?"

"It signified that she did not wish to be disturbed."

"Some husbands," Constance said tactfully, "would object to being locked out of their wife's room."

Montague gave a twisted little smile. "But I wasn't locked out. I have a key to that room too."

"Then why did she bother locking it at all?" Solomon said. "Who else was likely to disturb her?"

A slight pinkness stained Montague's cheeks. "No one. It was merely a sign to me. We had an agreement. You see, we both wanted to have children, but in Caterina's case, not just yet. She wanted to further her career first. I respected that."

So Caterina decided when they were intimate in order to prevent pregnancy… Was she as careful with Darrow? Not that it mattered. With a key, Montague could indeed have put the roses in his wife's room. There was just no reason for him to deny it.

"Did you have any visitors on Wednesday evening?" Solomon asked.

"No. I completed some work, then read until Caterina came home."

"Did you ever go to the theatre to hear her sing?"

"Often. But not every night."

"I suppose her dressing room was full of flowers from admirers."

Montague smiled. "Yes, it was, whenever I was there. I can see you wondering if I minded. I didn't. I was proud of her, and it was all part of her being who and what she was. I can see you also wondering why on earth such a vibrant creature chose me, a dull, middle-aged merchant, to be her husband. Believe me, I asked myself the same question many times. Kellar has made no secret of his disapproval. None of us may understand it, but the truth is, she loved me. I was her stability, as necessary to her life as she was to mine."

His voice cracked just at the end, and Constance propelled herself to her feet. "We are so sorry for your loss," she said. "And we thank you for your candor. We won't intrude any further."

In fact, she was desperate to get out of the house, which suddenly seemed full of Caterina's ghost and choked with the profound grief of the living.

Annoyingly, when they stepped out of the front door, the carriage was missing.

"John must be walking the horses," Solomon said.

Constance took his arm, still impelled to put distance between them and the house, and all but dragged him across the road to the gardens in the middle of the square.

"I believe in his grief," she said intensely. "He had nothing to gain from her death."

"Apart from the money he inherits, which will certainly be useful to his business."

"Even then, he said they were weathering the storm. Either he genuinely loved his wife, or he is the best actor in Creation. Sol?"

"Yes?"

"I tried to will myself into Caterina's shoes when Mary was explaining. I tried to imagine myself betraying you with some other man who caught my eye."

"And could you?" he asked lightly. He wasn't looking at her, but he cared about the answer. The very stillness of his arm beneath her fingers told her so.

"Solomon, I couldn't even imagine the man. For me, there can't be anyone else."

He pressed her arm closer against him, as if he understood the depth of her revelation. Last night's quarrel had been driven back into perspective. There had been so few of them that it had taken her by surprise. Their desperate lovemaking had shown her many things, chiefly that she could not lose him. But more than that, there could be no one else for her, ever, whether he was at her side or not.

"We never understand other people's relationships," Constance said. "Whores have lovers and husbands as well as clients. Some people love more than one man or woman at a time. Some people indulge in affairs that never change how they regard their wives or husbands. For all his worldly wisdom and apparent cynicism, I don't think Kellar understood her at all. If she strayed, he assumed it was Montague's fault, that there was a lack of... Solomon?"

He had stopped dead on the path, not even looking at her. Quite suddenly, she had lost his attention. Piqued, she followed his gaze to the bed of red roses beside her. It was a lovely display...

And the petals were exactly the same shade as the flowers in Caterina's room.

More than that, there were gaps. Stems cut precisely, as though with sharp scissors or secateurs, several from one plant, more from the one next to it. Slowly releasing Solomon's arm, she began to walk around. Flowers had been taken from four plants, and when she counted them, there were twelve pristinely cut stems.

"They're not Darrow's roses," she said. "Whoever put them in her room, they came from here."

CHAPTER SIX

UNTIL HE SAW the rosebushes with the cut stems, Solomon had been ready to throw in the towel, in the parlance of the prize fighter. There had seemed to be no other clues to collect and no threads of inquiry worth following. For reasons of his own, Kellar found it hard to accept Caterina's death, but there was no evidence pointing to anything other than the heart failure diagnosed by her doctor.

During their quick luncheon at the Silver and Grey offices, Constance argued, "It makes no real difference. We already decided Caterina herself had slipped out of the house at night to collect the roses. She could just as easily have crossed the road and picked them herself."

"She could have," Solomon agreed. "But if she was as careful of her rest, as Mary said, then why would she?"

"It would give us two bouquets of red roses," Constance said. "Is that not too great a coincidence?"

"Not for someone like Caterina. And in any case, we only have Darrow's word that he gave them to her and that she took them to the theatre."

"Why would he lie?" Constance demanded.

"I have no idea," Solomon admitted. "But I don't think we've solved the mystery of the roses yet. We can at least go to the theatre this afternoon and see if someone there can make sense of it."

She sighed. "I suppose so."

Solomon watched her eat in silence for a few minutes before he said lightly, "Tired of mysteries, Constance? Do you want to retire?"

She opened her mouth to deny it, then thought about it a moment longer. "No. I'm just not afraid of stopping anymore."

He raised his brows. "You were afraid to stop?"

"I thought if we did, I wouldn't see you anymore."

He reached across the desk and threaded his fingers through hers. "I thought up the partnership in the first place as a means of keeping you with me."

She smiled. "And a means of distracting me from the establishment."

"That too, though it didn't work out quite so well, did it? I didn't understand, then, what you were doing. Or even what I was feeling for you. I just wanted more."

To his delight, color seeped into her face. "So did I. I didn't trust the emotions, but I always seemed to trust you. We don't need the mysteries anymore."

"But do we *want* them?"

She searched his eyes, her soft, slender fingers caressing his palm. "I do. Just not this one. Do you?"

"In general, yes. And in the case of this one, I wouldn't feel right if we left it as it stands."

She sighed. "Neither would I," she admitted. "Though I don't have to like it." She rose and dragged his hand to her lips before collecting his plate and putting it with her own for Hat to wash when they were gone. "Then let's get it over with."

"In a moment," Sol said, standing and taking her into his arms.

In fact, it was about ten minutes before they emerged from the office and walked arm in arm to the opera house.

The front door of the theatre was closed, the notices outside still proclaiming that last night's performance of *Rigoletto* had been canceled, presumably out of respect for the dead. The date had not been changed to today, so perhaps Caterina's understudy was due to perform instead.

All of which sparked another suspicion in his mind. Was there not a huge amount of backbiting and jealousy amongst theatrical people? If foul play was involved in Caterina's death, was it not more likely to come from here than from the people who loved her at home?

The stage door, when they eventually found it and Solomon had battered at it for some time, was opened by a glowering porter who demanded belligerently, "What?"

Only then did he look Solomon up and down and take in Constance's presence.

"Are you leaving flowers for Mrs. di Ripoli?" he asked with greater civility.

"We have already paid our respects to her husband," Constance said. "On his behalf, we were hoping to speak to Mrs. di Ripoli's dresser."

"And her understudy," Solomon added.

The porter's frown returned, as though he suspected them of being journalists. However, it must have been a fleeting notion, assuaged once more by their appearance, for he opened the door wide for them to enter.

"Don't know if Miss Gentle is free—she's got a lot to do if she's to go on tonight, but Rose is in the dressing room…"

He led them into the bowels of the building, along a passage of many doors. Pieces of muffled music and several different voices drifted to Solomon's ears. He wondered if Darrow was here, too, rehearsing with the orchestra, or if he were no longer needed. In any case, without the attraction of Caterina, he probably preferred solo performances. He was too ambitious—and perhaps too good—to enjoy being lost in an orchestra.

The porter halted at a door with Caterina's name still upon it and opened it.

A woman stood by an open trunk, cradling an elaborate gown to her cheek. The large dressing table appeared to have been cleared of everything except a vase of wilted flowers. Other posies, in similar conditions, some shedding petals, some almost dried, were scattered all over the room on every available surface.

The woman lowered the dress, blinking at the visitors as though adjusting to present reality.

"They're from Mrs. di Ripoli's husband," the porter said to her gruffly. "Give me a shout if you need me."

The woman nodded vaguely and quickly addressed Solomon. "I haven't finished packing up all her things yet, but we'll send them to the house later this afternoon—unless you want to wait?"

"We haven't come for her things," Solomon said. "We just wanted to talk to you about Mrs. di Ripoli. My name is Solomon Grey. This is my wife."

"Rose Samuels," the woman said, dropping a slight, unexpectedly graceful curtsey.

"Your name is familiar," Constance said. "Don't you sing, too?"

"I used to," the dresser said. "Until I was ill. My voice never recovered. Now I dress the prima donna." She dropped the gown on top of the things already in the trunk and gestured toward the sofa by the window. "Won't you sit down?"

"Thank you. Did you know Mrs. di Ripoli well?"

"Since she came to England. My voice had already gone by then, and she understood how difficult that was. More than a mere loss of income, although God knows that matters too. She helped me accept and live with it. Especially after she was ill herself and thought her career too might be over."

"Then you were her friend as well as her dresser?"

"Yes."

Constance smiled. "Good. Then you will understand how the suddenness of her death might…disturb those closest to her. You were with her for the performance on Wednesday evening?"

Rose inclined her head. "Of course."

"Did she seem well to you?"

"Very well. She was excited and confident, as she usually was before and during a performance. And she was brilliant as Gilda…

But she was also happy."

Constance seized on that. "Had she been *unhappy* before Wednesday evening?"

The dresser waved that aside as though it was of little account. Or perhaps she regretted the words. "A little. Her life was complicated."

"In what way?"

Rose shrugged, now definitely uncomfortable. "Oh, juggling her professional life and her marriage. She naturally wanted to give her all to each, but that wasn't always possible."

She definitely knows about Darrow, Solomon thought.

Constance had obviously guessed the same, for she said, "Especially when added to another, less public relationship."

Rose flushed. "There is nothing in that. Foolish rumor."

"We have already spoken to Mr. Darrow," Constance said.

The dresser started toward them, then halted, clenching and unclenching her hands. "Oh. Mr. Montague doesn't know, does he? She never wanted him to know. That was why she broke it off. Or, at least, she was going to. I thought that was why she was happier on Wednesday, because she had finally done so."

"He played with the orchestra here on Wednesday evening," Solomon said. "Did he visit Mrs. di Ripoli here in her dressing room?"

"Oh, no, she never allowed that. She told me he just liked to be part of her performance."

"Did she say such things to other people?" Solomon asked.

"No, no, she was very discreet."

Except with Mary Webb and Rose Samuels. "Did he send flowers to her dressing room?"

"If he did, it was anonymously."

"On Monday evening, when she arrived at the theatre, did she bring flowers with her?"

"Monday? Yes, I think it was Monday she arrived with a dozen red roses. I put them in water for her."

Solomon looked around the room again. There were droopy

white roses and a multitude of other species, but nothing that resembled a dozen red roses in any condition. "When did she take them home with her?"

Rose raised her eyebrows in clear surprise. "She didn't. She asked me to throw them out on Wednesday evening because they were smelling bad—I'd forgotten to change the water, and roses don't really thrive in here. Not enough sun..."

Solomon exchanged a glance with Constance.

"Where did you put them?" she asked pleasantly.

"I squashed them into the dustbin outside."

The roses in Caterina's bedroom had certainly never been squashed. If she had brought them into her house, they had not been Darrow's.

"When you helped Mrs. di Ripoli to dress," Constance said, "did you ever notice marks on her person?"

Rose frowned. "What sort of marks?"

"Any sort—bruises, cuts, swellings..."

"No." Rose looked more bewildered than outraged. "Never that I can recall."

"Did you ever get the impression she was afraid of anyone?"

Rose smiled. "Caterina? Lord, no. She wasn't frightened of anyone or anything."

"Not even her husband?"

Rose paused, her lips already parted to reply. After an instant, she said, "Well, she was afraid of his not thinking well of her."

"You mean if he found out about Mr. Darrow?"

"Exactly."

"What about Mr. Darrow?" Solomon said. "Did she ever seem afraid of him?"

Rose shook her head emphatically. "Oh, no."

"Tell us," Solomon said, "about Mrs. di Ripoli's understudy."

"Ellen? She's talented—lacks just a little certainty in the upper ranges, and obviously she doesn't have Caterina's stage presence. But she has a very promising future, especially if she manages the part of Gilda tonight."

"Is she ambitious?"

Rose smiled. "Of course she is."

"Were she and Mrs. di Ripoli friends?"

Rose thought about it. "Not friends," she said. "I don't think Caterina noticed her much, though she was kind. Ellen admired Caterina, of course. You could almost see her learning from the prima donna, absorbing everything she could."

"Was she jealous?" Solomon asked.

"A little, I suppose. Who wouldn't be? Caterina had every-thing. Or seemed to…"

Constance rose from the sofa. "Could you possibly direct us to her?"

"I'll get her to come to you here as soon as she's free. I have things I should be doing for her in her own dressing room."

"She won't move here?"

"Not yet," Rose said firmly, and hurried off.

"Well," Constance murmured, sitting back down, "that's one theory gone. It seems our roses really did come from the square garden. Do you believe her that Caterina had ended the affair?"

"She didn't seem very sure, did she? Darrow did not appear to know it had ended."

"And Montague didn't know it existed. In which case, neither of them have a motive to hurt Caterina."

"Except her money, in Montague's case," Solomon said. "And it was only Kellar who peddled that theory."

Constance cast him an uneasy glance. "Kellar's mystery is becoming annoying. Again. I think we need to tell him we'll walk away from this unless he is completely honest and open with us."

"We don't know that he hasn't been. We just don't quite understand him."

At the sound of quick footsteps in the passage, they broke off their discussion. A young woman in her early or mid-twenties walked into the room. In appearance, she was Caterina's opposite, short and plump and ordinary. Though her voice when she spoke was definitely beautiful, despite her harassed expres-sion.

"Mr. and Mrs. Grey? I'm Ellen Gentle. Rose said you wanted to speak to me. Something about poor Mrs. di Ripoli?"

"That's right," Constance said.

"I can't stay for long," Ellen said. "Everything depends on me tonight, and I have to be perfect. For Caterina's sake," she added quickly.

"It must be very difficult," Constance said, "especially while grieving at the same time."

"Of course," Ellen said, though there was no real grief in her expression.

"We understand you learned much from Mrs. di Ripoli," Solomon said.

"I would have been foolish not to. I suppose everyone has told you I'm not yet ready for this role. They're right, of course. I will look and sound like the understudy. But I will have done it. And creditably."

"Were you friends?" Constance asked. "You and Caterina?"

"No. Not that she was ever unkind, and nor was I. She just…moved in a different world from me. She was the prima donna, I very much the understudy who was never supposed to be needed. But I think she liked that I *did* study. And it's as well, as things have turned out."

"I understand she sang well on Wednesday evening," Solomon said.

"She was brilliant," Ellen said. "She lit up the stage, the whole auditorium. She *was* Gilda, and she sang perfectly. It was probably her best performance, and I have watched them all."

"Did you congratulate her afterward?"

"Of course, though I doubt she noticed. She knew what she'd done."

"Did she celebrate with the rest of the cast?" Constance asked.

"Oh, no. She thanked us as usual and rushed off home as soon as she had changed."

"Was that usual?" Solomon asked.

"Yes, when her husband didn't come. She lingered more

when he was with her."

"You *saw* her leave on Wednesday evening?"

"Yes, I was at the stage door when she stepped into her carriage."

"Did she have flowers with her? Or a bag?"

"No, not that I saw. Why?"

"She must have had many admirers," Constance said without answering. "All trying to speak to her as she left, thrusting gifts into her hands…"

"She'd learned to avoid all that. With grace, too. She carried the double role very well."

"Double role?" Solomon repeated, although he knew perfectly well what she meant. He was trying to make her betray any intense jealousy she might feel, the kind that would surely be necessary if she had harmed Caterina.

"Prima donna and respectable wife."

"She had everything," Constance said, echoing Rose's earlier words.

But Ellen only nodded. "She seemed to." She shivered. "She was not so much older than me. How is her husband?"

Solomon thought more of her after that. Rose had not asked after Montague.

"As you would expect. Shocked, unable to quite grasp his loss."

Ellen nodded. "The funeral is tomorrow."

Montague had not mentioned that. The speed of the burial startled Solomon, though he said only, "Will you go?"

"We shall all go to the memorial service. And to the house afterward, since we are invited. To show our respect."

"Well, we might see you there," Constance said, rising to her feet. "Thank you for talking to us."

Ellen's brow twitched, as though she still wasn't sure exactly why she had been summoned, but she nodded politely before she turned to go.

"Oh, Miss Gentle?" Solomon said as she reached for the door.

"Where was it she lived?"

"Somewhere off Fleet Street, isn't it?" She glanced over her shoulder, frowning. "You would know that if you really came from her husband. Who are you?"

"You misunderstand," Constance said, picking up her leather bag. "Of course we know. The question was to see if you did. Have you ever been there?"

"No," Ellen said, her nostrils flaring. "None of us have, even Rose. I think Watson had better show you out."

"DO YOU REALLY suspect Ellen Gentle?" Constance asked as they walked back to the office.

Solomon sighed. "No. And if I did, I don't know what I'd suspect her of. No one seems to have wished Caterina ill. The doctor is convinced she died of natural causes. The roses most likely came from the square, probably picked by Caterina herself, during the night when she couldn't sleep for all the euphoria of her brilliant performance. The idea of murder seems to be all in Kellar's imagination."

"Why?" Constance asked.

"I have no idea. I vote he is our first port of call tomorrow morning."

"We could go tonight," Constance said.

He caught her gaze. "Or we could stay at home."

The wicked gleam he loved lit up her eyes. "We could. After office hours."

"Of course." He adjusted her hand on his arm, drawing her closer and caressing the skin of her wrist beneath her glove. "How far away is that?"

"Oh, an hour or two."

Solomon, responsible and conscientious man though he was, began to seriously contemplate how to remove Janey and Hat from the office early. Reluctantly, he decided the only excuses he could come up with were too blatant to be believed. He would just torture himself with anticipation instead. Even that held a strange pleasure, because she was his.

Until he thought of Digby Montague, sitting alone in his house in his bewildered grief, his joy taken from him in one unforeseen instant.

Every moment in this life had to be lived to the full, with no opportunity lost. Perhaps that was what had driven Caterina to follow her every whim.

CHAPTER SEVEN

CONSTANCE AND SOLOMON had just sat down to dine when the front doorbell rang.

Constance liked welcoming visitors to her new home, but in this case, she was conscious of faint annoyance. She couldn't work out quite what irritated her, though it seemed to be a messy tangle of different things: last night's argument and its wildly delicious aftermath, Solomon's eyes, and Caterina's death. She did not wish to be disturbed.

Neither did Solomon, from his expression, so they carried on eating their soup, which was very good. Constance knew that Bibby—recently taken on from the establishment as cook's assistant—had made it herself and was waiting anxiously for their verdict.

Lottie the parlor maid scratched at the dining room door. "Sorry, ma'am, sir, but a Mr. Kellar has called. Shall I deny him or ask him to wait?"

Constance met Solomon's gaze. He gave the faintest of shrugs, but it was enough. Get the matter over with now and the rest of the evening was theirs.

"Show him in here, if you please, and set another place."

Kellar entered with all his usual urbanity. "Oh, forgive me! The girl did not tell me you were dining."

"Join us," Constance said, indicating the chair on her other side. "We have just begun, and there is plenty of soup."

Kellar let himself be persuaded, while Lottie set the place

before fleeing to warn the kitchen in time for the second course, and Solomon poured another glass of wine.

"The soup is delicious," Kellar said. "My compliments to your cook."

"I shall tell her," Constance said, happier with him already. There had always been something beguiling about Kellar.

He made pleasant small talk until the soup course was removed and the duck brought in. Only when the servants had left again did he say why he had come.

"I only meant to call in for a moment," he said, "to ask how your investigation progresses."

Solomon picked up his knife and fork. "We have found no evidence of any cause of death other than the doctor's opinion, nothing to justify an autopsy. Nor have we met anyone who wished her ill."

Kellar took a sip of wine and paused, twisting the stem of the glass between his long, shapely fingers. "You don't believe me about Montague."

"We're not even sure *you* believe it," Constance said wryly. "Beyond disliking the man, you have no real reason, and you are not a fool."

Kellar inclined his head in sardonic appreciation and set down the glass. "You may be right. Although do you not find the haste of the funeral somewhat indecent? We have run out of time for any autopsy now."

"I doubt it matters," Constance said. "Montague seems to be just filling his days in a slightly desperate manner. You gave us no indication that Caterina was afraid of him."

"I don't believe she was," Kellar replied.

"Then you never heard of them quarreling?"

"No…"

"Did you see any sign that he ever beat her?"

"Good God, no! I would have intervened long before this if I had ever imagined such a thing. What makes you ask that?"

"One person's hearsay," Constance said vaguely.

Kellar drummed on the table with the fingers of his left hand. "What about the lover?" he asked abruptly, proving his interest was more than merely dislike of Montague.

"Darrow? He too seems to have been devoted. Caterina, however, may have been at least considering breaking off the relationship, which might have maddened him, theoretically. But there is no evidence he left his own home, let alone entered hers. There is no evidence of any wrongdoing at all. Even the roses seem to have come from the square. The simplest explanation is that she picked them herself during the night."

"In her nightgown?" Kellar said dubiously. "I'm not sure I believe that."

Constance shrugged. "Again, there is no evidence one way or another, but everyone we have spoken to said she was excited by her success that evening—"

"With cause," Kellar agreed. "She was splendid."

"Isn't it possible that this excitement prevented her from sleeping? And I'm sure she was quite capable of dressing and undressing herself."

Kellar frowned. "Isn't it more likely that Montague picked them and took them to her?"

"Before murdering her?" Solomon asked. "How? Anyway, he denies giving the flowers to her, though he admitted he had a key for his wife's door. He was perfectly open."

Kellar continued to eat with evident enjoyment, as though they were conversing about everyday matters that did not trouble him. And yet he wouldn't have begun this if he were not deeply concerned.

"What about the pillows?" he asked at last.

Constance had not forgotten about the pillows, but they seemed the sort of oddity that would never have an explanation. "Who knows? The propped-up pillows could have fallen during the night and she pulled one under her head while still asleep."

"Placing the other neatly beside her, also in her sleep?" Kellar said blandly. "Pillows can be used to kill, you know."

Constance shivered. "We do know. We have investigated such a case. I looked, as it happens, and there was no sign of tearing on any of the pillowcases, or of damage to her fingernails, which were quite elegantly long."

"If she was asleep, she might not have struggled," Kellar pointed out.

"If she was asleep," Solomon retorted, "how did the killer get in? If it was Montague, he must know her preferred pillow arrangement. Why would he make such a mistake?"

"People do, in the heat of the moment."

"I thought he was too dull to have heated moments?" Constance argued.

Kellar laughed and laid down his knife and fork.

"I think," Solomon said, "it is time you told us the true reason for your suspicions—which, frankly, aren't borne out by any evidence whatsoever. The truth, Kellar, if you please."

The man's eyes widened only slightly, but Constance did not believe in his surprise. The mystery of the man had beguiled her in Venice. She had even wondered at one point if he was her father. But for an instant, she saw him clearly, an aging man with a lifetime of deviousness behind him, whatever his role for the government he served. His friendship, his help, were always conditional, and she doubted she would ever know what those conditions were.

In that moment, she did not like him at all.

"You are manipulating us," she said. "Why?"

She could not even trust her sudden sense of his vulnerability because, frustratingly, he was not looking at her. But at the doorway—where her mother stood.

Oh, for the love of... Trust Juliet to interrupt at this precise moment! Now what were they meant to do?

But Juliet appeared to be up to the challenge. Dressed in her usual, flowing, tentlike garments of many colors, she threw up her hands in horror.

"Bless me, dearies, I never knew you had company," she

exclaimed. She had never called Constance *dearie* in her life. "Silly girl just told me to go in. I'll see meself out again and come back tomorrow."

And with that, she did indeed whisk herself out of the door, closing it behind her as softly as she had opened it.

Constance closed her mouth and, with an effort, refused to be distracted. In fact, distracting *him* from the brief interruption was now imperative.

"Well?" she demanded of Kellar, who was looking as bland as ever.

"Well, *what*, my dear Mrs. Grey?" he asked. "I asked you to do something for me and you agreed. Do you accuse all your clients of manipulation?"

Constance thought of Angela Lambert and her ghost, of Barnabas Lloyd and his entire family, and said, "Only those who are guilty of it. If you really want the truth, if you really want us to pursue Caterina's death any further, you have to tell us exactly why you are suspicious, and what she was to you."

He curled steady fingers around his wine glass without lifting it. There was nothing about him that spoke of unease, let alone lies.

"I don't know why I'm suspicious," he said seriously. "I just feel it in my bones, as I told you at the outset. As for what she was to me, I told you that, too. I knew her parents and helped her escape from trouble in Rome to England. I am fond of her, and I feel responsible for her."

"Were you her lover?" Constance asked directly.

His face broke into smiles. "Of course not. She could be my daughter."

"Is she?" Solomon asked.

Kellar still looked amused. "No. Though her mother and I were closer than you might approve of, I did not even meet her until Caterina was thirteen years old."

"But you had an affair with her mother?"

Kellar lifted his shoulders. "What can I say? I am an imperfect man."

"Stop it," Solomon said sharply.

For the first time, Kellar betrayed the faintest hint of surprise. One finger shifted very slightly on his wine glass. Then he released it and leaned back in his chair.

"I don't know what it is you suspect me of," he said, "but it is clearly getting in the way of the investigation. In the course of my diplomatic career, I have done many things for queen and country that I cannot speak of. Some would, indeed, be reprehensible were they not for that greater good."

As if mechanically, he reached again for his wine glass and this time took a drink. Because he needed it? Or was he just giving himself time to think what to say?

Kellar lowered the glass from his lips and gazed into it. "Traveling players, singers—entertainers of all kinds make excellent couriers of information and private messages. As things grew more turbulent in 1847, Caterina's father tried to step away from our arrangement. I…used his wife's affection for me to maintain their role in my communications. Early in 1848, they were both killed by Roman government forces. I don't know whether or not it was their connection to me that led to their deaths, but I felt responsible for Caterina in more ways than one. That was why I took her out of Italy and brought her here to be safe."

"And you still feel responsible," Solomon said. He hadn't taken his eyes off the other man's face.

Kellar nodded. "Perhaps you are right to question my judgment, even my pride. After all, I brought Caterina here to be safe. Her parents' killers were never brought to my idea of justice. I probably drink wine with them nowadays." He looked up at last, catching Solomon's steady gaze. "But my instinct stands. Something is wrong about Caterina's death."

"Did you love her mother?" Constance blurted. She wasn't even sure why it was important, though it probably had something to do with Juliet.

Kellar's gaze fell again. He set down the glass.

"No," he said. "But I was fond of her."

"Do you believe him?" Constance said abruptly.

They were in their bedroom, preparing for bed in companionable if thoughtful silence.

Solomon dropped his cuff links on the dressing table and pulled his shirt over his head. "I believe there is truth in amongst all the words. I don't think he ever lies outright."

"But he is deceiving us?"

Solomon sat on the bed to remove the rest of his clothes. "He wants us to continue the investigation. He admits to being ruthless in pursuit of his goals. If there is deceit, I can't see what it is, or what his purpose might be."

He rose, naked, and prowled to the washstand. His skin glowed like dark gold in the candlelight. Her muscles tightened in inevitable desire. But he was her husband and there was time for everything.

Constance, who had been brushing her hair long enough to make it stand out from her head like a fuzzy golden halo, threw down the brush and paced discontentedly to the bed. She climbed in and admired the glistening droplets of water on Solomon's long, lean body. He dragged the towel across his broad shoulders, down the rippling muscles of his arms and chest to his flat stomach and narrow hips...

She swallowed and, with an effort, rediscovered her thread. "He wants to keep looking after her because he still carries guilt over her parents. All he can do now is bring whoever is responsible for her death to justice. He doesn't want to accept that no one is responsible, because then he is useless. He is a very complicated, convoluted man."

Solomon threw down the towel and paced toward her, large and predatory. God, he was beautiful. And she adored the glittering heat in his eyes, as if he had hungered for her for days. And yet last night...

Desire flooded her. *Oh yes, last night...* And now there was *this* night.

He sat on the edge of the bed, gazing at her. "We have been trying to prove him wrong. What if he's right?"

"I'm not sure we'd ever prove it."

"And what," Solomon said slowly, "if *he* is guilty of the murder?"

Lust vanished along with her breath. "Then...we would never prove that either." And since Kellar was the one who had instigated the investigation, he would be the only one who was never suspected of the crime. "Oh, Solomon..." She seized him by the shoulders for comfort. "And he saw Juliet! Do you think he recognized her?"

"She certainly did her best to put him off the scent. I have never heard her sound quite so Cockney."

In spite of her sudden fear, a breath of laughter caught her by surprise. "And he showed no sign of recognizing her, did he?"

"No." Solomon appeared to have lost interest in the matter. He was idly stroking her nape, bending his head toward hers.

Even before his mouth touched hers, desire rushed back, making her gasp as she drew him down with her. He covered her whole body in one long, sensual caress. Other people's old relationships ceased to matter. There was only the truth of their own, constant, urgent, and unbearably sweet.

JULIET SILVER OPENED her shop not long after seven o'clock the following morning. That was not unusual. She lived right above her place of business and saw no reason to waste any opportunity. She often caught new customers that way, people on their way to work, others returning from a night shift, or gentlemen who had not quite made it to their own beds.

At the very least, she could combine thinking time with industry as she polished her treasures and rearranged displays in the never-ending quest to attract visitors to her shop.

No, it was not unusual for her to unlock the shop door so early, change the printed sign to *Open*, and wrestle the tempting display table of pretty but worthless knickknacks outside. She then decided which pieces needed to be better displayed, and which should be made to shine.

What made this Saturday morning different was that she had difficulty focusing on either thoughts or work. Not even when her old business in Seven Dials was being threatened by the most ruthless of criminals had her stomach been this tightly knotted. Juliet was rattled.

She snatched up a silver tray with its matching teapot, sugar bowl and cream jug, and carried them to the back counter. She squeezed behind and sat on the stool, laying out her cloths and her newly mixed polish. Then she set to work with feverish intent.

What the devil had prompted her to seek Constance out last night? There had been no reason for it, beyond the fact she hadn't seen her daughter for a week and felt the urge. It wasn't as if they had ever lived in each other's pockets, at least not since Connie had turned so wayward…and Juliet had turned so disastrously to the bottle. There was no point in dwelling on which had come first. But it was ridiculously important to Juliet that the new rapprochement between them remained, even grew.

Solomon Grey—*beautiful man*—had been good for Connie in many ways, softening those prickly edges, protecting her. *Most* of all, protecting her. In all conscience, Juliet could step back now, go her own way without worrying about her daughter. Except that it was Solomon who had made the shop possible, and she didn't really want to be anywhere else. And except that she seemed to *like* keeping her eye on Constance, now that she no longer had to.

Only what in God's name was the girl doing on such intimate terms with Sebastian Kellar?

More to the point, what was he doing here in London?

She had known him at once. The shock had gone through her like a lightning bolt, and she had fled with all speed. Thank God she had retained enough sense to exaggerate both her movement and her speech.

She moved the cloth further to the right of the shining tray and gazed at the reflection of her own plump, saggy face and her impossibly blonde locks. No, there was nothing there to remind him of the woman, the girl, she had once been.

She shied away from that girl. It was one of the rules she lived by—forgetting the past and concentrating on the present. Anything else led to debilitating self-pity... And yet Sebastian Kellar's handsome, clean-shaven, young face kept intruding, painting itself over the older, bearded countenance of the distinguished man dining at Connie's table. Old tenderness, forgotten desires, foolish hopes, and bad decisions... Lots and lots of bad decisions. Followed by worse ones.

She rubbed harder at the tray, sweeping around its ornate edges and using her nails to push the cloth into each tiny crevice.

Nowadays, her decisions were better. She had trusted Solomon because Connie did, and they were both right. Hard work had replaced gin in her life. Pride in her business and pride in her daughter had given her hope, and a certain contentment she would guard jealously, especially from Sebastian bloody Kellar.

In Venice, he had seen Juliet's young face in Constance. She would not dwell on that either. That past could not impact this present, but she had to consider the future too. Should she warn Constance about him? Perhaps Solomon would be more susceptible to her advice.

"You are manipulating us," Constance had been saying when Juliet blundered into the dining room. *"Why?"*

Why indeed? Was he somehow involved in whatever mystery Constance and Solomon were investigating? Connie was naturally suspicious—Juliet had taught her to be so—and had clearly seen that much about him, but she could not know the rest.

Having polished the tray to within an inch of its shining life, Juliet turned her attentions to the teapot.

She would find Connie again later, either at the Silver and Gray office, or at home in the evening. Either way, the shock of seeing Kellar would not happen again. Forewarned was fore-armed. In the meantime, she had work to do, customers to serve, for the bell over the door had rung and a woman and her child had come in talking about gifts for someone's birthday.

Juliet smiled and let them browse alone for a little, while she attended to her polishing. The delight of her shop was the unexpected, and she always waited to see what attracted individual customers before offering suggestions and choices.

Gerry, her longtime general factotum, would be in soon to help, though not Marissa, the girl she had taken from Connie's establishment. Marissa didn't work Saturdays. She went home to her family in the country each week, now that she had a respectable job and a decent room she shared with another shop girl.

A shadow fell over Juliet. She hadn't been keeping track of the woman with the child.

"Juliet," said a voice that jolted through her.

The teapot landed too hard on the tray and she whisked her suddenly nerveless hands into her lap, where they gripped each other.

Smugness always led to disaster.

She forced a smile to her lips and raised her eyes to his. She wanted to die of humiliation.

"Sebastian," she said, just as though she had seen him a couple of weeks ago. She even sounded pleased. "How are you?"

There was a pause. The years had added gray to his hair, and more lines to his face, especially on his forehead and at the corners of his eyes and mouth. But the overall effect was one of distinction rather than deterioration. His skin was browner, bronzed by warmer sun than ever shone over England. And his blue eyes still gleamed with intelligence and humor.

Yes, three decades had been kind to Sebastian Kellar. They had all but destroyed Juliet. It struck her suddenly that this was the closing of the circle for her, and perhaps for him. He had remembered her, had recognized her even at Connie's house. But now, this close, he would no longer want to. Relief flooded her. There was nothing she had to do or say, just be herself. It didn't matter.

"How am I?" he repeated. "Overwhelmed, I think. It suits you, this setting."

Whatever she had expected, it was not that. In desperation, she resorted to her professional manner. "Are you looking for something in particular?"

A smile flickered across his face. It might have been understanding. Or mockery. "Actually, I was looking for you."

How the devil had he found her? Surely Connie had not blabbed? She *would* not, not without asking, and she never had. But then, she had never told Juliet that Kellar was in London…

"No, I didn't ask your daughter," Kellar said, as though he'd read her thoughts. Damn him, he had always been too good at that, too. "She is too protective to have told me. She is a very beautiful and interesting woman."

"She is. Solomon is devoted to her."

"And she to him. It is an odd arrangement, but a very charming one."

Juliet raised one supercilious, painted brow. "What do you mean by that?"

"Oh, come, Juliet," he said gently. "One doesn't have to be in London long, or ask many questions, to discover who Constance Silver is."

Then he knew, and there really was no more to hide. So she laughed. "You'd need to have asked in some shockingly low places to discover me."

"I have been in London some weeks."

During which time he had found Constance and uncovered

her double, if not triple, life and tracked Juliet to her place of calm and safety. A chill of sudden fear passed over her.

She slid off the stool. "Excuse me. I have customers…"

"Juliet."

He didn't touch her, force her in the slightest, but she paused, aware of nothing but him and the tension cramping all her muscles.

"It is good to see you again," he said.

And at that, finally, she could turn and laugh in his face. "No, it isn't, Sebastian. Goodbye."

CHAPTER EIGHT

Constance woke in the morning with the urge to buy Solomon a gift.

It wasn't his birthday, and they had never been in the habit of giving extravagant presents to each other, just little, personal things, and the balance was certainly in Constance's favor.

She needed to speak to her mother today, and the last time she had been in the shop, she had seen a silver and lapis lazuli signet ring that she'd thought Solomon would like. Why had she not bought it for him at the time? Because he was not a showy kind of man, and she hadn't been sure he would wear it. But he would value it as her gift. And the deep blue would be stunning on his elegant hand…

She sat up quite suddenly.

"Solomon? What if Caterina *did* pick the flowers that night, but not for herself? Could she not have meant to give them to her husband?"

Solomon opened his eyes. "What, a guilt offering because of her affair with Darrow?"

"Maybe. Husbands do it often enough. But it could just have been part of her euphoria that night that she wanted to give him something? Perhaps she dismissed Darrow because her true love was her husband, and she wanted to show that. Either way, it makes sense. She wasn't hiding the roses. They need not be any kind of riddle. Just a surprise good-morning present."

Solomon rubbed his eyes and levered himself up beside her.

"Twelve red roses?" he said doubtfully. "Exactly the same gift as Darrow had given her two days before?"

Put like that, it didn't sound quite such a good idea. "They were different flowers."

"But the square is not their property. Stolen flowers hardly make a meaningful gift."

"Do you think she would regard such a thing? I can see her doing it, a wild, impulsive gesture of love."

Solomon put his arm around her shoulders. "You really have grown terribly romantic since you married me. Is this your final effort to be rid of the case?"

She frowned. "Actually, no. I think it's the beginning of a new effort. Kellar is right about the pillows. And I think we need to find out if anyone living around the square saw who picked the roses that night. Also, we need to investigate all our chief suspects more thoroughly, especially whoever picked the roses."

"And who are our chief suspects?" Solomon spread his fingers out from her shoulder and counted them off as he spoke. "Montague, because it would have been easiest for him— although the maid, Mary Webb, is also a possibility there; I just can't see a motive. Darrow, because he was dismissed, or because she threatened his career in some way—only, how did he get into the house? We've never examined the back of the building to see how easy it would be to climb up to Caterina's room. We've been too busy trying to prove she *wasn't* killed. But if Darrow could get in that way, so could other people."

"Like Ellen Gentle the understudy," Constance said, "although I doubt it." She took a deep breath, looking up at him. "And Kellar."

Solomon nodded. "And Kellar. We need to know more about everyone. And I think we should test the medicine, to make sure it just hasn't been replaced with water."

"How on earth do we do that without involving the police?"

"I believe I have a chemist working for me."

"Of course you do," she murmured. "The harder part will be

extracting the medicine, if it hasn't already been disposed of. Fortunately, the funeral is today, so we have an excuse to be at the house. Preferably while everyone else is out of it."

WHILE SOLOMON WENT to his office at St. Catherine's Dock to set off inquiries into Digby Montague, Constance called at her mother's shop.

It was open early, as usual. Gerry was wrapping an expensive-looking parcel for a gentleman at the counter. Juliet was in the middle of the shop looking colorful and exotic as she extracted something from a display case to show to a young couple in worn, barely respectable clothing. Her gaze darted at once to Constance as soon as she entered.

Was that relief in her mother's eyes? Unease prickled through Constance. Was Juliet in trouble again? Had her past caught up with her somehow? Or was she worried because she had seen Kellar last night?

The slight jerk of her head directed Constance to the back of the shop. On her way, she noticed the lapis lazuli ring still in its cabinet, its old, carved silver setting contrasting with the dazzling blue of the center.

Gerry spared her his usual boyish grin and a nod from the counter while he accepted payment from his customer. The parcel was indeed expensive.

Constance opened the door to the back room, sat down at the table that was no longer so rickety since Lenny Knox had repaired it, and helped herself to a butter biscuit from the plate in the middle.

Five minutes later, Juliet bustled in and sat down opposite. "I'd send Gerry for tea, only he's busy. It's unbearable in here if you light the stove in summer. I'm glad you called in—I want to speak to you about your visitor."

Constance blinked. "That's fortunate. I want to speak to you about him, too." And she had doubted her mother would co-operate, considering how close-mouthed she'd been when first told of their meeting in Venice.

"He knows who and what you are," Juliet said abruptly. "He made it a point to find out. I don't know why. But you need to be careful. He's not quite the harmless, amiable gentleman he appears. He can be dangerous, Connie."

"In what way?" Constance asked.

"*All* ways."

Constance waited, but that seemed to be all her mother had to say on the matter. She leaned forward. "Ma, you need to be more specific than that. He's up to something and we need to know what."

"What you need is to keep out of his business," Juliet retorted.

"Why? What do you know about him?"

"Nothing for thirty years, but people don't change that much."

"Then what happened when he was young? He said he wanted to marry you."

Juliet shrugged, though her mask of carelessness did not quite work. "He *said* he did. He said a lot of things. He appears to *be* a lot of things. A perfect gentleman in every way, witty, knowledgeable, observant, remembers everything he ever hears—a bit like you. But he ain't your father, so never think it."

Constance, who had thought it for a heady few minutes in Venice, said impatiently, "I don't. I'm too young. What did he do to you?"

Juliet's painted eyebrows flew up. "To me? Nothing. But I once saw this *gentle*man beat up two others quite brutally, and haul one off in a waiting carriage."

"To the police?"

"There was no police force in those days, but no, not to the law at all. A man was found dead that night, two streets away."

"You can't know it was the same man," Constance argued.

"He sounded it by the description in the newspaper. A foreigner, he was."

"Did you ask Kellar about it?"

"He brushed it off, claimed he'd been attacked, which might be true, but he was too damned efficient about the business for a gentleman."

"Is that why you refused to marry him?"

Juliet actually blushed, a rare enough sight to knock Constance completely off balance. "No. I was young and stupid enough to find it exciting. He was, you know. A bit like your Solomon in his own way, understated, if you grasp my meaning? I actually liked the element of danger… I was too sheltered in those days to understand what it meant."

"So why didn't you marry him?"

Juliet waved that aside.

"I need to know, Ma," Constance said. "If it wasn't violence, what was it? Did he lie? Manipulate? Steal? Entertain other women?"

"I did see him with another woman once. He didn't introduce us, but I wasn't jealous by nature. No, it was my own pride. He assumed I would go to America with him, when the Foreign Office posted him there. I was only a penniless companion, but he'd no right to assume. I let him go alone. Actually, I didn't think he would. But he did."

Constance hesitated. Her mother had never been so open, never told her anything about her past before. "He said he wrote to you and you never answered."

Juliet's gaze flickered. In among the surprise, there might have been regret. "Never got any letters," she said with studied carelessness. "I'd been flung out of the house by then for immoral behavior."

"With him?" *Of course it was.*

Constance had grown up believing her mother had been born into the same world as she, a world of squalid poverty, prostitution, and survival by any means, most of them criminal. But Juliet had been well enough born to be companion to a lady, and her fall was similar to several other women whom Constance had helped over the years. Elizabeth Maule for one, and she called Lizzie her friend. Juliet, she had despised and loved in equal measure.

"The first of many," said her mother.

"Why did you not come with me to the establishment?" Constance blurted.

To her surprise, Juliet actually answered. "Because I wanted you out of that trade, and because I had my own business."

"And pride. Again."

"Laughable, ain't it?" Juliet's Cockney accent was more pronounced again.

Constance shook her head. "No."

Juliet's gaze fell. Constance's hostility and rudeness never upset her mother. But apparently her kindness did.

"You called him manipulative last night," Juliet said, brisk again. "Why? What's he trying to get you to do?"

"Investigate the death of an opera singer whom he rescued from the revolutions in Italy."

"And you're doing it? Walk away, Constance."

"I don't think we can. Look, we don't entirely trust him. Even in Venice we suspected he was more than a diplomat. I think he does the dirty work our government cannot be seen to be involved in. This business with Caterina di Ripoli could be some kind of elaborate plan to get us to prove he wasn't involved in the death when he was. But we have one advantage."

"What?" Juliet demanded.

"He doesn't know we are investigating him too."

FROM HER MOTHER'S shop, the lapis lazuli ring in her bag,

Constance walked briskly on to the Silver and Grey office, where she summoned Janey to her room.

"I want you to go to Eagle Square," Constance said, "just behind Fleet Street. Speak to the servants and anyone else you can find who lives there. We want to know of any odd movements, comings or goings at number eight Eagle Square, on Wednesday evening and very early Thursday morning. Also, a description of anyone seen cutting stems of red roses in the square garden."

Janey took such instructions in her stride these days. "Anything else?"

"Yes. Find out what the neighbors say about the residents of number eight—a Mr. and Mrs. Digby Montague. Mrs. Montague was an Italian, who died on Wednesday night, also known as Caterina di Ripoli, the opera singer."

Janey's eyes widened, as though she had heard of her, but all she said was, "I'll start now, will I?"

"Yes. The funeral service begins at eleven, with, I believe, baked meats afterward at the house. It might be a good time to find servants unsupervised."

"I suppose you and himself will be at number eight?" Janey said.

"I suppose we will."

Constance, already dressed in funereal black, occupied herself with the post on her desk, and signed a few of Janey's letters until Solomon arrived in the carriage.

"Well?" she asked, striding along the hall to meet him. "What did you learn?"

"That Montague is putting a brave face on things but is living on a knife's edge. One more run of bad luck, and the general opinion is that he'll go under. I have people verifying the details, but it's most likely true. I have another associate to speak to, but he was out of town this morning. What did you learn?"

Constance preceded him into his office. "Juliet doesn't trust Kellar. It seems he has always done the Foreign Office's dirty work and is good at it. He is as manipulative and underhanded as we imagined in Venice and, according to my mother, is not above extreme violence. She suspects him of killing a man even before they parted."

"Parted?" Solomon said. "Then he really did have an understanding with her?"

"I don't think they understood each other at all, but certainly there was an attraction and a proposal."

Solomon's eyes were as perceptive as ever. "What else?"

"She's disturbed by his presence. He found her quite deliberately, and he knows all about me. And I think she's…frightened."

"Of Kellar?" Solomon said sharply.

"I'm not sure," Constance said. She knew she was being evasive, but the habit of keeping her mother's secrets was hard to break, even with him. "She seemed more worried about me."

Solomon threw his hat on the desk. "I wish I knew someone important in the Foreign Office."

"I do," Constance said. "And I think we should make use of him. But first, to Eagle Square."

THEY TIMED THEIR visit well. Caterina's funeral service should have been well underway, and they were not likely to be disturbed by Montague or the other mourners. At the same time, it was almost feasible for the servants left behind to believe they had come straight from the church.

"Mr. Montague should not be long," Constance said breezily as soon as a rather harassed-looking Nancy let them in.

As she had hoped, the servants were busy laying out the funeral meats, and were thoroughly glad to leave Constance and Solomon to their own devices. They gathered that Collins the butler had gone to the funeral, representing the staff, which meant even the boot boy was pressed into service helping Cook and carrying things.

Having shown them to the spotlessly clean drawing room, Nancy fled again.

Constance did not bother sitting down. Solomon opened the drawing room door a crack and then walked quietly out. Constance closed it behind her and followed him upstairs to Caterina's room.

It felt empty in a way it hadn't before, as though Caterina's spirit had finally left through the open window. Or because the roses had finally gone too.

The trunk Constance had last seen in Caterina's dressing room at Covent Garden stood by the bed.

Solomon went straight to the window, lifted it higher, and peered out. A rush of cooling air whisked around the room. Constance walked to the cupboard where Caterina's medicine had been kept, praying it was still there.

It was. She took it all, every measured powder wrapped in paper, sweeping them into her small black bag. She placed two handkerchiefs and her purse and comb over the top, just in case the bag opened accidentally, and then closed the cupboard again.

There was nowhere in the room they had not looked on the first occasion they were here, except beneath the mattress. Solomon came to help her lift it.

"Well?" Constance asked. "Is the wall climbable?"

"It might be, though if the window were closed, Caterina would have had to let him in. We need to look more closely from below."

Constance nodded, sweeping her hand beneath the mattress and finding nothing. No love letters or threatening notes or empty papers that had once contained powdered digitalis.

"Letters," she murmured, as Solomon lowered the mattress again. "There were flakes of charred paper in the grate when we were first here..." They were gone, now, the hearth thoroughly cleaned. "Do you think Caterina burned Darrow's letters after she ended their relationship?"

"Or he did after he'd killed her?"

"One of them must have destroyed them. After all, how do you conduct a secret liaison without communicating? No one that we can find carried messages between them. How did they know where and when to meet? Was it written in stone? Every Monday at three o'clock, at this friend's house?"

"Perhaps they communicated only through the friend," Solomon suggested. "Or perhaps Kellar is completely deluded and the poor woman simply died naturally."

Or he was having them pursue shadows for no reason they could fathom.

They left Caterina's room and, on impulse, Constance caught Solomon's arm and tugged him further along the passage to the room next door. She pressed the latch and they went in.

This was obviously Montague's room, left neat and tidy. Something glinted on the bedside table. Caterina's wedding ring. The sight was indescribably sad. She turned away. Solomon pulled open a few drawers.

"If he kept private letters from his wife, they're not here," he murmured. "But…" He stood aside to allow her a glimpse of the open middle drawer above the dressing table. What looked like a complete set of house keys lay there on a large ring. Beside it, unlinked to anything, was a solitary key.

"Caterina's door key," Constance said. She had a sudden vision of the man in his shining white nightgown, carrying the key and a single candle, drifting like a pale ghost through the darkness from this room to his wife's, silently unlocking the door, setting down the candle, sitting beside her on the edge of the bed while he reached for one of the propped-up pillows and held it over her face, pressing harder as she began to struggle in blind terror…

She shuddered, blinking the horrific vision away. What would it take for a husband to *do* that to his wife?

She went to the window that looked out onto the square. "He could have seen whoever picked the roses, if he didn't do it himself. But he wouldn't have seen anyone climbing up to Caterina's window. Or heard, probably."

"Why would he pick roses and murder his wife?" Solomon asked.

"He could have left the roses for her before she was murdered. *If* she was murdered. This is a *stupid* case, Sol."

He took her hand and led her out of the room. As they approached the staircase, the voices of the servants below drifted upward, an older woman's voice, presumably the cook's, issuing orders and the maids answering.

Constance and Solomon slipped out of the front door apparently unnoticed. Solomon pulled it almost shut behind him, and they hurried round the side path to the back garden.

It was walled and enclosed in almost complete privacy. An elm tree and an apple tree blocked the view from the houses on either side, and a high wall at the end meant she couldn't see the mews lane and its lower buildings beyond. And behind that seemed to be a faceless, non-residential building, perhaps a warehouse or offices.

As they approached the house and the first ground-floor window, a luxuriantly spread table was visible, a white-capped maid rearranging dishes to make room for others. Solomon stepped back out of range of any casual glance from within, tugging Constance with him. One of Caterina's windows was immediately above.

The old elm tree grew a few feet from this end of the house, its knobbly trunk sticking out toward the building before bending back toward the garden wall and the house next door. The face of the Montagues' house was uneven. Constance reckoned she could climb up to Caterina's window via the tree easily enough, though perhaps not in a billowing silk-and-lace gown and crinoline.

Solomon, with no such impediment, jumped, catching one of the overhanging branches, and hauled himself up to stand on the knotted bend of the tree. From there, he climbed to the next branch and inched his way over to the wall of the house, just above the dining room window. He found the first foothold easily and reached up to grasp the sill of Caterina's window. A second later, he pried up the sash, opening it slowly as wide as it would go. Then he climbed on to the sill to look inside, gauging, presumably, how easy it would have been to enter the room quietly. He then closed the sash again to where it had been set before and quickly retraced his steps to descend.

He wasn't even out of breath as he brushed his hands together to dislodge dirt. Constance brushed down his coat and one knee with her gloves. No words being necessary, they then walked back to the front of the house, where it was simple to push the door open and close it again behind them.

Collins the butler stepped out from the dining room and paused, gazing toward them with one eyebrow raised.

CHAPTER NINE

CLEARLY, COLLINS HAD dashed back from the funeral to attend to his duties at the house. And he did not look pleased to see them.

"A little fresh air," Constance said breezily. "Tell me, Collins, is there a rule regarding the flowers in the square? Are residents allowed to pick them?"

The butler's nostrils flared. "No, madam. The residents have an agreement not to, so that we may all enjoy the gardens equally."

"And do all the residents keep to that agreement?" Solomon asked.

"*We* do, sir," Collins said. "I can't speak for any other household." He inclined his head and retreated back toward the kitchen, glancing at his pocket watch as he went.

Constance and Solomon returned to the drawing room, from where, a moment later, they heard footsteps in the passage and the opening of the front door. Montague had returned.

Perhaps he needed a few moments alone, for when the drawing room door opened, it was to reveal only a middle-aged couple Solomon had never met before.

The woman looked surprised but recovered quickly, advancing with her hand held out and her expression at once solemn and gracious. "Forgive me, we meant to be here to welcome Digby's guests. I'm his sister, Mrs. Potter. This is my husband. Digby has asked us to act as his hosts for the day, in case he is not quite up to the challenge."

Solomon introduced himself and Constance, and they all shook hands.

"How is Mr. Montague?" Constance asked.

"Cast very low," Mrs. Potter replied briskly. "Quite under-standably."

Solomon had the impression she didn't find it understandable at all. Her face, like her mourning dress, was somewhat severe, her lips thin by temperament as much as nature's gift. Her eyes, while shaped like her brother's, lacked his friendliness. A woman of hard practicality, perhaps.

"Such a beautiful and talented lady," Mr. Potter contributed. Perhaps he was the softer side of the couple, or just had the imagination to hide his lack of sympathy.

Their conventional, almost mundane words in the circum-stances sounded peculiarly rehearsed. Neither was overwhelmed by their sister-in-law's death. They had not, Solomon guessed, approved of her in the first place.

But then, much like Solomon, Montague had married some-one regarded by most as inappropriate. A woman who performed on the stage would never be good enough for stifling middle-class respectability. In the eyes of the world, Caterina's profession put her almost in the same category as Constance. Montague had defied convention and the disapproval of his family to marry Caterina. And she had not even had the grace to give up the stage. That said a great deal about Montague's strength of feeling for his wife.

"We advised him to wait longer before burying her," Mrs. Potter added, addressing what some, including Kellar, might have regarded as unseemly haste. "After all, she has friends scattered all over the country—and abroad, of course—who might have wanted the chance to attend, but he wouldn't hear of it."

"Needed to be doing something," Mr. Potter pronounced. "Poor fellow."

Or he'd needed to bury her quickly before an autopsy could be or-

dered? How did a world-defying love turn to murder within three years? Because murder needed strong feeling...

"Does he have more than his work—and his family, of course—to help sustain him through these next difficult months?" Constance asked. "Good friendships? Special interests?"

"I'm sure his music will be enough," Mrs. Potter said. "Though, of course, that was how he met Caterina, so..."

"He is a musician, too?" Solomon said in surprise. He remembered the piano and the violin in the drawing room, but had assumed they were Caterina's, either for personal use, or for her teachers and accompanists.

"Oh yes," Mrs. Potter said. "Quite a distinguished one, actually, although, of course, only in an amateur sense. He used to play in an orchestra in London. And of course there was that quartet in India—very highly thought of. Ah... You will excuse me." Mrs. Potter flitted back toward the door as new arrivals could be heard in the hall.

"Did he spend long in India?" Solomon asked before her husband could hurry after her.

Mr. Potter paused again. "A few years, in his youth. Learning the tea business, don't you know. Not recently, though. Since old Montague died, he's been needed here at the head of the ship, as it were. Well, I suppose he should..."

As he made leaving motions, Constance caught his eye and smiled dazzlingly, with inevitable effect. "Mr. and Mrs. Montague's was a rare match," she said encouragingly. "Unusual."

Mr. Potter nodded at once in instant, almost slavish agreement. She could have suggested black was white at that point and he would have bent over backward to prove it for her. "Indeed, it was not quite what we had hoped for Digby, especially in his mature years. His first choice was more *appropriate.*" He smiled quickly, adding hastily, "But not to be."

"His first choice?" Constance pounced.

"Oh, don't misunderstand me," Mr. Potter begged. "This was years ago, and of course Caterina was a very fine woman in her own way."

"He was married before?" Solomon asked. Why had they not thought of this? Montague was not a young man, after all.

"Oh, no, not *married*," Mr. Potter said. "But he was engaged—oh, some ten years ago now—to a charming girl, Sophie Worthington. Of the banking family, you know."

"She changed her mind?" Constance asked with sympathy.

"No, no, she seemed very devoted. Sadly, she died, a mere few weeks before the wedding. Poor Digby has not been lucky in love. As the vulgar put it." His gaze flickered to his wife, who was glaring at him from across the room, and he gave Constance a last, wistful smile before he excused himself and went to do his duty by the other guests.

The room had filled up quickly during this conversation, with somber people dressed uniformly in black, speaking in hushed voices. Solomon remembered why he hated funerals. But, as previously agreed, he and Constance now parted ways in order to speak to as many people as possible and learn what they could.

He introduced himself to a group of people who appeared to be Montague's neighbors in the square, largely a mixture of tradespeople, some highly educated, some not so much. Several had grown up together with Montague and appeared genuinely appalled by the sudden death of his lovely young wife.

When Solomon mentioned how happy the couple had been, everyone nodded in agreement. Because it was expected of them? Or because they genuinely believed it?

Montague himself entered the room inconspicuously, clearly with his emotions well under control, and began to greet people, moving from group to group. Carl Darrow, who had entered with a theatrical group that included Geoffrey Reid, Ellen Gentle, and the dresser Rose Samuels, appeared to offer his quiet condolences along with everyone else, and Montague accepted them with dignified thanks, as he did all others. Clearly Darrow also had himself well in hand, for Solomon saw no sign of animosity in his posture. He was keeping very much in the background for once.

"Sir?" Mary Webb offered him a choice of drinks from her tray. Although this was hardly part of her job, she was obviously making herself useful, as required. Solomon took a glass of wine from the tray and stepped back from the neighbors to give himself a modicum of privacy with Mary.

"A quick question for you," he murmured. "Did your mistress go to sleep that night with her window open or closed?"

"Open a crack, as usual," Mary replied.

"As it is now?"

She didn't even ask him how he knew. She just nodded and excused herself to move on.

"Are you by any chance Mr. Grey?" asked a well-modulated female voice on his other side.

Inevitably dressed in black but with a certain theatrical flair in the dark lace of her collar and cuffs, she had the kind of stoutness he associated with opera singers, along with a strong-featured, beautiful face. She could have been any age, but Solomon guessed somewhere in the thirties. More than that, she was vaguely familiar, though he could not place her.

He inclined his head. "I am."

"I'm Marianne Locke. I sing."

He smiled. "Quite beautifully, in my opinion. I am honored to make your acquaintance. Were you a friend of Mrs. Montague?"

"I was indeed. Carl Darrow told me you have been asking questions about her. As if you think her doctor was wrong."

"It is as well to be sure," he said vaguely. "Would you agree with me?"

Her eyes flickered. "I might." She opened her plain black reticule and extracted a business card, which she handed to him. "This is hardly the time or the place, but perhaps you and your wife would call upon me?"

"Would tomorrow suit?" Solomon said at once. A quick glance at the card was enough to assure him that her house was where Caterina had met Darrow.

"After two o'clock," she said, inclining her head before she drifted away.

Interesting. She was the first person they had encountered in this case who had sought them out, so presumably she had something important to say.

Turning, he caught sight of Kellar for the first time, on his way out of the room. Constance was casually following him at a distance. Montague, still doing his duty, left one group of people and moved toward some men Solomon thought were musicians—Darrow's friend Reid was among them. But as though sensing scrutiny, the widower changed direction and approached Solomon instead.

"Thank you for coming," he said, offering his hand. Solomon took it, and it slid free almost at once. "I didn't really expect you. I assumed from our last conversation that your questions—or Kellar's—were satisfied."

"There are just a few trifling matters that niggle at us," Solomon said. "Perhaps you can help us clear them up, although this may not be the best time."

"There is no good time," Montague said bleakly. "But at least let us walk as we talk. I don't want her memory sullied."

Solomon cast him a surprised glance as they strolled to the edge of the room. "Neither do we. Do you think it's even possible?"

"With words like *murder* floating in the air, yes," Montague said in an intense murmur. "What is it you want to know?"

"The roses," Solomon said. "They seem to have come from the garden in the square."

Montague had already told him he hadn't put the roses there. He merely looked very slightly irritated, without the guilt of a man caught in a lie. "We don't take flowers from there."

"Who does?"

"No one. In theory, though, I have heard people complaining about it from time to time. To be honest, I never paid much attention. I have less trivial things to occupy me."

"You obey the rules," Solomon said. "From talking to people about her, I see your wife as a more rebellious spirit."

A smile flickered across the widower's face. "She was." The smile was already dying.

"My wife had the idea that Mrs. Montague, wakeful that night for whatever reason, slipped outside during the night and cut the roses herself in order to give them to you first thing in the morning. Does that sound like something she might do?"

Montague blinked rapidly. "Yes," he whispered, and buried his face in his barely touched sherry glass.

"Thank you," Solomon said. "I don't suppose she was a climber?"

Montague lowered his glass, frowning. "What on earth do you mean?"

Solomon smiled. "My wife likes, in private, to remind herself of a wild childhood by climbing trees and so on." More like drainpipes, stone walls, and roofs. "The dignity of adulthood can be frustrating for her. I wondered if your wife was the same."

Montague looked baffled. "I never saw her do such a thing, and she never mentioned it. Besides, after her heart issues, she would have surely been foolish to take *excessive* exercise."

It didn't seem to enter Montague's head that his answer kept the mystery open. Again, not the act of a guilty man. Solomon imagined Montague's feeling for his wife to be much like Solomon's own when he had first seen Constance—dazzled and overwhelmed by beauty and the force of desire. He wondered now if Montague had ever got beyond the heady brilliance to an understanding and deeper love of the woman beneath, flaws and all.

"But she could easily have slipped out of the house for five minutes without anyone hearing?" Solomon asked.

"She probably could, but I doubt she did. She knew the importance of rest to her career and, latterly, to her health. She was very strict about sleep."

"Even though, by the accounts of everyone, she seemed particularly euphoric after her performance that night?"

To give him his due, Montague considered that, and again came the flicker of a tragic smile. "There was a mischievous streak in her—rebellious, you called it—and she had a loving nature. She might have taken those few minutes to fetch forbidden roses, just to surprise me in the morning. Is that all that troubles you?"

Solomon decided frankness might work. "Apart from the arrangement of the pillows, and Mr. Kellar's certainty that something is wrong."

"That," said Montague, "is down to Kellar's own arrogance. He wanted Caterina to depend on him alone. He is jealous."

Solomon's stomach gave an uncomfortable twist. He had been here before with suspicions of Kellar, which had then proved to be untrue. "You mean he wanted to marry her himself?"

Montague gestured impatiently with his free hand. "He was more like a doting father—no man would have been good enough for his precious girl. And, of course, there is snobbery. Kellar is a gentleman. I am merely in trade."

Something else to ask Juliet, perhaps—was Kellar really the gentleman of birth and breeding he always seemed? Exactly who were his antecedents?

"Will you excuse me?" Montague said with perfect politeness.

Solomon inclined his head. "Of course."

Montague moved away to some other people, who had clearly already helped themselves from the buffet laid out in the dining room. The figure of Carl Darrow caught Solomon's attention. He stood alone, his expression solemn, as suited the occasion, but not betraying the profound grief of the previous day.

It was a good act. But Solomon felt sure that was all it was. There was something just a little lost and entirely vulnerable about the violinist. And then Geoffrey appeared at his elbow and the impression passed.

Solomon strolled on, listening to the hushed conversations about Caterina's great talent and Montague's touching devastation. He decided to look into the dining room. First, though, he sought the cloakroom to wash his hands, which still bore traces of dirt from the garden and the windowsill.

As he left the cloakroom again, two men were crossing the hall to the front door. Montague, showing a valued guest out. Only the guest in question was Darrow. Intrigued, Solomon paused by the cloakroom. Neither man had seen him. They appeared to be talking together with perfect courtesy. Whatever Darrow's animosity, he was hiding it.

Montague opened the front door, ushering the other man out. "I'll walk with you to your hackney."

Darrow did not demur, and a twinge of unease twisted through Solomon. Impossible to tell if the tension he sensed came from himself or the men in front of him. From Darrow, he thought suddenly. The man was definitely uncomfortable, his shoulders rigid and held just a little too high.

If he had killed Caterina, in some moment of mad rage at her rejection, what fury might he harbor toward her husband? Surely no harm could come to the man in broad daylight…?

Montague did not close the front door tight. Solomon strolled after them, as though also enjoying a moment of fresh air. Among the array of carriages waiting in the street, the grubby old hackney was easily recognized. Two people were already inside—Reid and an unknown young woman.

Solomon slowed, tilting his head toward the sky, although he kept his gaze firmly on the men in front, who halted by the hackney door. As Darrow opened it, Montague inclined his head to the other passengers and offered his hand casually to Darrow.

"I know she thought a great deal of your music," Montague murmured.

Darrow could do nothing but accept the hand, but there was an almost imperceptible pause before he did. And then he twisted round to put his foot on the step.

It would have been easy to miss, but Solomon was watching minutely. With perfect timing and lightning speed, Montague kicked one leg from under the younger man, who fell sprawling face first onto the hackney floor.

Montague, already turned away, didn't appear to notice either the fall or the exclamations within the carriage. He merely walked calmly back in the direction of his house. Certainly, he did not glance at Solomon nor appear to see him.

And yet the moment changed everything. It meant Montague knew very well that Darrow had been his wife's lover. And revenge, however petty, even on such a day as this, was sweet.

⫸⫷

"He knows," Solomon said abruptly, when their carriage had picked up Janey around the corner from the square. "He knows about Darrow."

"Montague?" Constance said, frowning. "What makes you think so?"

Solomon told them about the incident by the hackney.

Constance, staring at him, seemed as stunned as he. "This gives him a motive of passion… Not only that, we have misunderstood him from the first."

"And if he led us to that misunderstanding," Solomon said grimly, "then he is far subtler and a far better actor than we have given him credit for. Kellar could be right about him."

From the back-facing seat, Janey was scowling at them. "He ain't evil just 'cause he thumps a man who's touched his wife."

"But he didn't thump him," Constance said. "He tripped him in such a way that only he and Darrow should know who was responsible, while causing the man maximum embarrassment in front of his friends and the waiting coachmen. It was humiliation for Darrow while keeping Montague's own, and his wife's, reputation unsullied."

Janey grimaced, clearly finding the attack tame and trivial. In her world, her old world, it was. But not in Montague's.

"Did you speak more to Kellar?" Solomon asked Constance.

She sighed. "Yes. But he said nothing about Montague—he couldn't really, in those surroundings. I tried to make him talk more about Caterina and her parents, and he seemed to—up to a point—but the man is *impenetrable*. From everyone else, I really just confirmed my view of Caterina as a charismatic, vital woman who drew people to her like moths to a candle but was close to very few. Even Montague's sister had nothing bad to say about her personally. Did you learn anything from the neighbors, Janey?"

"They're respectable people," Janey said with a cheeky grin, "though not top of the trees like us. Their servants ain't so snooty neither, and most were happy enough to talk. The Montagues are well thought of, and she much admired. Some of the mistresses try to copy her style of hair and dress, with sometimes hilarious results. About the roses, I only picked up one clue—don't know how useful it is."

"Go on," Solomon said.

"One of the maids at number twelve heard her master grumbling about someone stealing flowers from the garden in the middle of the night. He's got a bee in his bonnet about it, so she didn't pay much attention, but she thinks it was Wednesday night he saw someone in there, and Thursday morning at breakfast he was complaining about it."

"Did he see who it was?" Constance asked eagerly.

"The maid didn't believe he did. But he blames it on someone called Arthur Wainright at number two. They've been feuding for years, according to her, so she don't believe it. Says Wainright's an amiable old codger and would only do it to wind Mr. Jones up—Mr. Jones being the master at number twelve."

"But it is definitely a man this Jones claims to have seen?"

"So his maid says."

Constance looked at Solomon. "Then it wasn't Caterina who

took the roses to her room."

"If Jones is right and didn't just dream the whole thing," Janey said.

"I don't suppose," Solomon said, "that you managed to speak to anyone at the Wainright house?"

"There was a manservant there found the whole thing amusing, said Wainright and Jones had grown up together and never agreed on anything. I tried to get him to say whether it was him or his master, but he only laughed, claims his lady friend would wallop him for bringing her a dozen red roses because she'd assume he was making up for some guilt and had stolen them besides."

"We'll call at number two tomorrow," Constance said with the kind of vagueness that meant she was thinking of several things at once. "They all bear more investigation."

"Who?" Janey asked.

"Montague," Solomon said. "Darrow. And Kellar."

CHAPTER TEN

WHEN CONSTANCE ARRIVED at her disreputable establishment off Grosvenor Square that evening, she had two tasks in mind. Solomon, who had correspondence to deal with and particularly wanted to write to his brother David in Paris, had not come with her. Often, he didn't—his form of tact and trust and keeping his own promise of her independence.

She valued that in him. And yet she missed him. She wanted to spend the evening at home with him, and sleep late on a lazy Sunday…

But everyone at the establishment greeted her with their usual fervor. Although they were increasingly capable of managing without her—indeed, had done so for the two months and more she had been away in Venice—her presence tended to lift the evening for both staff and guests.

She knew this without arrogance. She had worked damnably hard for a decade to perfect her professional, sparkling persona. Like Caterina, she dazzled men and drew them in. And also like Caterina, she still managed to maintain her distance. For Constance, it was a deliberate part of her charm, the alluring butterfly too elusive to be caught. Until Solomon. Only Solomon, who had always seen beneath the bright feathers, and yet still loved her.

Had Caterina picked the wrong husband? Or the wrong lover? The very existence of the latter should have proved the former, and yet life was complicated and often messy, and

Constance could not be sure.

She had arrived early at the house in order to talk to Edith before the evening's party got underway. She found the girl already in the main salon, alone, playing soft, sweet phrases on her violin. Her face lit up at once, and she lowered the bow.

"Evening, ma'am!"

"Edith," Constance said, sitting beside her on the sofa. "I've come to pick your brains again. About Carl Darrow. Where did he study?"

"At the Royal Academy, I think."

"Do you happen to know when? Or how old he is?"

Edith's eyebrows flew up. "No," she said blankly. "But he can only be twenty-four or -five at the most, don't you think?"

"Do you know anything about his family background? Where he comes from?"

"We only ever spoke about music." Her brow twitched. "He might be from Manchester originally—he mentioned it once in my hearing—but I don't think he can have lived there since he was a child. He doesn't sound northern, does he?"

"No. No, he doesn't." *But then, I don't have to sound as if I come from the gutters of Seven Dials, either.* "Was his affair with Caterina di Ripoli common knowledge?"

Edith's eyes widened. "Not to me!" She sighed. "Of course, I don't move in such rarefied circles, do I?"

Constance smiled. "Not yet." She rose. "I think the first of our guests is arriving."

Hastily, Edith sprang up too, raising violin and bow to begin her repertoire of the evening, a gentle, charming background to the ultimately mercenary transactions of the salon.

The evening was as familiar to Constance as breathing. She laughed and chatted according to the tastes of her company. She flirted while she watched the rest of the room, performed introductions, and made sure the wine flowed in just the right quantities to make a relaxed and civilized evening. She had no illusions about the nature of the enterprise, and nothing had changed, and yet…she felt curiously detached from it. It may have been Caterina's case that was distracting her, or the thought of Solomon alone at home, where she would rather be. And vague discontent because neither of the men she sought had turned up.

It wasn't as if she could beard them at home or at their offices. She wasn't even sure how they would greet a visit from Solomon.

She was just about to give up and go home when Sir Francis Fanshaw walked into the salon with a familiar gleam in his eye.

"Constance, my jewel! How delightful!" he exclaimed, taking her proffered hand and bowing over it punctiliously. "It's an age since I've caught even a glimpse of you."

"Nonsense, you just don't notice when your eyes are all on Deborah."

Sir Francis laughed. "Trust me, you are too modest. Where *is* Deborah?"

"Around," Constance said. "Before I let you go to her, I want to ask you if you know one Sebastian Kellar, a diplomat lately posted in Italy."

Something flickered in Sir Francis's good-natured eyes. She couldn't quite read it, and the next instant, the expression had vanished. "I know Kellar. Good fellow."

"Then he is valued by the Foreign Office?"

"Without doubt."

She gave him a few more seconds, but he merely smiled and sipped the wine presented to him by Max the footman.

"You are reticent," she observed.

Sir Francis laughed. "My dear, I am always reticent about the office. Work is a dull subject for a Saturday evening in such company."

"And you have a duty of confidentiality that I would never ask you to break. My interest is more personal. What sort of a man is he? Besides a good one."

"A trustworthy one, of course. Good company, well read,

knowledgeable in all sorts of matters."

"Is he from an important family?"

"He is a gentleman, if that's what you mean. Gentry stock. I thought such issues didn't interest you?"

"They don't as a rule. I just find him…elusive."

"He does travel around a good deal," Sir Francis said. "Or he did. He is being considered for a highly important, London-based post. He says he wants to settle down at last. And, of course, it would be a wonderful promotion for him. A reward for years of loyal service, if you like. Is that what you want to hear?"

"I don't know," Constance said honestly. "Is he married, Sir Francis?"

Sir Francis's eyebrows flew up. "Not to my knowledge."

Constance drew him away to an even quieter corner. "Confidentially, Sir Francis, has he ever been in trouble in his career? I'm thinking particularly around 1848."

Sir Francis hesitated, though whether over his memory or some knotty problem of ethics was unclear.

"There was some mess in Rome," he said at last.

"Was that when he brought Caterina di Ripoli here?"

His face smoothed into a relieved smile. "You know about that already? He pulled some strings he probably shouldn't to make it happen, but he is such a useful man, he was forgiven."

"Then *the mess in Rome* was already forgiven?"

"There was nothing to forgive," Sir Francis said. "Arguably, he risked too much bringing the girl here, but he felt responsible. One likes that about him."

One did—if it were true. Or was the full story not yet revealed?

"This position in London," she said. "Will he get it?"

"Probably," said Sir Francis, smiling right past her as Deborah walked seductively across the room toward him.

Constance bowed out gracefully and sent for her carriage.

SOLOMON WOKE ON Sunday morning with the feeling that all was well in his world and was about to get considerably better. With a low growl of hunger, he reached for Constance—and found only the cooling patch of bed where she had lain.

He opened his eyes, aware of the sunbeam spreading through the half-opened curtain. In its light, Constance sat at her little escritoire, dressed only in her nightgown, busily writing. For several seconds, he let himself just appreciate her in silence, then he rose from the bed and padded naked across to the desk, pulling the curtain fully closed as he went.

She glanced up smiling. "Solomon."

"Constance. Writing our notes?"

She generally did, with precision and conciseness, not because she could not remember every word she heard or read, but because it helped them both see patterns from unlikely or even conflicting facts. From their very first case together, when they had co-operated from defensive self-interest, this was how they had worked. And yet this time, she blushed.

"No, actually. I'm just experimenting."

"With what?" he asked. He could see it was a list of some kind, but gentlemanly tact prevented him from reading it without her permission.

"With the names of people who might conceivably accept an invitation from me without disgracing you."

Surprised, he glanced down, and she picked up her piece of paper and handed it to him. He skimmed down the names. "Tizsas, Lord and Lady Trench, the Swans...Zenobia Paul...Jason Madly?"

"I like him, now that he's given up the notion of taking me to bed. Besides, I wondered if Mrs. St. John might come with her daughter."

Both Madly and the St. Johns had been involved in the mystery of the two bodies found on the establishment doorstep a couple of months ago.

"I don't know if they'll come," Constance said. "I'm trying to work out how disastrous it would be if everyone on my doubtful list stayed away. What do you think?"

She sounded almost nervous, and he realized how much she was trying. Her instinct was against this party, but she was prepared to try her best to make it work, to please him. And perhaps because something had shifted in her mind, maybe the sad ending to the Montagues' marriage, or just from her natural generosity.

"I think it's an excellent list," he murmured. "I'd like to add a few more names and see what you think."

It was the right thing to say. And to do. He was still inclined to lay down the law, however benign and well intentioned, and that was neither fair nor sensible where Constance was concerned.

He let the paper flutter to the desk and placed his hands on her shoulders. Bending, he kissed her cheek and her nape, heard the familiar catch in her breath. Slowly, he drew her to her feet and against his naked body for a long, slow kiss. And then another. It was she who made the first tiny move toward the bed, and that was all the invitation he needed. He swept her up in his arms and laid her on the pillows beneath him.

Everything else could wait.

AT PRECISELY TWO o'clock that afternoon, Solomon and Constance knocked on Marianne Locke's front door. She had rooms with their own separate entrance in a larger building. It would, Solomon reflected, make a discreet meeting place for lovers. If Caterina had been seen entering the building, she was obviously calling on her friend. If anyone had noticed Darrow, well, he could have been visiting any number of other people.

The singer opened the door herself. Interestingly, she wore black again, although it was a different gown from yesterday, more modest and comfortable.

"My wife," Solomon said with the usual tingle of pride. When he had first met Constance, he could never have imagined saying those words, let alone being proud of them. What foolish assumptions and prejudices misdirected the brain…

"How do you, Mrs. Grey?" Marianne led the way into a cozy parlor. A piano occupied one corner of the room, which was decorated in pleasant autumnal shades of green and brown and gold. "Do sit down. I'll fetch us some tea."

She must have had everything prepared, because she returned only moments later bearing a tea tray. A sliced cake already sat on the low table conveniently placed between a sofa and two armchairs. Whatever the singer had to say to them, she had not invited them for a scolding.

While the tea was infusing, she said, "Carl—Mr. Darrow said you called on him with questions about Caterina, at Mr. Montague's request."

"With Mr. Montague's permission," Solomon corrected her. "Our questions were inspired by the concerns of another friend of Caterina's."

"Mr. Kellar," Constance said. "Perhaps you know him?"

"We have met. Caterina was very fond of him. I believe he was a family friend who helped her escape from Italy during the late revolutions."

"Then you understand his concerns about her death?" Constance said.

"I understand his grief. I'm not sure I understand what his concerns actually are. Darrow seemed to think you doubted her death was of natural causes. Which naturally troubles both of us."

"Is Mr. Darrow angry with us for these questions?" Solomon asked. The violinist had certainly avoided both of them quite adeptly yesterday.

"No, he is angry with Mr. Montague," Marianne said ruefully, "having tried and convicted him in his own head. If indeed that much thought was actually involved."

"Do *you* believe Mr. Montague could have harmed his wife?"

"He doted on her. He is a gentle man."

Not so gentle that he could resist tripping the man who had cuckolded him. Plus, Marianne hadn't actually answered the question.

"Mrs. Locke, was Caterina afraid of her husband?" he asked bluntly.

"Oh, no. I'm sure she had no cause to be."

"Not even if he *knew* about her relationship with Darrow?"

Marianne's lips parted and closed again. She had made up her mind to tell them something—why else would she have invited them here?—but it was not easy for her to say. No doubt loyalty and past promises made it so.

She sighed and picked up the teapot. "He did know."

"What makes you think so?" Constance asked.

"Because Caterina told me. That was why she decided to end the affair with Darrow."

"Was Montague threatening her?" Solomon leaned across the table to take the cup and saucer from her and passed it to Constance.

"I don't believe so." Marianne concentrated on pouring a second cup. "He is not that kind of man. It was her own decision. She could not bear to hurt him."

Constance frowned. "Then why did she begin the affair in the first place?"

Marianne gave Solomon his tea and poured some for herself. "Impulse. The same reason she did most things. And attraction. Carl is a handsome young man, and she loved his music. A slice of cake, Mrs. Grey?"

"Thank you." Constance accepted the plate and helped herself. "Then in her mind, at least, if her husband didn't know, she wasn't hurting him?"

"Something like that," Marianne said.

"You disapprove," Constance remarked, "and yet you allowed them to meet here."

Marianne stirred sugar into her tea. "I was her friend and I knew her. She would have met Carl anyway, one way or another, no doubt recklessly and causing massive scandal as well as a public breach with her husband. Here, they were as safe as they could be until the affair had run its course."

"You assumed it would end?" Solomon said. "Was there no chance that Caterina would come to prefer Darrow?"

"No, I don't believe so. Her husband was her rock. If it came to a choice, she would always choose him. Carl knew that."

Solomon sipped his tea. "When did Montague find out?"

"About a fortnight ago. Or, at least, that's when Caterina learned that he knew."

"How did she find that out?" Constance asked. "Did he tell her in so many words? Or did she confess to him?"

"No, I think he told her that he knew. According to Caterina, she assured him passionately of her love and promised to end the affair."

"When?" Solomon asked. "When exactly did she do that?"

"That," Marianne said carefully, "is really what is bothering me, and why I wanted to talk to you. She told me a couple of weeks ago that she would end it that very day when she met Carl—which I had already helped her arrange for Monday the twenty-seventh of June. I offered to stay here for moral support while she delivered his congé, but she insisted she would be better alone, so I went out. And then, only a couple of days later, she asked me to arrange another meeting, for Tuesday, the fifth of July."

Solomon set down his cup. "Then she didn't end it after all?"

"I don't know. She told me she had, but that there was some 'difficulty' she needed to resolve."

"And she met him again on that Tuesday?"

"I assume so. I went out as usual to give them privacy, but I never saw her again."

"Were there no signs that they had been here?" Constance asked.

Marianne met her gaze frankly. "The spare bed had not been used. Nor was it on the previous occasion. She was keeping her word."

"And did you discover what the 'difficulty' was that meant she had to see Darrow in private again?"

"No. But by all accounts and my own observation, her performance at the opera was spectacular on Tuesday evening, and especially so on Wednesday. She was happy. I would say she had somehow solved the difficulty."

Constance leaned back against the cushions. "Or," she said slowly, "she had arranged to run away with Darrow."

⫸⫷

THE COVENT GARDEN shop bearing the sign *Curiosities and Antiques, prop. J. Silver* was closed.

Kellar was not surprised. It was Sunday, after all. Since he had never in his passing surveillance seen Juliet leave the premises after the shop was locked up for the night, he presumed she lived in the rooms above it. He had seen lights up there yesterday evening, but it had not been the right time to call.

Daylight was less threatening. She was more likely to open the door. And then…

Keeping his mind on the current steps in his plan, he halted decisively outside the solid wooden gate that he suspected led to some kind of service lane. It didn't.

Opening it, he found himself in a small yard behind the shop. It was paved and well swept, and all around it were pots of beautifully scented flowers and herbs, contrasting vividly with the usually rank London air. Memory tried to distract him: a much younger Juliet kneeling by a flower bed, the sun on her golden hair, as she weeded the soil and cut chosen stems to brighten a house that was not hers. The scents of hyacinths and roses came back to him, mingling with rosemary and sage.

The plan, Kellar.

He knocked on the door, not so loudly that he would startle her, but not too timidly either. He wanted her to hear. Then he stepped politely back, so as not to loom. He had the feeling she would shut the door in his face if he loomed, and then where would the plan be?

The downstairs window showed him a little kitchen with a table and a couple of chairs—probably the back of the shop.

He heard movement beyond the door and caught his breath. A key was inserted into the lock and turned. Two bolts were drawn back. None of it was hurried, not even the opening of the door.

Juliet Silver wore a bright floral-print gown whose principal color was orange. She hadn't painted her eyebrows or any other parts of her face, which betrayed more than her years. Life had not been kind to Juliet. But a trace of the young woman and her bold courage echoed in that direct, open gaze.

She didn't even look surprised. "Sebastian. I thought it would be you."

He took off his hat. "May I come in?"

Everything depended on her answer. Well, not everything. He still had an alternative.

Her eyes remained on his. He had to make an effort not to flex his fingers, ready to push open the door if he had to.

She moved the door suddenly, pulling it wide. "Well, don't just stand there. I have five minutes before I need to go out."

No, you don't. Smiling, he stepped inside and closed the door.

CHAPTER ELEVEN

M RS. PHILPOT, CARL Darrow's landlady, recognized them with a grunt of welcome and gestured for them to go straight up.

Constance more than half expected Darrow to be nursing a thick head—either from falling on it yesterday or from an excess of alcohol. Or both. Certainly, she couldn't hear the violin, though there were some massively complicated scales coming from the piano in the sitting room.

Darrow practiced mornings, she remembered. Geoffrey Reid had the afternoons.

When Solomon knocked, a grumpy "Enter" snapped from within, seeming to confirm her suspicions.

However, Darrow sat at the table by the window, busily writing. He was in his shirt sleeves, but as soon as they walked in, he sprang to his feet and reached for his coat. His eyes were clear, despite a rather colorful bruise around one eye.

"Sorry," he said, bowing to Constance. "An argument with a hackney floor. It won."

"I thought it was Mr. Montague who won?"

He paused. "What do you mean?"

"My husband saw him trip you."

Darrow blushed, suddenly looking much younger.

"Why lie?" Solomon asked.

"Wouldn't you?" Darrow retorted. "What else could I do? There aren't so many reasons for a bereaved husband to attack another man on the day of his wife's funeral. I chose to preserve her reputation—and mine. I don't care about Montague's, though I daresay he wouldn't like to be known as a cuckold."

He swung away, waving one hand toward the comfortable chairs. "But you saw him, Mr. Grey. You saw how violent he is? *And* how he covers it up with such civility for the benefit of observers? No wonder Caterina was afraid of him."

"Would it surprise you to know," Constance asked, sitting down, "that no one else believes she was afraid of her husband?"

"No," Darrow said. "She told me things she told no one else."

"She told Marianne Locke that she was ending her relationship with you," Solomon said.

Darrow frowned. "But she didn't," he said blankly. "Why would she say that? Why would she *do* that?"

"Because her husband had found out," Solomon said. "And she chose him over you."

If he had hoped to surprise any ugliness out of Darrow with such a brutal statement, he was disappointed. Darrow just looked bewildered. "But I could swear Montague didn't know, not before the funeral…" His eyes widened. "Would Marianne have told him that very day? I know she disapproved and wanted me out of Caterina's life… But I never thought her capable of such hurtful behavior."

Neither did Constance, though appearances were often deceptive.

Darrow shook his head, staring down at the carpet. "No, she wouldn't," he answered himself. "I thought him too dull to find out, but I must have been wrong…" He raised his head suddenly. "*That* was why Caterina finally agreed."

"Agreed what?" Constance asked.

"To come away with me. We planned it all last Monday and this Tuesday. We were to leave on Friday, after her evening performance. She was so happy…"

Constance met Solomon's gaze.

"Where were you going to go?" he asked.

"Back to Italy. She missed home and sunshine, and she was desperate to get away from Montague."

"And you were both willing to abandon your promising careers here in England?"

Darrow smiled. "In matters of music, England is nothing compared to the entire continent of Europe. The world is much bigger than London."

"And you were both prepared to face any difficulties Caterina might have had with the governments in Italy?"

Darrow shrugged. "She didn't believe it would be an issue."

"Will you go by yourself?" Constance asked.

He shook his head, once more morose. "I don't know. It wouldn't be the same without her."

Solomon stood up. "Well, we're sorry for disturbing you. Thank you again for your honesty. Er… Why didn't you tell us this in the first place?"

Darrow met his gaze without fear. "Because it's none of your business. And because, even then, I was trying to protect her memory." His lips twisted. "And yes, my own reputation."

⇥⇥✕⇤⇤

"THEY CAN'T BOTH be right," Constance burst out almost as soon as Mrs. Philpot had closed the door behind them.

"They can both *think* they're right," Solomon replied. "Both Darrow and Marianne seemed genuine to me, but they don't necessarily have all the facts."

"Neither do we," Constance complained. "Only Caterina did, and she can't tell."

Solomon ushered her toward the carriage, which had just appeared around the corner. "Perhaps she can. We need to look more closely at everything she did, everywhere she went and everyone she spoke to from the Monday she was supposed to end things with Darrow, to the day she died."

"That's more than a week," Constance protested.

"It won't be easy. But her life seems to have been more of a bubbling cauldron than we realized. Some man picked roses in the square—"

"If Janey's informant is accurate," Constance interrupted.

"As you say. Someone certainly entered Caterina's room, possibly via the window, and left her twelve red roses."

"And disturbed her pillows," Constance added bleakly. "Someone was in her room who shouldn't have been. They may or may not have killed her, but it's looking increasingly likely. Let's visit my mother."

Solomon's eyebrows rose, though he gave the order to the coachman and handed her inside. No wonder he was surprised. She had almost frightened herself with her sudden urgency.

"You want to ask more about Kellar?" he asked.

"Yes." Though she had no specific questions. She just needed to see that Juliet was safe and was trying to justify it. "We have three real suspects in Caterina's murder. Montague, Darrow, and Kellar. Of the three of them, Kellar is by far the subtlest. If Caterina died because she knew something about him, something that would damage his ambitions for this new position he's pursuing, then it's quite possible that Juliet knows it too."

Solomon took her hand in a strong grip. "It doesn't follow at all," he said gently. "If Caterina knew anything to his discredit— and we don't know that she did—then it was about something that happened decades after Juliet last saw him."

"True," Constance allowed, yet the speed of her heart didn't slow, and the knot of worry in her stomach did not unravel. Rather, it seemed to be tying and retying itself into bigger and more complicated tangles.

It was not far to her mother's shop, and she jumped out of the carriage before Solomon could move. She went straight through the gate to the back door. Somehow, she prevented herself from battering on it like a mad thing. Even so, her knock was loud enough to earn Juliet's wrath.

And yet no one answered. The knot in her stomach dived deeper, seemed to fill her whole body. *Damn you, Ma, don't do this to me...*

She knocked again and stepped back. "Juliet!" she called at the upper window.

Solomon took her place at the door and turned the handle. It swung open.

"She would never leave it unlocked," Constance whispered. *"Never."* Juliet had known too many thieves and casual "borrowers" in her life to give just anyone easy access to her shop and her home.

"Wait here," Solomon said quietly, and went in.

Of course, she followed him.

DIGBY MONTAGUE SAT on his late wife's bed, his violin and bow in one hand, and gazed around the familiar room. He should probably feel the presence of her spirit here, at least some echo of the woman who had been his wife only days ago. He should be able to imagine her here with him. It would be some comfort.

He had come up here to play to her, as if that would somehow connect her to him once more. She had liked him to play to her, even though his skill was so imperfect. Sometimes she had sung along with him, not in her full, operatic voice that could reach the furthest corners of the largest theatres, but softly, sweetly, just for him. He wanted to remember that, to feel it again.

But the emptiness glared back at him. Still silence battered at his ears. She was not here. There was no point in playing.

Imagination had never been his strong point. But then, he'd never needed imagination with Caterina. Her reality was overwhelming enough. His beautiful wife, vital, talented, and deeply, humanly flawed, had been wiped from the Earth in an instant, leaving nothing behind.

Except her money.

And the insulting suspicions of Sebastian Kellar, who had made it so difficult to get at her money while she was alive.

Well, there was no denying that it would be useful to Digby now.

He found himself staring at the naked pillows on the bed. Reaching out, he touched one, smoothed it as though preparing it for her lovely head.

No more.

Unbearable to be here. He was a practical man, and he had work to do. She had been such a distraction to him since he had first encountered her. He had been so helpless in her power, so doting that he had neglected his business. The loss of one shipment should not have been this catastrophic. But with hard work—God knew he needed that to keep the nightmares at bay— and Caterina's money, he would save Montague and Son. That would be his legacy. And hers.

He sprang up and strode from the room, abandoning his violin like a sacrificial offering. He rushed downstairs to his study, where he penned a commanding note to his solicitor.

AT SOME POINT, climbing the stairs with terror in her heart, Constance's hand had crept into Solomon's, for she became aware that he now held it with comforting firmness. Whatever she had to face at the top of the stairs, it would not be alone.

But still the fear could not be squashed, the sheer impossibility of life without her maddening, infuriating mother…

"Ma!" she called sharply. "Juliet!"

They entered her pleasant sitting room together. Constance saw her at once, sprawled on a sofa, her plump fingers curled as though around the glass so close to her on the table. Or the half-empty gin bottle that stood beside it.

The familiarity of her mother's pose—she had found her like this dozens of times in childhood and beyond—should have eased her alarm. It didn't. She pulled free of Solomon and flew to her mother, dropping to her knees, grasping her hand, groping for a pulse.

At least Juliet's eyes were closed, without that dreadful, blank stare of death. Beside her, lying flat on the sofa, was a bright red cushion.

"I can't feel her pulse!" Her voice shook with panic. "Sol, I can't—"

Solomon bent over her mother and gently took the hand, his fingers sliding over Juliet's wrist.

"She's fine, Constance. She's asleep."

Constance gasped, falling back onto her heels. She grasped her hair in both hands, tugging in an excess of relief and fury and old memory.

"Damn you, Juliet, wake up," she said harshly. "Drunken old tart, *wake up!*"

Juliet snorted, one hand groping blindly as though for Constance's voice. Or for the bottle. Constance seized the bottle and stoppered it before springing to her feet and removing both glass and bottle from the room. She was still shaking.

When she returned, moments later, her mother was hauling herself into a sitting position and smiling at Solomon. "Hello, my son! How did you get in? She been picking my locks again?"

"No, you left the damned door open," Constance said. "What were you thinking of?"

The smile faded from Juliet's lips, and from her slightly bleary eyes. The veils came down, as they often did. It had taken Constance a long time to realize that—that her mother was not the open, amiable book she showed the world.

"Must have needed a lie-down," she said vaguely.

Abruptly, the anger drained out of Constance. "What happened?"

Juliet rubbed her forehead, as though it hurt. "Oh, nothing. I had a visitor and a drink. Reminded me of old times."

There had only been one glass.

Memory came to Constance's aid. "I'll make tea."

There were no teacups by the basin either. No teapot waiting to be washed. The kettle was cold. Constance filled it from the tap and set it on the stove. She could hear Juliet's voice from the sitting room, with occasional interpolations from Solomon.

Impossible to know how much she'd had to drink. She had always been adept at hiding her drunkenness from Constance. Until she reached the comatose state, of course. Until then, the only clues were generally the care with which she enunciated. Oddly, although Constance hadn't guessed it at the time, this was when she betrayed her original accent. Drunk as a wheelbarrow, one could only control so many things at once.

While Constance gathered the necessary accoutrements onto the tray, and spooned tea from the old caddy into the pot, she calmed herself and began to think.

"Bless you, Connie," Juliet said comfortably as Constance brought the tea tray into the sitting room. "Just what I need, a good cup of tea."

Constance served her first, which was only polite. "What did Kellar want?" she asked casually.

Her mother didn't pause as she reached for her teacup, but the faint twitch of her lip acknowledged the hit and told Constance she was ready for the question. "Oh, just to talk over old times."

"What did you discuss?"

Juliet grimaced before taking a sip of tea. "Nothing. After thirty years with our lives gone in such different directions, there was very little to say."

So she'd sent him away with a flea in his ear—if she'd let him in at all. "Did he mind?"

"Don't see how he could have," Juliet said carelessly. "It's obvious I'm not the same girl he knew decades ago. I expect it was a relief to him. His responsibilities are at an end."

"Then he *is* a man who takes his responsibilities seriously?" Solomon asked.

Juliet shrugged. "He used to."

"Did he tell you," Constance asked, "that he has applied for a position in London?"

Only the faintest flicker of her mother's eyelid betrayed her surprise. If Constance hadn't been watching her so closely, she would have missed it.

"No," Juliet said without apparent interest. "He didn't stay long."

"He brought this case to us," Constance said. "Caterina di Ripoli's death. And we don't know why, because now we consider him one of our three suspects. Is he capable of killing?"

"Most people are, for the right reasons."

"Even if the victim was a woman?" Solomon asked.

Juliet smiled at him affectionately. "A life is a life."

"The thing is," Constance said, "until we know he didn't do this, you mustn't endanger yourself with him."

"Don't be daft, Connie. He's got no reason to kill me."

"HE DOES," CONSTANCE said half an hour later as the carriage finally took them toward home. "Kellar does have a reason to be rid of her."

Solomon understood her immediately. "A man stepping into a prominent role in a government office does not need embarrassments from his past getting in the way. It's a cold reason to kill."

"We've been thinking of this as a crime of passion, because of the roses, but when you think about it, if Caterina's death really was murder, then it was very well calculated. There is no actual evidence to show that she was murdered, let alone who killed her. I think that points to Kellar. But even if it doesn't, I think he went to see Juliet to make sure she wouldn't blab to the world that she—the eccentric shopkeeper, one-time fence and whore— was once almost engaged to the great Sebastian Kellar."

Solomon was frowning. "And she reassured him?"

"If he's prepared to take the chance."

"He took an interest in us," Solomon said slowly, "made a mighty effort and risked his own neck to try to save your life, because you are Juliet's daughter."

"Maybe. But I can't forgive him."

"For what?"

"For *bothering* Juliet."

"Was she bothered?" Solomon asked gently. "It seemed to me that *you* were the one upset."

"Oh, she was bothered," Constance said with certainty. "She might have thrown him out after one minute or even ten, but she was upset enough to forget to lock the door behind him, to knock back a cartload of gin, and fall asleep. She hasn't drunk like that in years, not in the daytime anyway, and certainly not since you found her the shop."

Solomon sat up straight, staring at her. "You think he *threatened* her?"

Constance shook her head. "That's not his style, is it? He's not some underworld villain from the East End. I doubt he makes threats at all, just acts when he considers it necessary."

"Then what upset her?"

"*He* did. His existence, his presence." And how far she had fallen.

THERE WAS NOTHING, Juliet reflected, like a daughter's contempt to make a drunken old tart pull herself together.

She had needed the gin for her nerves after Sebastian's visit.

She hadn't meant to slug quite so much, though in truth she had needed the sleep too. Still, Connie's disapproving face could curdle the milk as well as sober the most legless of topers. And despite the slightly woolly head, Juliet was stone-cold sober.

She hadn't invited him to her sitting room, or even her kitchen for a cup of tea. But then, he hadn't asked. He had only stopped to issue an invitation to dine. At a public place, too.

"A quiet eating house," he had called it.

She had known he would come back after his visit to the shop. But she certainly hadn't expected it to be for that reason. She had probably gawped at him with her ugly old mouth wide open. Why the devil would he risk being seen with someone like her? It wasn't as if she had any beauty or even glamor left. She could dress and paint herself into an eccentric, even interesting person, but not one of Sebastian's class. At best, she was vulgar. At worst...

Well, there was no point in dwelling on the worst.

"I'll think about it," she had said, just to make him go. "But probably not. Goodbye, Sebastian."

To her surprise, even a certain amount of foolish pique, he had not lingered, merely smiled as if he understood perfectly, which he probably did, the bastard. Then he had placed his hat back on his handsome head and departed, closing the door behind him.

Juliet had headed straight back upstairs, forgetting even to turn the key in the lock, and seized the gin with shaking hands. *Stupid, stupid.* She let Constance down too often through gin, when life had seemed unbearable and all she had was a couple of hours of oblivion. That wasn't true, of course, and even when she behaved appallingly, she had never forgotten that what she had was Constance herself.

Trust the girl to turn up the only time she didn't want her around. She had done that as a child, too. As if she sensed her mother's shameful weakness from afar and bolted back home to catch her at it. Still, Connie's astringence had had its sobering effects, along with Solomon's calm yet powerful presence.

She would not be dining with Sebastian Kellar.

Really, she would not.

CHAPTER TWELVE

ON MONDAY MORNING, Solomon and Constance left the house together in the carriage, and went first to a building near the river, where he dropped off the powders they had purloined from Caterina's bedroom. Even so, they still arrived early at the office, armed with Constance's updated notes—and a plan.

Over tea in Solomon's room with Janey, and with Lenny Knox, who had turned up on the off chance of a day's work, Solomon outlined the campaign.

"The aim is to find out as much as we possibly can about Caterina's movements between Monday the twenty-eighth of June and the night of Wednesday the sixth of July, when she died. We need to know everywhere she went, everyone she spoke to, who visited her, what her state of mind appeared to be after every encounter."

Janey's jaw dropped. "Get away, guv'nor. You need a whole army of peelers for that, and even then you'd never get *everything.*"

"We're hoping we'll get everything that stands out," Constance said. "And it's not as daunting a task as you think. She led a busy life, but mostly in predictable places. Her home, the theatre for both rehearsals and performances, the house of a particular friend. She was not a great socialite, except in her own immediate circle."

"Start at the theatre in Covent Garden," Solomon instructed

them. "We've already spoken to her dresser, Rose Samuels, and to her understudy, Ellen Gentle, but not in such detail. Bother everyone you can think of, from stagehands and doormen to singers and dancers, even passing hackney drivers."

He passed a letter across the desk to each of them. "To vouch that you are asking on our behalf, if it proves necessary."

"And what are you going to be doing?" Janey asked cheekily. "Writing reports?"

"No, much the same as you, only in Eagle Square," Constance replied. "Starting with your rose thief at number two."

IN FACT, IT was Solomon's privilege to approach the accused rose thief at number two, while Constance went straight to Montague's house.

The house was newer and probably a little smaller than Montague's, its owner, Arthur Wainright, a small, cheerful man of few pretensions and a pronounced East London accent. He was dressed in well-made clothes of decent quality but old-fashioned cut that somehow suited him. Solomon had seen him at the funeral on Saturday, but wasn't sure the man remembered him.

"Mr. Grey?" Wainright said as though in surprise as he ushered Solomon into what was clearly his office. A cluttered desk strewn with papers and ledgers took pride of place, and the chairs were not built for comfort. "What can I do for you?"

Since Wainright appeared to be a plain, open man, Solomon opted for the same approach. "I have come on what might seem a trivial and impudent quest. Understand, I have no authority to ask, let alone act upon what you might tell me. The matter bears on another that is more important."

Wainright looked intrigued, and gestured Solomon to sit on the visitor's side of the desk before taking his own chair. "Ask."

"Did you, by any chance, pick some roses from the square

during the hours of darkness on the night of last Wednesday to Thursday morning?"

Wainright's eyes gleamed. "Old Jonesy at number twelve complaining again? He blames everything on me, from dogs fouling the gardens to his own leaky roof. I don't have any dogs and I keep my own roof in good repair."

"But do you pick the roses?"

"I have done, largely to annoy him, so always when he's at home and watching."

A faint hope flickered in Solomon's mind, but even if Wainright was the rose thief, it didn't explain how his or anyone else's flowers had got into Caterina's bedroom. "Was he watching on Wednesday evening?"

"I don't know. I like my own comforts too much to go out in the middle of the night. I rise early. Work, you know."

"What is it you do, Mr. Wainright?"

"Carter. Rent 'em out nowadays, with or without drivers. Does very well for me."

"I'm glad to hear it. To be clear, my informant did not definitively accuse you. He just said he saw the figure of a man picking roses at about two in the morning. If it wasn't you, I don't suppose you saw who did do it?"

"Didn't see anyone at all. I was sound asleep at two in the morning. Who wouldn't be? Except a gentleman of leisure like yourself."

Solomon smiled. "You would be surprised. Do you have much to do with your neighbors the Montagues?"

"We say good morning and good evening. We don't dine together. Though I was over there on Saturday to pay my respects. You know that. You were there too." Wainright sighed. "Such a tragedy. Poor lady."

"Did you see Mrs. Montague out and about much?"

"Can't say I did. Occasionally, of an evening, I'd see her going out or coming in. Heard her more often—practicing, I suppose. Voice like an angel. I saw her once in the theatre…"

"When was the last time you saw her here in the square?" It was the first of many times Solomon was going to have to ask the questions, sort the accurate from the vague and build a timetable of Caterina's movements. At least Wainright seemed happy to help. Not everyone would be so accommodating.

SURPRISINGLY, MONTAGUE HAD again gone to work. Since he clearly had not rescinded his instruction to co-operate with Constance, she was able to interview each of the servants again. They didn't like it, of course—they had work to do, apart from anything else—but the hint this was all for their master's peace of mind seemed to remove any reluctance to talk. Which was interesting. They didn't just feel sorry for their master, they liked him, were protective of him.

Did a man like that—a distant man who inspired devotion in spite of himself—really decide to kill his wife? His very reserve made it hard to judge.

Even before she spoke again to Mary Webb, the other servants had helped her build up a schedule of Caterina's outings and returns to the house.

She had exercised her voice at home most mornings, sometimes with an instructor, sometimes alone. In the afternoons, she generally went to the theatre or met friends. Often, she did not come home until after the evening performances, but sometimes she returned earlier, often with purchases made at the shops. It seemed that on Wednesday the twenty-ninth of June, the day after she was supposed to have ended her affair with Darrow, she had left home in the carriage before luncheon, with the intention of shopping, though she had returned with no purchases.

"Did Mary Webb go with her?" Constance asked Collins the butler.

Unusually, Collins was not sure. "She might have. If madam

required her presence on her outings, Miss Webb usually came home late in the afternoon to attend to her duties here. She didn't usually accompany her to the theatre."

"Thank you. Tell me, did Mrs. Montague seem at all agitated or different in any way when she came home on the evening of Monday the twenty-seventh of June? Or at any time after that?"

"No, madam." The butler's supercilious face relaxed slightly. "But then, she *was* different, if you like, *every* time you saw her, sometimes livelier and laughing. At others more subdued. Sometimes talkative, at others more thoughtful."

"And on Monday the twenty-seventh?"

"I really couldn't say."

He wasn't being obstructive, she thought. He really couldn't remember all his mistress's moods. Times and destinations were things he remembered better.

"And the week that she died," Constance said. "Everyone tells me she was very happy on Wednesday night. What about Monday and Tuesday?"

Butler frowned in thought. "Monday, she seemed…preoccupied," he said at last. "I don't recall Tuesday. She was tired, I think, but contented."

"One last thing, Collins. You have been employed here for some years?"

"Indeed."

"Do you recall Mr. Montague being betrothed to another lady, some ten years ago?"

"Miss Worthington. Of course."

"Another tragedy poor Mr. Montague has had to face," Contance said with genuine sympathy. "I suppose he was very much upset by that, too."

"Naturally. It was so sudden, and she was so young…"

The familiarity of his phrase caused a chill to skitter down her spine. The words had been used so often about Caterina's death.

"How did Miss Worthington die?" Constance asked.

Collins spread his hands. "No one knows. She was found dead

in her parents' garden, as though she had just stopped breathing."

Just like Caterina... Her chill became a thrill of excitement. Dear God, no wonder Kellar was suspicious. Why had he not told them this in the first place? She wanted to bolt from the house, find Solomon immediately and tell him this stunning fact.

Montague... It had always made more sense. He was in the house, could easily have unlocked his wife's door—after picking the roses, perhaps as a reason to be welcomed into the bedroom. She was unfaithful and he needed the money...

And if she had been planning to run away with Darrow, she could, thanks to Kellar, have found a way to take her money with her.

On top of which, Sophie Worthington's death could well be why Caterina had been afraid of her husband.

Solomon needed to know.

But there was more to learn here first, armed now with this new knowledge.

She put her notebook away and stood up.

"Thank you, Collins," she said calmly. "Where will I find Miss Webb?"

"In the mistress's room."

THE MAID WAS packing her mistress's clothes into a trunk. The theatre trunk was no longer in the room.

"A sad task," Constance remarked.

Mary cast her unfriendly glance. "You again. Can't you let the poor lady be? She's dead."

"If she wasn't, I'd have no cause for these questions, would I?"

"You've no cause for them now," Mary retorted. "All you're doing is upsetting the master."

"Do you think so?" Constance asked. "Don't you think he'd

be equally upset whether we asked questions or not? He did give us permission, after all."

Mary sniffed and lovingly laid another folded gown in the trunk.

"Were you and your mistress aware that Mr. Montague had been engaged to be married about ten years ago?"

"Of course," Mary said indifferently. "Some people just have bad luck."

And others make their own. "Did it concern your mistress?"

"Concern her?" Mary turned from the wardrobe to face Constance. "What do you mean?"

"Someone told us that Mrs. Montague was afraid of her husband. Since it was not an impression we had gained before, I thought you would be the best person to ask."

"Afraid of him? Of course she wasn't." Mary stared at Constance, derision slowly fading from her expression until she didn't look quite so certain. "Afraid of losing him, maybe."

"Then fear wasn't why she locked him out of her bedroom?" Constance asked.

"I told you, that was no more than a sign of her wishes. He had a key to get in if he chose, and she was happy with that. They trusted each other."

All the same, Mary was thinking about it, perhaps considering certain events in the light of such a possibility.

"Did you ever see unexplained cuts or bruises on your mistress's body?"

Mary stared at her, affronted. "Of course not! What are you trying to imply?"

"I am trying to find out the truth. Were you aware that Mr. Montague knew about her liaison with Carl Darrow?"

"Oh no," Mary said, her hand flying to her mouth in clear distress. "She would have hated that!"

"But she knew that he knew. Or so she told her friend Mrs. Locke, to whom you took Mrs. Montague's note for Mr. Darrow. Look, I need your help. Come and sit down with me. Tell me about Mrs. Montague's mood on Monday the twenty-seventh of June."

Mary blinked. "How am I supposed to remember that?" All the same, she sat down, watching as Constance consulted her notes.

"It was a day she left the house early, as though she were going shopping or calling on friends. She won't have taken you with her because she was going to Mrs. Locke's home."

Mary frowned with the effort in remembering. "There was one morning that week—it might have been the Monday—when she was quiet. Thoughtful, I'd say. And the same evening, she seemed much…grimmer."

"As though she'd done something she hadn't liked? Was she angry? Worried? Sad?"

Mary shook her head impatiently. "I don't think so. More…*determined*."

Determined to do what? To keep her word to her husband and give up Darrow? Or to leave her husband and bolt to Europe with her lover?

"Did she ever say or do anything that implied she might go away for a time? A holiday? Or a visit to a friend some distance away?"

"No, I don't think so. We didn't know how long the opera would run."

But then, it seemed Caterina confided different things to different people. Her reticence might have been because she had no intention of leaving. Or because she wasn't taking Mary with her when she went—afraid, perhaps, that Mary, by accident or design, would betray her to Montague?

Constance met the maid's doubtful gaze. "Help me build a picture of her last days. Collins and Nancy say she left the house a little after midday on that Monday, the twenty-seventh. Is that your recollection?"

Mary nodded.

"What time did she return to the house?"

"After her performance. Just after eleven, I think, and she came up to bed shortly after."

"Did she lock her door after you left her?"

Mary thought about it. "Yes. Yes, I think she did."

Constance wrote it down. "Good. Now, what about Tuesday the twenty-eighth? How was she then?"

"Brisk," Mary said. "She went out after luncheon and took me with her. She intended to buy a birthday present, she said, after calling on a friend. In the end, the visit took too long and we went straight to the theatre. The carriage took me home and returned for her later."

"Whom did she visit?" Constance asked. "Mrs. Locke?"

"No. It was an old music teacher, George Martin."

"For another lesson?"

"Not that I heard. Besides, she wouldn't want to strain her voice before the evening's performance. She has a better teacher now, but she regards Mr. Martin as a friend, values his opinion. He's a pleasant old bird, sharp as a tack. I expect they just got talking."

"Where does he live?" Constance asked.

"Theobalds Street."

"And when did she come home from the theatre that night?"

"At the usual time, give or take a few minutes."

"Did she lock her door?"

"I think… Actually, I'm not sure. I can't remember."

"Very well, let's move on to Wednesday the twenty-ninth, a week before she died…"

BY THE TIME she left Mary, Constance had a fairly full account of Caterina's movements to and from home. It was nowhere clear enough to offer an explanation, but she was satisfied with the beginning.

It seemed that on Monday the twenty-seventh of June, the day Caterina was supposed to end her relationship with Darrow, she had instead locked her husband out of her bedchamber. And she had been grim and determined. Was she planning her escape because she suspected Montague of murdering his betrothed ten years before?

Descending the stairs, Constance intended to go out into the square and wait for Solomon to emerge from whichever house he was currently in. Only the hall was empty, and the door to what looked like Montague's study was open.

Montague was out at his office. None of the servants would see her.

She would never get a better chance.

She darted into the room and straight to the big mahogany desk.

Montague was a tidy man, and an oddly impersonal one for the passionate Caterina di Ripoli's husband. No papers were left on his desk, only a stand of pens and inks. No clutter of keepsakes and personal items, no books except what looked like business ledgers. Two landscape pictures graced the walls. No comfortable chair for reading or resting, not even one for visitors. This was strictly a work room.

Constance quickly tested all the drawers, finding them all unlocked, which spoke of a certain amount of trust in his household, apart from one.

The unlocked drawers contained blank paper and spare ink, an appointment book, a few letters waiting to be answered or copied, and another complete set of house keys. Constance flipped through the appointment book, in which he seemed to have recorded largely business meetings, but a couple of entries mentioned visits to the theatre and supper with Caterina. A few dinner parties had been attended and hosted in the spring, presumably before the opening of the current opera. And one Sunday dinner with Kellar was noted starkly, shortly after his arrival in England.

Yet Kellar was more familiar with the house than that. Had he visited often in the past? Or had he called on Caterina in the mornings, while her husband was out at his office?

More carefully, Constance read the entries for the days between the twenty-seventh of June and the sixth of July, but there were no scheduled suppers with his wife noted, or any unusual meetings. Very little seemed to have been entered after the sixth, as though Montague's efficiency had taken an understandable knock.

Replacing the book exactly where it had been, Constance closed the drawer and set about picking the lock of the middle one on the left-hand side. Hurried footsteps in the hall made her pause, her heartbeat racing. Kneeling on the floor behind Montague's desk was not a comfortable position to be found in.

She jumped up and hurried to the fireplace, keeping her eye on the study door. The footsteps moved on into the drawing room. The maid dusting, no doubt. Constance slipped back to the desk and returned the handy little tools to the lock. A second later, it clicked.

Keeping alert for any movements across the hall, she slid the drawer open. Only two small bundles of letters nestled within, tied with ribbon. Intrigued, Constance lifted one and untied it carefully.

A quick glance showed her each letter was written by the same hand, that of Sophie Worthington. They seemed to be replies to his, modest love letters containing a touching air of excitement that ran all through their courtship and betrothal. Sophie seemed to have been young, lively, innocent. And she very much looked forward to marrying dear Digby.

Constance moved to the last letter in the bundle, the most recent. But she found no trace of disagreement, no quarrel between the pair that might have resulted in murder. Memorizing the address from which the letters had been written, she quickly retied the bundle and replaced it in the drawer.

The other, smaller bundle was correspondence with Caterina.

The letters stopped after their marriage, as if, after that date, she had never gone very far without her husband. These were much shorter than Sophie's letters, but much more effusive and frank from the beginning. She sent him a thousand passionate kisses, missed him every moment they were apart, lived only for the sound of his voice and the terribly few hours spent in his arms.

Both sets of letters were moving in their different ways, but Caterina's made Constance feel particularly guilty for prying. More than that, they niggled at her certainty that Montague was the murderer of both women. She could see no reason for him to kill Sophie. It wasn't as if he had married anyone else around that time. Caterina was not yet in England. Also, the mere fact that he had kept those letters—and only them—showed a softer, more sentimental side to the man that did not fit with murder. And he locked up the letters like a symbol of that hidden side, revealed only to his loves.

In a hurry now, she retied Caterina's letters and placed them beside the others before closing the drawer and using her tools to spring the lock back into place.

The awareness came upon her slowly. No sound disturbed her, no movement at the corner of her eye caught her attention. She simply felt uneasy, which she did anyway for invading the privacy of someone's dead loves—even if he was a murderer. And then she knew she was being watched.

Her stomach dived as she dropped the picks into her bag and rose slowly to her feet.

Digby Montague stood in the doorway watching her.

CHAPTER THIRTEEN

S HE COULD NOT tell how long he had been there, but she saw no point in losing the rest of her dignity by lying. So she said nothing. Neither did he. After a long, tense moment, he moved with deliberation and closed the study door.

Suddenly, she was glad of the desk between them. Her skin prickled all over. She altered the grip on her bag, which could double as a useful weapon in a crisis, and calculated the time it would take her to reach the bell rope.

"Did you read them?" Montague asked, his voice expressionless.

"Some of them," she replied. "I'm sorry. This must seem to you an intolerable invasion of your privacy."

"It should," he agreed, taking a few steps further into the room. "But, in fact, I find it hard to care. Whether or not you read them, my wife will still be dead. I take it Kellar is now convinced beyond all doubt that I killed her?"

"Kellar's convictions are a mystery to us too." No harm in reminding him that she and Solomon came as a pair. Used to spotting the signs of violence in advance, she could see no warning of it in Montague. Yet her body reacted on its own, every nerve alert and ready. Monague could have killed two women and got away with both. Right now, it wasn't much comfort to know that if she became the third, Solomon would hunt him to destruction. At the very least.

"If anything," Constance said, feeling her way, "the letters would appear to stand in your favor. But I would not have read them if we didn't have grounds for suspecting you. To put it vulgarly, you have most to gain from your wife's death, and your business is in need of funds. You would have had no trouble entering her room, with or without roses. And you have not been truthful with us."

"I see no reason why I should be," he said frankly. "You have no authority, and I have every right to keep my private life just that."

"Be assured that if you have done no wrong, your secrets are safe with us. My main reason for reading your letters is our discovery that the late Miss Worthington died in a disturbingly similar manner to your wife."

Montague's lips twisted into a bitter smile. "I thought Kellar must have ferreted out that fact. How much worse do you imagine it made me feel to see Caterina like that? Suddenly dead with no reason, no cause, a nightmare that repeats as though I'm cursed."

"You?" Constance said coolly. "It is the women who are dead. And you never told us about Carl Darrow."

Montague gave a quick, impatient shrug. "What honorable man would publicize his wife's shame and his own?"

"When did you discover she was involved with Darrow?"

He moved toward the desk and dropped into the hard chair at its other side, rubbing a hand across his face. "I knew from the way she spoke of him, another interest, another fascination. And I knew from her distraction when it actually began." The corner of his eye twitched. "He was not the first, but I doubt she was aware I knew about the others."

"Why did you tell her you knew about Darrow?"

"Because I had had enough. I couldn't go on constantly looking over her shoulder for yet another man. I wanted my wife to *be* my wife. Perhaps I should have spoken before, but…she was like some wild, rare creature not subject to the laws of the rest of the world. She needed her freedom to follow her heart, and I knew I held a piece of her that no one else ever would. They were passing ships. I was her rock."

While he spoke, Constance had moved subtly and now stood by the bell rope. Sitting, he was less threatening, but she did not like his unfocused stare. And his sudden, rare openness set her teeth on edge. It was almost as if he were acting.

"Someone else called you her rock," she commented.

"Steady but dull. And yet Caterina's needs were not the only ones to be considered. The affair with Darrow went beyond her usual two weeks, and I had had enough."

Constance caught her breath. Was this to be a confession? And if so, would she get out of this room alive?

She took a firmer grip of her bag, felt the bell rope nudge against her arm. "So what did you do?"

"I told her. It was a Sunday, and we were both free all day. We walked in the park and talked, and it all came out. I told her I had reached the end of my tether, that she had the choice of ending the affair or leaving me, because I could stand no more. She wept, appalled that she had hurt me, and promised to see Darrow the very next day to break everything off between them for good."

His eyes refocused on Constance, and she inched her fingers near enough to grasp the bell rope.

He said, "I further told her there were to be no more men, that she had to keep her vows to me or make a clean break, because I would live like this no longer. She agreed."

Constance licked her lips. "And this conversation took place on Sunday the twenty-sixth of June?"

He blinked, as though surprised by the detail. "Yes. It must have been."

"Did she tell you afterward that she had spoken to Darrow and ended things between them?"

"Yes. She told me the next evening when she came home from the theatre. She smiled and made a fuss of me."

But locked you out of her room...

"Then she seemed happy?"

"Not *happy*," he said consideringly. "But contented enough. As though she knew she had done the right thing. But she was not a machine. She could not turn her affections off with a lever. She had to adjust to his absence."

"And did she?"

He nodded. "I believe so. Gradually through the next week she seemed happier and happier until, by the last Wednesday, she was positively euphoric, and it went deeper than her brilliant performance at the opera. I think she found an unexpected new fulfilment in fidelity, in the new closeness it had brought us."

Or in her new resolve to run away with Darrow?

"I was enough for her," he said. "I shall always be glad of that."

"Thank you for your honesty," Constance said, although she was far from certain it was genuine. "Tell me, did Caterina know about your previous betrothal?"

His eyes widened. "Of course."

"Did she know how Miss Worthington died?"

"Hardly. Even the doctors didn't know that."

"Did she ask about it? Did she ever seem frightened of you?"

His brow smoothed, his lips curling into a bitter little smile. "You mean, did she suspect me of murdering poor Sophie, and did she fear she was my next victim? Hardly. I believe I would like you to leave now."

This fitted so perfectly with Constance's wishes that relief flooded her. All the same, she gave his chair a wide berth and her bag-wielding hand remained poised. As she placed her fingers on the door latch, he spoke once more.

"Mrs. Grey? You will not be admitted again."

She opened the door and went out, crossed the hall to the front door, and walked into the sunshine. Her legs were shaking.

Where are you, Solomon?

Instinctively, she walked in the direction they had left the carriage. It waited under the shady branches of a chestnut tree at the corner of the square, the coachmen leaning on the trunk and chatting to a couple of other men. He straightened as soon as he saw Constance coming and walked toward her.

"Where is Mr. Grey?" she asked.

He nodded behind her. "Just coming, ma'am."

Spinning around, she saw Solomon crossing the garden and forced herself not to run to him. But he knew her, and her disquiet must have shown, because he instantly took her hand, threading it through his arm and drawing her with him along the path, their bodies very close together.

Constance soaked up the comfort of his nearness like a sponge. "It's Montague," she blurted, and poured out everything she had learned about the unexplained death of Sophie Worthington, her discovery of the letters, and being caught by Montague, who had at least answered her questions before forbidding her his house.

Solomon listened carefully, as he always did, then said, "But you don't believe him?"

"I couldn't shake off the feeling that he was *acting*."

He nodded. "People do act, of course, when they have something difficult to say. Sometimes it's easier to say as someone else. If you see what I mean. Especially for someone as private as Montague."

"True," she said doubtfully. "Then you don't think I'm right?"

"About his killing Caterina and possibly Sophie too? We still have no real evidence that a murder took place, but if it did, Montague would certainly be top of my list now."

Just telling him seemed to have calmed her nerves. Her discoveries and her fright slipped back into proportion.

"What have you learned?" she asked.

"Frustratingly little. Our alleged rose thief denies the charge, says Mr. Jones at number twelve blames him for everything. Apparently, Wainright does cut flowers from the square simply to annoy Jones, but he did not do so in the middle of Wednesday night—Thursday morning. I have a few sightings of Caterina's comings and goings to add to her schedule, but nothing more. Most people were more interested in discovering the reasons behind my questions than in bothering to cover anything up. They're curious but not maliciously so. As far as I can tell."

"Are you finished here? Shall we call on Kellar?"

"I think it is time."

"Past time," Constance said grimly, thinking of her mother's agitation the day before. "I shall enjoy taking him by surprise."

KELLAR HAD NEGLECTED to give them his address, which now seemed more suspicious than when they had first noticed the oversight.

"He might well be at the office looking for us," Solomon pointed out as the carriage pulled up just off Picadilly. "He must want to be kept informed."

"But does he?" Constance asked as Solomon reached forward to open the door. "He hasn't come to us since Thursday night, and he could hardly ask much at the funeral luncheon. If he's guilty, I can't really understand his stirring up this investigation in the first place. Can you really see him climbing up to Caterina's bedroom window and letting himself in?"

"Yes," Solomon said frankly, handing her down from the carriage. He nodded to the coachmen, and Constance took his arm. "He is very fit for a man of his years, and the climb is not arduous. That there is no evidence of foul play fits his character and the skills we suspect him of possessing. And he could well be using us as we first suspected, just to prove his innocence. Then there is the reason for keeping his address secret. Simply the habit of a man who tends to make enemies?"

"Possibly. I'm certainly glad to know Francis Fanshaw. A man can't apply for such a prominent position without an address, after all." And Sir Francis, fortunately, had seen no reason to keep it secret. "Actually," she added thoughtfully, "I doubt he wants *me* endangering his reputation by visiting him."

"What a shame," Solomon said, halting to knock briskly on what they believed to be Kellar's front door.

It was opened by a tall, thin manservant with a face as veiled but considerably less friendly than Kellar's.

"Mr. Kellar, if you please," Solomon said, proffering his card. "The matter is urgent."

The servant took the card without looking at it and made a very slight bow. "Please follow me."

Constance suspected they would be abandoned in a reception room while Kellar nipped smartly from the house, but it seemed she maligned their host. The servant led them straight to a parlor, where Kellar himself stood in front of the empty fireplace.

"Mr. and Mrs. Grey, sir," the manservant announced, still without apparent reference to Solomon's card.

He saw us arrive, Constance thought, *and he's quite prepared for us*. The man was annoying.

Kellar advanced upon them, smiling, hand held out, quite the consummate diplomat. "You will join me for luncheon, won't you? I am about to sit down, and there is plenty for three."

"In that case, thank you, we will," Constance replied, and they followed him through to the cozy dining room, where Kellar was an attentive host, holding Constance's chair and waiting for them both to sit before he assumed his own place between them at the head of the table.

The same manservant brought in a tureen of soup and several other dishes, which he left on the table before withdrawing discreetly. Kellar himself served the soup and offered Constance a glass of wine.

"Thank you, no," she said. "We have more to do this afternoon." And one needed all one's wits around Kellar.

"Ah. Then you doom me to drinking alone, unless I can persuade you to a small glass, Grey?"

"No, thank you," Solomon said.

Kellar let them appreciate a mouthful of excellent, creamy vegetable soup and a bite of delicious herb toast before he said, "Well, how does your investigation progress?"

"Interestingly," Solomon said. "It seems you could well be right that Montague had something to do with his wife's death."

Kellar paused for an instant with his soup spoon halfway to his mouth. "You have evidence?"

They didn't answer immediately. Instead, Constance said, "Why didn't you tell us that Montague's betrothed had died in similar circumstances?"

This time, Kellar laid his spoon in the bowl. Constance could have sworn he was surprised, though whether by the news or by their discovery of it, she could not decide.

"I didn't know," he said slowly. "I merely sensed something about him that I did not care for. Caterina told me nothing about an earlier betrothal, merely denied that he had been married before."

"It does not appear to be a secret. The servants speak of it openly."

Kellar picked his spoon up again. "When you say similar circumstances, what exactly do you mean?"

Constance told him the little she knew.

"Interesting," Kellar remarked.

Constance could not quite read the expression that flickered briefly through his veiled eyes. Consternation, perhaps, or guilt. Hoping to keep him off balance, she said, "Why do you keep bothering my mother?"

Kellar blinked. "Bothering her? Dear lady, I happened to wander into her shop one day and on another I knocked on her door to call, as one occasionally does upon old friends. Consider yourselves, comfortably calling on me today. And since we are questioning each other—why did you not introduce her when she blundered into your dining room on Friday?"

"I wasn't sure she wanted to speak to you," Constance said.

"Neither was I," Kellar replied. "Hence my brief visits."

"And what did you learn from those brief visits?" Constance asked frostily.

The hint of a smile tugged at Kellar's lips. "That she doesn't seem to be sure either."

"Then we can take it that is the end of the matter?" Constance said, sounding for all the world like an overprotective parent. Part of her wanted to laugh. Most of her was far too uneasy.

"Probably," Kellar said vaguely.

"But you still haven't answered my question," Constance pointed out. "Why did you go there? You even knew *where* to go, and neither of us told you that. You can't have expected to find your Miss Silver running a curiosity shop in Covent Garden. And don't tell me it was an accident, because I wouldn't believe you."

Kellar smiled, lifting his wine glass and turning it in his fingers. "Of course it wasn't an accident. Why *wouldn't* I seek her out?"

Constance laid down her spoon, meeting the challenging, yet humorous gaze. "Cards on the table, Mr. Kellar. You know who and what I am. I'm sure you can guess who gave me the idea. Juliet is doing better than she has in twenty-five years, and I won't have her...bothered."

She almost said *upset*, but that would perhaps have betrayed too much.

"You love your mother," Kellar observed.

"That is not the point at issue," Solomon intervened. "What interests us is why a gentleman in pursuit of an important Foreign Office promotion should start visiting a lady of questionable reputation."

"Nicely put," Constance said without taking her gaze from Kellar.

"Thank you," Solomon returned. "The other thing that concerns us is what Caterina Montague might have known about you that you wish to keep silent. And yes, the two questions *are* connected."

Kellar caught his breath, his eyes dancing. "Oh my goodness, I have become a suspect! That, I did not foresee."

"No, you foresaw acquittal," Constance said coldly, "well before accusation."

"It seems I was wrong. How did I do it?"

"You could have persuaded her to let you in through the front door. After all, she knew and trusted you. Or you could have climbed up through her window while she slept. You knew where her bedroom was."

Kellar stood and began to collect the bowls, which he placed on the sideboard with the soup tureen before lifting the lids from the remaining dishes on the table.

"You are very thorough," he remarked. "I commend you. But in this case, you are quite, quite wrong. I would never have hurt a hair on Caterina's head because, you see, I hold myself responsible for her parents' deaths."

It was simply said, without obvious emotion or urbanity. A simple fact. Either he was telling the truth or he was the best actor never to walk the stage. Constance inclined to the former.

Judging by Solomon's next remark, so did he. "You will appreciate that we have had dishonest clients before. If you truly want our help, you must tell us the whole truth. Do you want our help?"

"Yes," Kellar said, resuming his seat. "More than ever, now."

"Then tell us," Constance said, "about the last times you saw Caterina alive. From Monday the twenty-seventh of June."

"Allow me to help you to some cold meats while I try to remember…"

"WHAT DO YOU think?" Constance asked when they had left Kellar's abode.

"That we took him by surprise, both by finding his home and

by our discoveries about Caterina."

Despite the calm neutrality of his voice, she knew he was troubled, and she shared that unease. "Why would he be surprised?" she wondered aloud. "He was the one who suspected murder in the first place. Whatever his reasons—and I do mostly believe in his guilt over her parents—did he expect us to be such poor investigators?"

"Perhaps he did," Solomon said slowly. "Perhaps, as we thought, he really did employ us to find nothing. Which means there must be something to find."

"Insulting." Catching sight of the carriage ambling toward them, she halted. "But why would he think so little of us? He knows we found the killer in Venice."

"I have no idea. The trouble is, I still like the man. I don't believe he lies to us. He just keeps things back, probably from habit."

"Are you ruling him out as Caterina's killer?"

Solomon made a frustrated gesture with one hand as the carriage came to a halt beside them. "We have no evidence one way or the other. But if he killed Caterina to keep her quiet and preserve his reputation, why would he then go anywhere near Juliet, whose company could ruin him at least as effectively?"

Constance shivered. "He could have hurt her, in the flat. He had the time. She's used to taking care of herself, but…"

"But he left when she bade him. Which implies he is indeed a man of honor."

"But we have no proof. Montague is still our likeliest suspect. Where now?"

"The Royal Academy of Music," Solomon said, "as we originally planned. We have been neglecting Darrow."

Perhaps, but it didn't take two people to talk to his teachers at the academy. Not when everything was pointing toward Montague as the culprit. "Why don't I let you off at the academy," Constance suggested, "while I go and speak to the Worthingtons about their daughter's death?"

SOLOMON HAD SOME sympathy with Constance's eager pursuit of Montague. He did indeed seem the likeliest suspect. But his own tidy nature required a closer look at all suspects, and they knew considerably less about Darrow than about the other two. Of course, he was much younger and there would be less to find, but a school was bound to be less biased in its opinions than friends.

The Royal Academy of Music was just off Hanover Square. Made from three old houses knocked into one, it appeared to be a maze of low doorways and passages that resembled tunnels more than hallways or corridors.

Solomon discovered the administrative office more by luck than anything else, and explained to the elderly gentleman he found there that he would like the opportunity to speak to the teachers of the violinist Carl Darrow.

The man's eyes widened. "Darrow? I have heard him play. A most promising young talent. But I don't believe he was one of our students. I would surely have recalled him, being a violinist myself."

The old gentleman might well have been a violinist, but he also resembled most people's idea of an absent-minded academic at best. At worst, an aging old man whose memory had wandered off with the years.

"Could you possibly check your records?" Solomon asked politely, just as a younger man entered the office.

The old fellow beamed. "Of course! Mr. Vallance here will help you. The gentleman is looking for Carl Darrow's instructors. He isn't one of ours, of course, but best to be sure. He might have come for a few lessons…"

The younger man marched over to a formidable array of cabinets. "What year do you believe he left the academy?"

"I'm not sure. 1852 at the latest, I would say, possibly a year or so before that."

The clerk, if such he was, looked irritated, but opened the second drawer from the top of the last cabinet in the row. After a moment of rummaging, he shut the drawer again, moved to the next cabinet, and repeated the process.

This went on for some time, without explanation. Eventually, the young man strode across the office to more ancient-looking cabinets and carried on.

Eventually, he swung around to face Solomon. "I have looked back over ten years, and there is no Darrow in our records at all."

Solomon, who had begun to suspect as much, said hopefully, "Could some member of staff have removed them temporarily? Perhaps to write a character reference or some such?"

"His registration would remain. He never matriculated here, and was never taught here, even on short courses." The faintest of smiles dawned, and the young man cast an almost affectionate look at his ancient colleague. "Besides, if Mr. Laurel doesn't recall him, he never stepped through our door."

⚜

CHAPTER FOURTEEN

T HE ADDRESS IN Kensington from which Sophie Worthington had written her love letters was not a modest one. A detached house, it was the largest in the leafy street. Constance was glad she had worn something more decorative than her severe office gown. It was quite possible, of course, that Sophie's parents had moved in the decade since she had died.

A butler opened the door to Constance's ring, and she presented her business card, asking for Mrs. Worthington. To her relief, he invited her to wait in a comfortable reception room while he established whether or not the lady of the house was at home.

Constance looked out of the window and wished she had used her personal card rather than the Silver and Grey one. Many people found "inquiries" to be both repugnant and impertinent. If she was denied, she supposed she could always write, although there were no guarantees of an answer, and she would be reduced to the time-consuming process of meeting the lady or her husband "by accident."

A rustling at the door caused her to turn just before it opened and a modestly but fashionably dressed lady in dove gray walked in. The woman was somewhere in her fifties, with neatly pinned, almost-white hair. Her posture was erect, her manner curious rather than outraged. Her eyes bore that sad, faded look of the bereaved, even when they smiled.

"Mrs. Silver?" she said. "I am Mrs. Worthington. What can I

possibly do for you?"

She didn't invite Constance to sit, which was quite understandable.

"First, please forgive my intrusion," Constance said pleasantly. "I am investigating a lady's recent death and hoped you could provide me with some answers."

Mrs. Worthington's eyebrows flew up. "Why? Am I acquainted with this lady?"

"I would be surprised. You have probably heard her name, Caterina di Ripoli, otherwise known as Mrs.—"

"Montague," Mrs. Worthington interrupted. "Digby's wife. I could not attend the funeral, but I sent flowers."

"Then you and Mr. Montague are still close?"

"No, not really. Just a card at Christmas, and we notify each other of weddings and funerals. I was glad when he married, though the lady was a curious choice from a worldly point of view."

"Did you attend the wedding?" Constance asked.

She shook her head. "I didn't think that would be appropriate."

"Did he notify you of Mrs. Montague's death? Or did you learn about it in the newspapers?"

"He wrote to me. Mrs. Silver, I am at a loss. What is it about the poor young lady's death that you are *investigating*?" There was a very slight emphasis on the last word that may have signified contempt for the work or for Constance herself. "She died of a weak heart, did she not?"

"Is that what Mr. Montague told you?"

"Yes. It was in the papers, too. Are you saying it is not true?"

"She did have a heart irregularity," Constance said carefully, "successfully controlled by her physician's treatment. She was healthy enough to sing the main part in an opera six nights a week and to practice rigorously every day. To all intents and purposes, she was a healthy and active young woman. And yet she apparently died in her sleep."

Mrs. Worthington's eyes fell.

"It was like that with your daughter too, was it not?" Constance said gently.

The lady raised her eyes again, and this time they were outraged. "What are you trying to imply?"

"The similarities are on the bare surface. I am trying to find out if they go deeper. Let me tell you the circumstances of Mrs. Montague's—"

"I don't wish to hear about them!" Mrs. Worthington snapped. "Are you some kind of ghoul? A reporter for some disgusting scandal rag?"

"No, ma'am. I am rather desperately trying to find the truth about one young woman's inexplicable death."

Mrs. Worthington waved one dismissive hand, swinging away from Constance. "Sometimes death is not explained. God just takes his own and we are left to cope with it, to make sense of it."

"That is what I am trying to do," Constance said at once. "Make sense of it. And, if possible, prevent it from happening again."

"You are not a doctor!"

"No, I am not. But I can observe, and I can think. So can you. Mrs. Montague went to sleep one night, apparently happy with her whole life. She was found dead by her maid in the morning. There were no marks on her body, no obvious signs of bodily distress or poisoning. But her pillows had been moved into a position in which she never slept. Somehow, a vase of roses had made their way into her bedchamber during the night, probably cut from the garden in the square opposite the house. Does any of that sound remotely familiar to you?"

Mrs. Worthington moved away from her and sat down. Distractedly, she waved Constance to the chair opposite.

"Only in the suddenness. My daughter was found in our own garden, where she had been reading. I thought she had fallen asleep in the sunshine and took her hat out to her. She didn't want to damage her skin so close to the wedding. But she wouldn't wake up…"

"It was you who found her?" Constance asked.

Mrs. Worthington nodded. "She looked so peaceful… I dropped the hat over her face—as a joke, you know, to wake her—but she didn't stir. Though she was still warm to the touch, I could not rouse her. I shouted into the house for them to fetch the doctor immediately, and then my husband and Digby ran out and Digby felt dementedly for her pulse, for a breath, and found none. The doctor came quickly, but I already knew my daughter was dead."

She ended on little more than a whisper.

Constance had to swallow before she said, "Mr. Montague had been with your husband before they came out to join you after you shouted?"

"What?" Mrs. Worthington blinked, as though making belated sense of Constance's question. "No. No, we were expecting him, but he hadn't yet arrived. I think he just came in and saw Stanley—my husband—bolt out of his study. He followed him, of course, sensing the emergency. He still had his hat in his hand when I saw him." Her lips twisted. "Foolish, the little things one remembers about such huge, shattering events…"

"They can be," Constance said, "and sometimes they are very helpful. I'm sorry to ask this of you, but could you possibly show me where this happened?"

Mrs. Worthington stared at her, jaw dropping. But something had changed. Outrage had vanished from her eyes, and wary curiosity had taken its place.

She closed her mouth and nodded. "Very well."

Constance followed Mrs. Worthington through the house to a sunny parlor with French doors to a colorful garden. They stepped onto a close-cut lawn and walked toward a large, well-established pear tree.

"It was summer then, too," Mrs. Worthington said. She pointed behind the tree. "That is where I found her. From the parlor, I could only see her legs and feet, and the sun was shining directly onto them…"

"And you found her lying down? On the grass?"

"On a red tartan blanket. I still have it, though I never use it."

"Was she on her back or her front?"

"On her back, with her eyes closed. Her book was open beside her."

"Was her head on a pillow?"

Mrs. Worthington shook her head. "No… She had brought a cushion to sit on, though she must have tossed it aside when she lay down. Usually, she sat on the cushion with her back against the tree trunk. Ever since she was a child…"

Constance's stomach gave a twist of recognition. "Where was the cushion when you found her?"

"A few feet away." Mrs. Worthington pointed toward a bed of bright, sweet-scented roses. "Just by the flower bed, lying carelessly, as though it had been knocked or thrown there without attention."

Constance imagined a faceless young woman, little more than a child, sitting reading, with her back against the tree. The soporific effect of the sun on this contented girl could have caused her to move position, stretching out on her back, shoving the cushion aside with her right hand.

She looked around the garden, saw the path around to the front of the house. There was a tall old gate that had probably once been used to keep children safely corralled. She could imagine Montague walking up that path and through the gate, as silently as he had entered his house and his study this morning. Keeping to the same path, he could easily have kept himself from view from the parlor, where Mrs. Worthington had been sitting.

Had Sophie already been asleep when he approached the tree? Had he picked up the cushion and simply held it over her face until she stopped breathing? If so, would her mother not have noticed the frantic kicking of her legs as she fought to save her own life?

Surely it was more likely that he found her in her usual position, with her back against the tree. She was probably delighted to see him. Perhaps they had kissed and he had swept her, lover-like, onto his knee, still hidden by the tree while he seized the cushion she had been sitting on and smothered her with it. He was a big man. He could have controlled her thrashing without moving that cushion.

And when she was dead, he had simply smoothed out any grimace or sign of distress from her skin. Closed her eyes. Perhaps he had even picked up escaped feathers from the cushion, from her nose and mouth and hands, replaced fallen pins from her hair, and then laid her out on the blanket so that only her legs were visible from the house, and hurried back down the path. Perhaps he had taken a short walk to calm his breath and his nerves. Or just gone straight to the front door and rung the bell…

"Was there a postmortem examination?" Constance asked.

Mrs. Worthington nodded. "The doctor advised it because there was no obvious cause of death. But it revealed nothing. She was perfectly healthy. Just…dead. There was no obvious signs of disease, but the coroner did say there was much they still had to understand about diseases of the heart and the brain…" She gave a helpless little shrug. "The cause didn't really matter to me. It would not bring my daughter back to life."

"No," Constance agreed. "I am sorry. Where is your husband's study, where he heard your call for help? At the back of the house?"

"It looks onto the side. My husband is dead too, you know. He never really got over Sophie's loss. I think he was glad when the lung fever took him the following winter."

Constance's heart twisted. "I'm sorry," she said again. "You have had much to contend with."

"So has poor Digby," Mrs. Worthington said. "He did not harm my daughter, and I very much doubt he harmed his wife. If that is what you are thinking."

It was. It still was. "Where is the back door? To the kitchen?"

"At the side also."

"So there is no kitchen window at the back of the house?"

"No."

"And what time of day did this happen? In the afternoon?"

"I found her at half past two o'clock."

When the servants would have finished their housework and were preparing for tea and dinner, and showing any callers into the parlor or the drawing room Constance had glimpsed at the front of the house.

"What time did you expect Mr. Montague to call?"

"He came most days, around three, earlier if he and Sophie had planned some excursion."

"Then he was not hard at work at the office every day?"

"I think he played truant sometimes. But he had begun to look a little tired and drawn. I suspect he began early and returned to the office in the evenings, even after concerts and parties."

"He was a devoted suitor?"

"He was."

"And Sophie, was she equally devoted?"

"It was a love match. My husband would have preferred her to marry a banker like himself, of course, but he bowed to her wishes. We both liked Digby."

"Did she ever give you any indication that he frightened her in any way?"

"You mean was he over-amorous?" Mrs. Worthington said wryly. "If he was, she never told me."

"In any way at all," Constance repeated.

"No," Mrs. Worthington said. "She was eager to marry him."

"Did they ever quarrel?" Constance asked.

"Occasionally. Little squalls, quickly over on both sides."

"In the week before she died," Constance said, "did she seem different in any way? Worried? Distracted? Euphoric, even?"

Mrs. Worthington shook her head. "No. She was an even-tempered girl, in love, and looking forward to her wedding."

Yet there was a motive somewhere, Constance thought grimly. However, she would not find it here.

MONTAGUE HAD NEVER set foot in a police establishment before. He had no real idea what went on there. But he had once met a superintendent of police whose place of employment was at Scotland Yard, and he remembered the man's name. He had definitely been a gentleman.

"Mr. Galsworth, if you please," he said, presenting his card to the rough fellow in uniform who had just batted a crowd of grubby urchins out of the way to get to him.

The name worked like a charm. Galsworth must indeed be a senior figure, for the rough fellow straightened even further and snapped across the room, "Mr. Galsworth in his office?"

"Yes, sergeant. No further appointments this afternoon."

"Come with me, sir, if you please." Abandoning the disconsolate urchins, the sergeant marched across the hall to the stairs and Montague followed him, his heart racing.

He knew he was taking a chance. It had cost him several hours to work out the best course of action, for he knew not to act on impulses born of anger. And he had been furious to find that woman poking about his desk, outraged by the invasion of his privacy, the abuse of a permission he had granted like a fool. Kellar should have known better, for though Mrs. Grey spoke like a lady, she was no more than a thief, a burglar, with all the little tools of her grubby trade. He wanted her arrested, slung in prison, hanged.

And yet she was married to Solomon Grey, whom he had no desire to offend. Grey could well be a means to stabilize his business, and he could think of no inoffensive way to tell him to rein in his wife's criminal impulses. No, that would come better from some officer of the law.

Which brought its own risks. The last thing he wanted was to have the police taking an interest in Caterina's death. Dear God, no. He was walking on a knife's edge…

The sergeant left him for a mere moment to present his card to the superintendent, before Galsworth himself came to the door, his hand held out in welcome.

"Montague, my dear fellow. My sincere condolences on your loss. We were so saddened to hear of it."

"Thank you," Montague said mechanically, allowing himself to be ushered into a large office—a little functional, perhaps, but Galsworth had added a few homely touches: a couple of decent landscapes on the walls, a photograph of his wife and children on his desk.

"They'll bring tea," Galsworth said, indicating the visitor's chair on the near side of the desk, "though I'm afraid you might not recognize it as such! What brings you to me today?"

"I've had a bit of a run-in with someone," Montague said diffidently, "someone who has taken advantage of my trust and my state of mourning to commit what I can only call a crime." He threw up his hand to forestall Galsworth's immediate outrage. "No, I don't want her charged. I don't want Caterina's name associated with scandal of this nature. But I cannot allow the incident to pass, either."

Galsworth was frowning. "What exactly did this woman do?"

"I found her kneeling in front of my desk, applying instruments I can only imagine to be lockpicks to the drawer."

"My dear fellow!" Galsworth exclaimed. "How did she even get into your house?"

Montague sighed. No acting was necessary here to produce the kind of tolerant annoyance he had always felt for Kellar. "It was the fault of a family friend who had become something of a father figure to Caterina after the death of her parents. He actually helped her to come to this country with her inheritance intact. He was fond of her. I don't doubt his sense of loss, and so when he began looking for answers to the suddenness of

Caterina's death, I humored him. I allowed him to send a couple I thought respectable to ask more questions of my household and the doctor who had treated my wife."

"Did they learn anything…concerning?"

"Nothing that we did not already know. They kept harping on the roses found in her room. Roses. I ask you, what harm could roses have done her? I think it was just an excuse to keep poking around the house. But I have had enough, Galsworth. I want them to leave me and my household alone."

"Quite right," Galsworth said, gratifyingly downright. "Have you told your servants not to admit them?"

"Of course. But as I said, she has lockpicks."

Galsworth's eyebrows flew up. "And you think she might… But that is outrageous! But you know she has used devices already."

"Which is why I thought a word—perhaps not from you, but from someone relatively senior—might deter them. If they know the police are informed, they will surely desist and leave us in peace."

"It's the least a grieving widower can expect," Galsworth said, clearly incensed. He snatched a piece of paper toward him and reached for a pen. "Who exactly are these people?"

Montague was prepared. He fished Silver and Grey's business card from his pocket and passed it across the desk.

Galsworth frowned. "Silver and Grey… Why do I know those names? Yes, they have figured in a few reports that have crossed my desk. Leave it with me, Montague. I have just the man to put them in their place."

Montague allowed himself to shift in his chair and made his smile both uncomfortable and apologetic. "Grey is one Solomon Grey, a rather important shipping magnate with his fingers in many pies."

"Political pies?" Galsworth asked sharply.

"Largely commercial, but we know how these things overlap. Wealth such as his brings power. This investigation sideline must be largely his wife's business. I can see no other reason for him to be involved in such a low enterprise. Naturally, I wouldn't mind his being made aware of her methods—without accusing him of anything that might adversely affect you." *Or me.*

Galsworth nodded sagely. "I quite understand."

"I have taken up enough of your time." Montague rose and held out his hand. "Forgive me for presuming on our slight acquaintance, but I did not know where else to turn."

Galsworth stood up and grasped his hand. "I'm very glad you did. As I say, I know just the right man to sort this out for you." He accompanied Montague to the door, where he addressed the constable outside. "Send Inspector Harris to me."

So it was done. The woman would be scared off and Grey informed without alienating him from Montague's business interests.

And Montague himself was free from suspicion.

⌥

CHAPTER FIFTEEN

S OLOMON, HAVING GIVEN up the search for Darrow's music school, changed tack and decided to visit instead his own valued associate, Thomas Halliwell, who had been out of town when he had last looked for him. The two men had done lucrative business together in the past, and Halliwell, like Montague, had considerable interests in tea.

"Grey, my dear fellow, an unexpected pleasure!" Halliwell greeted him, coming out of his impressive office to shake hands. "Come in, tell me what I can do for you. My man told me you called on Friday when I was away."

"I did."

"A brandy to celebrate?" Halliwell asked, walking to the cut-glass decanter on the mahogany cabinet.

"What are we celebrating?"

"Whatever you like," Halliwell said, chuckling as he poured. They took their brandies to the comfortable chairs by the fireplace, and Solomon said, "I'm interested in a tea merchant called Digby Montague of Montague and Son."

"Old and respected firm," Halliwell said.

"Do you do business with them?"

"Don't need to, so I never have."

"Do you hear credible rumors about his solvency?"

"For years, now, but he always bounces back. Sails a little close to the wind with selling his cargo and paying his creditors. Pity, because they have a couple of highly lucrative plantations in

India."

"You spent some time in India, didn't you?" Solomon said casually.

"I did. Still do, from time to time."

"Did you ever encounter Montague there?"

"No…" Halliwell hesitated, then added, "The first time I went was with my father about fifteen years ago, and I believe we just missed Montague. Though it's a huge country, a continent really, there's a network of British residents who make London gossips look like amateurs. I have no evidence that Montague ever did anything wrong, but he certainly earned their anger and contempt with some sort of scandal."

"How?" Solomon asked. "I don't suppose it involved a young lady who died suddenly?"

Halliwell raised his eyebrows. "Oh, no, she wasn't dead from what I heard. Just a lot poorer. She was a young widow, I believe. Some kind of swindle that involved her paying for tea Montague had already sold elsewhere. By the time the fraud was discovered, he had already sailed. I don't know the details, or even if these unsavory rumors are true, but I do know Montague had difficulty shipping his tea after that. As if the ship owners had turned against him. When they do ship it, they probably overcharge."

"Which would explain why his profits keep going down," Solomon said thoughtfully. "And why he can't weather the loss of a single cargo."

"It might," Halliwell said cautiously. "But it would be unkind to spread rumors I certainly can't substantiate. I never heard anything against the man since then."

"No, neither has anyone else." *And yet…* "Do you have a name for this widow?" Solomon asked.

INSPECTOR HARRIS OF Scotland Yard was not best pleased to

receive the summons of his superior. In his view, Superintendent Galsworth existed only to get in the way of police work. Therefore he only grunted in response and dismissed the messenger without lifting his eyes from the report he was writing about a particularly nasty murder in Whitechapel.

"Shouldn't you go now, sir?" said Sergeant Flynn, who was working at the other desk.

Harris spared him a glare.

"Get it over with," Flynn explained. "Then you'd have the rest of the afternoon for real work."

Harris threw down his pen—fortunately nowhere near his report, since the ink spattered for several inches across his desk. "Damn it, do you always have to be right?"

"He might have a more interesting case for us," Flynn pointed out.

Harris made a derisive noise, but all the same, he stood up. "You're right. Get it over with."

Accordingly, he marched out through the main office and on to the rarified corridor where Galsworth had his office.

"Ah, Harris," said Galsworth, looking up from whatever he was reading. It might have been a report, although Harris's theory was that no real work ever passed the superintendent's desk. Only that could explain its tidiness. "Got a bit of a knotty problem for you. What do you know about a firm called Silver and Grey?"

"They undertake private inquiries, sir," Harris said warily, for though he disapproved of the firm's existence on principle, he actually quite liked them in person.

And they had been useful in the past. Sort of.

"Honestly? Who the devil are they?"

"I have found them to be honest," Harris said carefully. "It's something of a side interest for Grey, who's quite a magnate of the shipping world, amongst other things."

"And the woman?"

"What about her, sir?" If Galsworth didn't already know,

Harris was not about to tell him that Constance Silver was a high-class madam.

"What's her background?" Galsworth demanded. "How does she come to be married to a fellow like Grey?"

"She is very beautiful, sir," Harris said uncomfortably.

Galsworth scowled. "Is she, by God? I have reason to doubt her honesty."

Harris could not imagine them ever meeting. "You do, sir? In what way?"

"She's harassing a friend of mine—poor fellow's only just buried his wife and came home to find this Grey woman kneeling in front of his desk, actually breaking into a drawer with a lockpick! Outrageous, Harris!"

"Indeed it is, sir," said Harris, just as if he hadn't done similar things himself. The trouble with Galsworth was that he was too far removed from the investigation of criminals.

"I want you to go and have a word with her," Galsworth. "Frighten her off. Threaten her with arrest and prosecution. Can't have her harassing decent gentlemen in mourning, can we?"

Certainly not when they're friends of yours, Harris thought cynically. Aloud he said, "Very well, sir."

"Might warn the husband what she's up to, too. Daresay he wouldn't stand for it."

Harris, who had a sudden urge to laugh, coughed to cover the fact. "I daresay he wouldn't, sir."

"Well, off you go, then. Make it your priority, Harris. Do it now."

It was already five o'clock and it was his eldest's birthday.

"Go yourself, mind," Galsworth warned. "I want her to know the full force of the law is watching her. She's not to go near Digby Montague or his house, ever again. Understood?"

"Perfectly, sir," Harris said calmly, and walked smartly out of the office. He'd do it too, but not at the expense of his son's birthday tea. He was going home. Tomorrow morning, he might let Silver and Grey laugh at him.

Returning to his office, he found Flynn still there.

"What do you know about a fellow called Digby Montague?"

Flynn thought, tapping a pencil against his cheek. "Married to the Italian opera singer, Caterina di Ripoli. Or he was. She died last week."

"Foul play?" Harris asked.

"No, weak heart, apparently."

"Then what the devil are Silver and Grey doing poking around the widower's house?"

Flynn's eyebrows flew up. "You think there's more to her death, then?"

"Silver and Grey would appear to think so. Or someone's paid them to entertain the idea. And someone else, presumably the husband, has pulled the 'old boys' strings to have them seen off."

"So, are you to see them off? Or investigate the case?" Flynn asked.

"I'm too busy to bother with either," Harris growled. "And so are you. Where's my hat?"

"Going to Silver and Grey's?"

"No, I'm going home. It's Will's birthday."

CONSTANCE WAS ALREADY back in her office, writing what she had learned into her notes and into the schedule of Caterina's doings in the nine days before her death, when Solomon returned.

"What did you learn?" she asked as soon as he entered.

"That Darrow never attended the academy. I trailed around several lesser schools and teachers, only one of which had dealt with him for a matter of six private lessons. No one I spoke to had even heard of him until eighteen months ago."

Constance replaced her pen in its stand. "Really? Then his rise to this level of prominence is quite…unusual. What does it mean, I wonder?"

"His talent is undeniable." Solomon threw himself onto the chair opposite her. "His origins, however, are obscure. Does that matter? I don't know. But why tell people you attended the academy when you didn't?"

"To hide where you really were?" She shrugged impatiently. "Or to hide the fact that he is largely self-taught. There is professional prestige in a good school."

"It still makes him a liar," Solomon pointed out, watching his wife rifle through her notes and add the lie to her notes on Darrow. "I also spoke to Thomas Halliwell, who has interests in India and tea, and he recalls rumors that Montague swindled a young widow out there. Whatever happened, and whether or not it was true, it turned the British in India against him. It probably affects his profits, even if it's lies."

"And if it is true," Constance said, "it certainly doesn't sit well with the honorable man everyone believes him to be. Could Caterina have found out about that?"

"Possibly. He couldn't afford his business to be attacked from this side too."

"Hmm... I don't suppose we can contact this widow?"

"She's still in India, so only by letter."

Constance sighed. "How inconsiderate of her. That will take weeks."

"What about you?" Solomon asked. "Did you find Sophie Worthington's family?"

"I found her widowed mother. And he *could* have killed Sophie in almost exactly the same way—using a cushion instead of a pillow. There was no reason for her death, no known health conditions that might have explained it. There was a postmortem that found nothing unusual. But there was no police investigation, no whisper of foul play. Mrs. Worthington will believe no ill of Montague. But he *could* have done it..."

Solomon listened to the details, occasionally asking questions. And was forced to agree. "He could have done it. It all adds up against him, and yet still we have no proof that he did anything to any of these women. Would he not guess that if his wife died in such a similar way, people might remember about Sophie?"

"If he got away with murdering Sophie," Constance countered, "why would he not use the same method on Caterina? What we don't know is *why* he would have killed Sophie. According to her mother, there was no hint of infidelity on either side. She would have brought him a very decent dowry, and Worthington, a senior figure in the banking world, would have made an extremely useful father-in-law. We need to dig deeper… Ah, that sounds like Janey."

Janey had entered with her key, calling cheerfully to Hat. "Guv'nors in?" she demanded, and a second later all but burst into Constance's office with Lenny in tow.

"Wotcher!" she greeted them. "Got *reams* of stuff for you from the theatre."

"Pull up a chair," Solomon invited Lenny as Janey threw herself into the one next to him.

Janey extracted a notebook from her bag—one Constance had given her for becoming an assistant rather than a mere receptionist in the firm—and leafed through several pages of notes, talking all the time. "Lenny spoke to the porter and a couple of the singers. I went round the stagehands, the dressers, and the understudy. And it's quite interesting. I ain't put it all into order yet, but you'll see her nibs was very busy during the time that interests you. The days she came early to the theatre, she didn't tend to stay there long. Got the porter to call her cabs, and he's got long ears." Janey grinned and fluttered her eyelashes. "I persuaded him to tell me where she went, me being so trustworthy and caring."

"Baggage," Solomon said appreciatively. "So where *did* she go?"

"The street names are in the book. Same street twice, and it wasn't a direction the porter had ever heard before. He knew the other address, though."

Constance raised her eyes from the book to meet Solomon's

gaze. "She'd found another place to meet Darrow, cutting out the disapproving Marianne Locke. She *was* going to run away with him."

"We don't know that," Solomon protested, although he had to admit it was a likely possibility. "She could have had another lover we haven't heard of, or she could just have needed the advice of a trusted friend."

"True," she agreed, but he could sense the excitement in her, as though they were nearing the conclusion and proof awaited only a step or two away. She returned her attention to the book. "This is good work. Well done, both of you. Let me copy it all into the overall schedule and see where we are…"

Her voice trailed off, her pen still while she gazed at Janey's notes, then referred briefly to her own.

"Same street," she said in triumph. "Look, Solomon—according to the stage doorman, Caterina ordered a hackney to take her to Theobalds Street twice, on Wednesday the twenty-ninth of June and Friday the first of July. And according to Mary Webb, she waited hours for her mistress outside a house in the same street on Tuesday the twenty-eighth of June."

"Three times in one week," Solomon said, frowning. "But she never saw Darrow so often."

"Mary never saw Darrow go into the house. I'm sure she would have told me."

"Would she have noticed?" Solomon said. "Waiting so long, she probably fell asleep. Or Darrow could easily have slipped in while the coachman walked his horses. Only…why would she change her habits?"

"Because she no longer cared about being found out. She was planning her escape."

"Why?" Solomon demanded. "We only have Darrow's word that she had agreed to go away with him, and we already know he is a liar."

"So is Montague, at least by omission. And you saw him attack Darrow at the funeral. There is anger in him, Solomon, however controlled. I *felt* it this morning."

"But there's no evidence," Lenny pointed out mildly, "against either of them."

"Lenny's right," Janey said.

Solomon sighed. "He is. Well, let's see if Darrow *could* have met Caterina at Theobalds Street on those days. He practices in the mornings, so it does leave his afternoons free in theory. That is for tomorrow. As is a visit to Theobalds Street. And we need to know if they had got as far as booking their passage to Italy or anywhere else in Europe. If Montague knew about that, then it really does give him a strong motive, so we should try to make a schedule of his movements, too. Could he have followed his wife? Inquired at the docks, or the Channel ports?"

The others nodded in agreement.

"What about your other suspect?" Janey asked. "This Mr. Kellar?"

Constance narrowed her eyes. "I would love to know his movements, too, but somehow, I don't believe our chances of learning them are very high."

JULIET HAD CHANGED into her newest gown. She had made it herself from some gorgeous scarlet silk that had come her way some years ago—most likely stolen, or at least with no duty paid. She could pretend it was her variation of the loose tea gowns that had lately come into fashion, though such garments were generally worn at home, not to go out and dine in public.

Not that she was *actually* going to go to meet Sebastian. Probably. She was merely testing out how she would look if she did go. She refused to apologize for what she was or what she had been, so *if* she went, he would see her in all her glory.

Well, at least, all her eccentricities. She had scrubbed the paint from her face and had not replaced it. Without it, she felt naked, vulnerable. But perhaps she looked better, too. Peering more closely into the glass, she noticed that her skin had improved in recent months. Less red and mottled. And her eyes were clearer. That, no doubt, was due to eating better, since she had a proper kitchen in the flat. And to a lot less gin.

There was nothing she could do about the plumpness and sagging of age.

How much did he know and guess about her life?

He had invited her to be seen with him in public—admittedly not by the kind of society he came from, but she had nosed around the eating house already and knew it to be a respectable place. The question was, how much harm would she do by going there? Harm to her own peace, harm to his life.

No, she would not go. It was not fair on either of them. If she stayed away, he would not ask her again. She knew that with certainty. He would take the hint, as he had when he left for America thirty years before. And peace would return.

If she went, God knew where it would lead. Nowhere good. She was no friend for the likes of him. He was still ambitious, on the verge of a prestigious promotion, according to Connie.

Which was another thing, of course. Constance and Solomon did not trust him. They appeared to suspect him of involvement in the opera singer's death. And Juliet could not put it past him. There would be a reason, of course, though she doubted it was one of simple ambition. Why then would he have invited Juliet to be seen in his company?

I would be death to his ambitions. But I could help Connie rule him out of their investigation...

And if she found he was guilty?

Well, Juliet was a pragmatist herself. It would depend on his reasons whether or not she would betray him.

It would be no betrayal. He has been nothing to me for thirty years. Connie is my life.

She stared at the bright, striking woman in her looking glass, and let her shoulders straighten. She had let her daughter down often enough, but Constance herself admitted that it was Juliet who'd made everything possible for her. She had taught the child to read and write and count, had drilled into her the various ways to stay safe from the scum of the streets and brothels. And if she had put certain matters off just a little too long and failed to stop her entering into prostitution—well, Connie had found her own unique way to both embrace it and rise above it. With a good and responsible man who loved her.

Oh yes, Constance was her pride and joy. And for her, Juliet would brave anyone or anything. Even Sebastian Kellar.

The question was, *should* she?

And was she using Constance as a mere excuse to go?

I could carry it off. At the very least, he'll know what and who I am. He will run a mile, and that will churn me up all over again. But that was always inevitable, and this way, I could help Connie. And when he does run... Well, I won't take to the gin again.

She turned abruptly and seized the red-and-cream hat, which she set on her head at a jaunty angle. She would go—and decide when she got there whether or not to stay.

Perhaps stupidly, she never doubted that he would be there. And he was, rising to meet her as soon as he saw her. She attracted a few glances and longer stares as she made her way toward him, but Sebastian bowed to her and held her chair, as though she were still a lady.

"What a striking ensemble," he said, his eyes twinkling. "You look lovely."

She laughed. "I know how I look, and lovely doesn't cover it."

"I had just made up my mind you wouldn't come."

"Well, you weren't completely wrong. I probably won't stay."

"Then why come at all?"

"Curiosity, of course. I've never eaten here before."

His lips twitched, reminding her unbearably of the secret humor they had once shared and thrived on. "Allow me to order.

And they do a decent claret, too."

He already had a glass at his elbow and now poured some from the bottle into the other glass. The table had been set for two.

"Very well," she said graciously. "If you tell me why you invited me."

"Why do you think? To remember the old days and find out how you are." He lifted his wine in a silent toast, and after a moment's hesitation, she raised her own and allowed the clink of glasses.

"And how do you think I am?" she asked.

"According to your daughter, better than for many years. But I prefer words from your own lips."

Juliet shrugged. "She generally knows what she's talking about, does Constance. For instance, she tells me you're about to be promoted to some new role of high importance."

"It's a home posting," he said deprecatingly, "and allows me to stay in one place. After thirty years of a nomad's life, I find I welcome it. Age catches up with us all."

"And just why, Sebastian, have you looked me up at the very time I could ruin your life?"

He smiled with something that looked alarmingly like affection. "No, you couldn't."

"Is that politeness talking?" she asked. "Because I very much doubt it is ignorance. You know how far I fell, and how damaging my company could be for a respectable man."

She thought his hand tightened on his glass, but since a waiter appeared and set a bowl of soup in front of each of them, he might just have been shifting it out of the way.

"May I know about that fall?" he asked when they were alone again.

"No," Juliet said. "I'm sure you've guessed enough."

He was silent for a few moments, while she ate her soup with an outward calmness she was proud of.

"I suspect it was my fault. Did the old besom read my letters?"

"Oh, no, I burned those. She read my diary—which was quite a feat, since I hid it beneath the floorboards. Clearly, she suspected, though she waited until after you had gone, and then out I went. Without a character, as they say."

"Why did you not tell me?"

"There was no point. I had chosen my bed, and I lay in it. Quite a lot, in fact."

A spasm crossed his face. She was fiercely glad of it, for the man generally betrayed nothing that he did not wish to.

"What of you, Sebastian?" she asked blandly. "Did you never marry?"

"No."

"But you were not celibate, were you? Was Caterina di Ripoli yours?"

"No. Though I did seduce her mother. And left them all exposed."

Though his expression did not change nor his voice waver, she sensed his guilt. He would do terrible things, but they still touched him.

"So you saved the child," she said with deliberate detachment. "Did you love her mother, then?"

"No." He didn't even hesitate. Perhaps he had expected the question. "I never loved anyone but you."

"Don't give me that," she snapped, her anger suddenly fierce. "I wasn't born yesterday, and I certainly don't need your damned platitudes."

"*Platitudes?*" He stared at her blankly, and then a hiss of laughter escaped him. "Straight for the jugular. You could always deprive me of breath one way or another. Why did you let me go without you?"

She shrugged. "I suppose I didn't want to go with you—enough."

"Did you never wish you had? Come with me, I mean."

"No. What would have been the point of that?" She set down

her spoon and leaned back in her chair. "The soup was good."

"Tasty," he agreed, finishing his own.

"Did Caterina know what you were?"

"She knew I was with the British embassy."

"But nothing that could damage you if it were made public?"

"Ah. You came as Silver and Grey's secret weapon. I should have known."

"The curiosity is my own."

"Then the answer is no."

"But I wouldn't know if you were lying."

"Yes, you would," he said. "Because I never lied to you before."

"You just don't tell the whole truth."

"Neither do you."

Her lips twitched. "Touché."

He smiled back and raised his glass to his lips. "I'm glad you came."

So am I, God help me.

With the arrival of the steak pie and fresh green vegetables, their conversation left such difficult personal matters for comparisons of plants in other countries and Juliet's attempts to grow flowers and herbs in pots in her tiny yard. There were a few funny tales shared, a discussion of music and drama—which inspired a sudden longing in Juliet to attend the theatre again—and even a more detailed account of his encounter with Constance and Solomon in Venice.

"She made less of it," Juliet said bleakly. "She always does."

"She has married quite the fierce protector. And they both protect you."

Wary of sliding back into the personal, Juliet finished the last of her dessert and thanked him for a very pleasant meal.

"It's time I went home," she added. "I open early in the mornings to catch the workers."

He nodded because, of course, he knew that already, and rose to his feet without trying to persuade her otherwise. He held her chair and placed her wrap around her shoulders. "You will allow me to escort you home."

His hands lingered just a little too long, light and warm. She remembered his touch with a totally unexpected spark of long-dead desire. Unable to breathe, she turned slowly to face him. Her heart clamored as though her whole life depended on the answer she gave now.

He was still a handsome and exciting man. And she knew only too well what she was. Confused by the past and by Connie's suspicions, she should not be in this position. And yet he had asked her, and she could say yes, and God knew what would follow from there.

But he *had* asked her. And it was only a short walk.

She drew a deep breath.

⭍

SOLOMON FOUND A larger-than-usual pile of post waiting for him at the breakfast table the following morning. Surprised, he sorted through the letters and found they were nearly all addressed to Constance.

He laid them at her place and opened his own while he ate. One was from his brother David, still in Paris but writing excitedly about coming home and that there was so much to tell him in person. Another was from one of his managers, and he folded it into his coat to read later. The last was a handwritten note from his chemist, which he broke open.

By then, Constance had come in, looking delightful in a wide-skirted gown of dark blue with a flattering V-shaped waist. He stood up and used the moment to kiss her good morning, as if there hadn't already been many such kisses. And more.

She returned the kiss with just as much enthusiasm.

"You are very popular this morning," he murmured, indicating the letters beside her.

Her eyebrows rose, but she sat down, allowing him to help her to egg and toast and coffee, while she regarded the pile dubiously, almost as if she expected each letter to explode. Intrigued, he sat back down and watched her take a bite of toast before all but forcing herself to open the epistle at the top of the pile.

"It's from Zenobia Paul," she said in surprise. "She has accepted our invitation for next Friday evening."

Solomon's eyebrows flew up. He hadn't known she had actually sent any invitations, imagining she was still agonizing over their lists of possible guests. Even the date of their soiree had only been tossed around between them rather than confirmed.

She grabbed the next letter. "Lord and Lady Trench have also accepted… And your Mr. and Mrs. Halliwell…" At last, she raised her eyes to his face with a peculiarly childlike wonder. "Solomon, they've *all* accepted. So far."

"Of course they have," he said comfortably. He suspected she might have sent the invitations quickly so that she didn't lose courage. And even then, it was probably to prove to him that she would either be ignored or refused. "And more will do so."

She still looked so overwhelmed that he reached out and covered her hand with his.

"There will always be people who reject us for one silly reason or another—the color of my skin or the gossip about you. But we have friends."

She blinked rapidly and swallowed, squeezing his hand in return.

"Did you ask Juliet?"

Constance's lips twisted. "I did. She won't come, of course, but I did send a card. To Kellar also, though I'll rescind it if we find anything against him. What of your letters?"

Remembering, Solomon unfolded the chemist's note and read it, before letting it fall back on to the table. "He found nothing. Every paper wrapping we found in Caterina's room held exactly the same dose of powdered digitalis, as prescribed by Dr.

Sorenson."

"Somehow I thought that would..." She trailed off as the door of the breakfast parlor opened.

"An Inspector Harris is here, sir," Lottie said. "From the police. I've put him in the morning room."

"Just bring him along here," Constance said, exchanging looks with Solomon, "and set another place."

But though he sat down opposite Solomon and accepted a cup of tea, Harris refused breakfast, saying he had already eaten. In fact, he looked embarrassed.

"I've been sent by my superintendent, Mr. Galsworth," he said bluntly. "It seems you've stood on the toes of a friend of his, and he insists you stop harassing him or face charges."

"What charges?" Solomon asked.

"Breaking and entering, burglary, breach of the peace, and I don't know what else. I don't know what you've been up to, but he means it, so be careful how you tread."

"Montague," Constance said, scowling. "For the record, his servants admitted me, he gave us permission to question his household, and I never stole anything."

"But he did discover you on your knees before his desk with a lockpick in your hand?"

"He might, but he didn't see me use it."

Harris let out a hiss that might have been anger or laughter. Even before they had begun Silver and Grey, he had been a friend and helped them in several of their investigations. But he was first and foremost a policeman, and Solomon would not underestimate that.

"We were asked," he said quickly, "to investigate the death of the opera singer Caterina di Ripoli. She was Montague's wife."

While the inspector drank his tea, Solomon explained the oddities of the case and their suspicions concerning Montague. "The thing is," he added, "he might have done it before. Ten years ago, his betrothed, Sophie Worthington, died in a similarly unexpected and inexplicable manner. I don't suppose you know anything about that?"

The story had brought a frown to Harris's face. "I'll see if there's any record," he said dubiously, "but I'll have to be dashed discreet or have a much better cause for suspicion if I'm to face Galsworth's wrath. In the meantime, seriously, don't alienate him. He can make life da—*very* difficult for you, and he will. Stay away from Montague's house."

Solomon nodded. Constance said, "Very well." But he knew they were both thinking the same thing. *They* had been banned from the house, but neither Janey nor Lenny had.

Then Constance took him by surprise, as she often did.

"I have no idea where you live, inspector, so I could not send you a card, but we are having a few guests on Friday evening and would be delighted if you and your wife could join us."

Harris looked startled. "Why?" he asked.

Constance laughed. "Because you have been a good friend and ally to us since before we began Silver and Grey. We are an odd couple with diverse friends, and the gathering is informal." Her lips quirked. "But respectable. We shall not embarrass you."

For the first time in their acquaintance, Harris blushed. He was an intelligent man of some education, but he did not generally move in wealthy circles. He was probably more at home with the rabble of the streets and Constance's girls than conversing with the likes of the Halliwells and the Trenches.

"Thank you," he said briskly, setting down his teacup and rising to his feet. "I'll speak to my wife."

Solomon walked with him to the front door and returned to find Constance gathering her wildly expanded notes into her bag. "What prompted that invitation?"

"Sorry," she said, pausing for an instant to rest her head against his arm. "I didn't confer with you first. I suppose I was just carried away! Besides, we both like him, and it came to me that we could do him a good turn for once."

"How?" Solomon asked blankly.

"Didn't you tell me that one of your favored guests was an

assistant commissioner of police, or some such thing? We might bring Harris to his attention."

Solomon began to laugh and threw his arm around her shoulders. "You are wonderful, you know."

CHAPTER SIXTEEN

"WE WANT YOU to take the train down to Dover," Solomon told Janey and Lenny. "Find out if Darrow and Caterina had booked a passage on any packet or other vessel sailing to the Continent. According to Darrow, they planned to leave London on the evening of Friday the eighth, so try to get hold of passenger lists from then onward. Tell them whatever story is appropriate, that your master has lost his ticket, or whatever, just to see if their names were ever listed."

"And if their names ain't there?" Janey asked.

"Go on to the next one. If necessary, travel to the next port and the next. I've listed them here for you."

Janey took the list from him, scowling at it. "Why don't you just ask this Darrow?"

"Because he lies," Solomon said, "and we haven't quite worked out why."

"You think he done it?"

"It's more likely he's the reason Montague's done it," Constance said dryly. "Either way, we need to know."

Lenny was peering over Janey's shoulder. "That's a long list," he said. "We'd never get round all those ports in a day."

"You might be lucky in Dover, but take tomorrow too, if you need to," Solomon said. "There are plenty of respectable hotels on the coast."

Lenny straightened, meeting Solomon's gaze. "That's not right, sir, for Janey."

Janey blushed rather painfully as though she expected everyone to laugh.

"*Respectable* hotel," Constance repeated mildly. "There is enough money for two rooms. Tell them you're brother and sister if it makes you feel better. But as Solomon says, with luck, you won't need to and can come home this evening."

"Why don't you two go?" Janey demanded.

"Because I'll be doing the same here in London," Solomon said, "and there are other lines to follow, like Caterina's friend whom she apparently visited three times in one week, probably as an alternative trysting place."

"And then she went back to Marianne Locke's again to meet him on the day before she died," Constance said. "There's something here we're not understanding, and we need to."

Janey shrugged. "We'd best be off, then."

"Take the carriage," Constance said, "collect anything you need from your respective homes on your way to the station."

"I got everything," Janey said quickly. "I come prepared."

It might have been true, but more likely she was keeping Lenny away from Constance's establishment, where she still lodged. Perhaps it was time she had rooms of her own somewhere else. Which would leave a vacancy for some other street waif.

Since they had no idea who or what they would find at the address in Theobalds Street, Solomon elected to accompany Constance before he began his trawl of passenger lists. As he picked up his hat, the heap of correspondence on the desk caught his eye.

"It's getting out of hand," Constance remarked, following his gaze. "I'll see what I can do today, if I get the chance. Unless I would be better employed searching passenger lists?"

"I can probably do it more quickly without wasting so much shoe leather," Solomon said wryly. "The correspondence might be a good idea, if nothing more urgent comes up. First, though, let's find out who lives on Theobalds Street."

They took a hackney to the end of the road and, since they did not have a house number, began by speaking to the tobacconist at the corner to try to establish who lived where.

Solomon bought a newspaper and some tobacco he would never use. Then, since they doubted Caterina and Darrow had met at a family home, he asked casually about a fictitious family called Grey, old friends he was sure lived in this street.

The tobacconist frowned. "Grey? Hmm, there's the Whites at number six, and Greens at number eleven, but I can't think of a Grey…"

"Wait, though," Constance said, "the family won't be called Grey, will they? Jane was his mother-in-law! Perhaps you know a family who lives with the wife's mother whose name is Grey?"

This elicited a few more house numbers and families, which they crossed off their mental lists before thanking the tobacconist for his help and departing.

They managed to cross off several more houses in similar fashion at the greengrocers', where they were fortunate enough to meet with the local gossip who knew everyone's business and was not shy about passing it on. In this way, they discovered a house that was completely locked up and empty, and another that was so full of people that it was never empty for a moment. Someone had lots of visitors, some had none at all except the woman herself, who liked to make sure the old dears were well.

With the houses left, there was nothing to do but knock on doors and say they were looking for Mrs. Montague, and was it true she was visiting the house?

At the first four doors approached, they encountered only blank headshakes. On the fifth, they were shouted at by the grumpy master of the house for wasting his time. The seventh door, nobody answered at all, so Solomon noted the number in his head to come back to later.

Number twenty-one was opened by a stooped old gentleman with wild white hair and a gray mustache. His expression, though distracted, was amiable enough. There was a speck of egg yolk on his lapel.

"Mrs. Montague?" he repeated in clear surprise at Solomon's request. "But my dear sir, have you not heard?"

At last! "Heard what?" Solomon asked, just to be sure.

"Why, that the poor lady is dead. It is a great grief to me." And indeed, there was profound sadness in his fading old eyes.

"We're so sorry," Constance said quickly. "In fact, we did know that she had passed away. But we understand she visited you several times in the week or so before she died. Could we possibly talk to you about her?"

The old gentleman looked from one to the other, his gaze sharper than had first been apparent. Then he opened the door wide. "Come in."

Constance and Solomon followed him into the house and into a pleasant but fading sitting room crowded with books and newspapers and sheets of music. A clarinet lay on the table; a guitar was propped against the wall. The connection to Caterina was obvious.

"My name is Grey," Solomon said, offering his card. "This is my wife and partner."

His bushy old eyebrows lifted as their host took the card, though he said only, "I'm George Martin. Some people call me 'professor,' though I'm not one. I just look the part."

"Wait," Constance said, recognizing the name. "Were you not Mrs. Montague's singing teacher?"

Martin wheezed out a laugh. "Nothing so grand. My talents are limited. My opinions are not! Fortunately, she valued those opinions. What are you investigating and what has poor Mrs. Montague to do with it? Please, Mrs. Grey, sit down."

"Thank you." Constance sat on the sofa, so Solomon sat beside her while their host lowered himself into the chair opposite, which, judging by its threadbare state, was his favorite.

"We are investigating Mrs. Montague's death, at the request of a family friend," Solomon began. "Perhaps you are acquainted with Mr. Kellar?"

"No. But I have heard his name. Was he not the one who brought her to this country?"

Solomon nodded. "He was. I imagine that is why he felt so responsible for her."

"The newspapers said it was her heart. Was that not the case?"

"We don't actually know. There are a number of oddities that we cannot explain. Pillows moved to positions she would not have chosen, a vase of roses that appeared as if by magic during the night. And, of course, the suddenness when she had appeared so well even the evening before. According to her doctor, her heart condition was well under control."

Martin narrowed his eyes. "What is it you think I can tell you?"

"You were not at the funeral?" Constance intervened.

Martin shrugged. "At my age, there are too many of those. And she was too young to die. Plus, it takes me all day to walk the length of the street."

They were all valid reasons to stay away.

"She visited you often?" Constance asked.

"Before she was married, yes. Or we went to concerts together. I often went to hear her sing, at various theatres all over the country. But my health is not so good these days."

"Our information," Solomon said mildly, "is that she called on you three times in the week before she died. That sounds quite *often* to me."

"It was unusual," Martin allowed, "for recent years."

"Was she alone?"

Martin nodded, lifting his brows in faint surprise at the question.

"On each visit?" Solomon pursued.

"Yes. What—"

"May we ask why she came so often?" Constance asked, so gently that it didn't even sound like an interruption.

Martin gave a slight shrug. "She wanted to go over old times,

I suppose."

"How long did she stay?" Solomon asked.

"A few hours, until she had to go to the theatre. We both enjoyed it."

"How did she seem to you?" Constance asked.

"Not ill, if that's what you mean."

"Happy?"

He thought. "Happy to see me, which is flattering for a lonely old man. I miss my concerts… But now I think of it unselfishly, she was a little troubled."

"Did she talk about her husband, her marriage?" Constance asked.

"Bless you, no. We talked mostly of music and musicians."

"Of Carl Darrow, perhaps?"

"Yes, sometimes, though I had little to contribute on the subject. I never heard the man play, always in the wrong place at the wrong time. But I have several of his notices and reviews."

"Then you never met Darrow?" Solomon asked.

Martin shook his head. "No."

Constance leaned forward. "Did she ever confide her reason for the trouble you noticed in her? Did you guess what it was?"

"No." Martin grimaced. "Looking back, I wonder if she knew she was dying and came to say goodbye."

⥲⥲⥲✦⥲⥲⥲

"WHICH IS POSSIBLE," Solomon said as they walked back up the street and went in search of a hackney.

"It's also possible that she was saying goodbye because she was leaving the country with Darrow," Constance pointed out.

Solomon sighed. "And probably more likely. Nothing else points to her being aware of imminent death."

"Except the fear Darrow mentioned, which he may have misinterpreted as fear of Montague."

Solomon considered that. "Possible. Whatever her reasons, there was clearly a bond between her and Martin. And we know now she did *not* go there to meet Darrow or anyone else."

"Providing Martin is telling us the truth."

"Do you think he's lying?" Solomon asked in surprise.

"No. Not really. But too many people are telling us partial truths—at the very least. We're missing something, Solomon."

"I think we are."

"Which doesn't mean Montague isn't guilty. He still has the best motive and opportunity. We just don't have the complete picture yet. Hopefully, you or Janey will find the missing pieces amongst passenger lists. I think I'll go back to the office and study the notes—in between dealing with that mountain of correspondence we've allowed to pile up."

"Good plan. I'll see you back there in a few hours—earlier, with luck."

But luck did not appear to be with him.

⇾⇾⇾⇥⇤⇽⇽⇽

KELLAR WAS FEELING uncharacteristically indecisive. Having taken care of Juliet and the main issue, there remained the problem of her daughter. Of Silver and Grey, who were disconcertingly sharp and persistent. He should have taken that into account after Venice.

This was one of his failings, of course. Being so successful in all his undertakings, he would have to be more careful not to underestimate other people. It was a form of arrogance, and he despised that.

He mulled the problem during a leisurely luncheon and the remains of his glass of wine.

No, it was best he make a call at their office before Constance took it into her head to visit her mother, which was certainly not what he wanted right now. And so he should remove her perception of the threat he presented. A little honesty was in order. Or, at least, partial honesty, in the cause of his own eventual triumph. He hoped.

He rang for his manservant.

"I'm going out, Jaffer," he said mildly. "And will dine at my club."

He walked to the offices of Silver and Grey, mostly because he liked to remain fit. The weather was a little too close, with drizzle in the air, so it wasn't a particular pleasure, but the brisk exercise did him good.

At first he thought the office was closed, for no one answered the door until his second knock, when it was opened almost at once by Constance.

"Your girl has left you in the lurch," he remarked, taking off his hat and stepping forward.

It was instinct to move aside in the face of such self-confidence, and she did. "Of course she hasn't. I sent her to buy cake, since I felt in dire need."

She closed the door behind him and led him into the second office, which appeared to be her own. "If you've come for news, I'm afraid we still have no solutions or evidence to offer you."

He wasn't convinced she would tell him if she did. Their last encounter had left him with few doubts about their suspicions of him. It would take more than money to lift those. So…

"Actually, I came to give *you* news," he said.

She took him not to the desk, where she had clearly been hard at work, for there were closely written sheets of paper scattered all over it, but to a group of comfortable chairs, where she invited him to sit.

"What news?" she asked with interest.

He smiled with as much boyish charm as he could muster. "More in the nature of a confession," he admitted, lowering himself into the chair next to hers.

Her eyes—incredibly beautiful eyes, reminiscent of Juliet's—remained veiled. "Why, what have you done?"

"I—er…started a fire where there was no fuel. I'm afraid I had no reason at all to believe Caterina's death was suspicious. I had an ulterior motive in involving you, and quite candidly, since I never liked Montague, I didn't mind in the slightest inconveniencing him."

Constance stared at him. "He had just lost his *wife!*"

"I thought you suspected him of murdering her?"

"I do," she retorted. "I've had a certain sympathy with murderers before. Are you telling me you just *pretended* to be suspicious?"

"Yes," Kellar said ruefully. "Sorry."

"But why?"

"I wanted to force an 'accidental' meeting with your mother."

Constance parted her lips. It was the only sign of shock he could see.

"It didn't work, of course," he said with a deprecating wave. "She fled, and I was forced to make our encounter more deliberate."

"You went to the shop, and to the house. Did that make the reason for her flight the first time any clearer?"

"You *do* have her sarcasm," Kellar said, pleased. "Anyway, I wanted to apologize and prevent you wasting any more time on the matter."

To his surprise, her lips twitched, as if she would laugh. That was like Juliet, too. Her eyes remained serious, though.

"Well, thank you for owning up. We will, of course, still charge you for this full day, too."

"I expected nothing less."

He waited for her to say more, to announce they were ending the case and would present their account. That she did not made him uneasy. He was uneasier still that he could not read her expression or her intentions.

She seemed to be waiting for him to take his leave.

"If you have nothing to add," she said eventually, "I'm afraid I have too much work to do to be able to entertain."

"Ah. Talking of entertainment, thank you for your invitation. I should be glad to come on Friday."

Constance rose. "I shall look forward to seeing you then."

It was rare enough for Kellar to lose control of any meeting that he was able to find it amusing. *Those Silver women.* "I too."

He rose, and a cushion tumbled to the ground. He bent and picked it up, gazing at it thoughtfully. He felt Constance's sudden tension and raised his eyes to hers.

He knew then. She didn't care whether or not he paid Silver and Grey. They would keep investigating. Unless…

"It's me, Hat!" called a voice from the hall.

Poor timing…

"I'm in here," Constance called, and one of the girls he remembered from his previous visits stuck her head around the door.

"Beg your pardon," she said. "I'll put the kettle on."

"Do that," Constance said, "but Mr. Kellar is not staying."

Apparently, he was not. He bowed gracefully and allowed himself to be conducted to the door.

⫸⫸⫸⫷⫷⫷

DESCRIBING KELLAR'S VISIT to Solomon a couple of hours later, Constance shivered again.

"You didn't believe him?" Solomon asked, frowning.

"I don't honestly know. He seemed sincere enough. He always does. I just found myself wondering why he was telling me, and why now. Is he trying to stop us investigating at all, because our inquiries will eventually lead to him? Or does he just want us to believe that he is so devoted to Juliet that she is perfectly safe with him?" Her eyes widened. "Oh, Solomon, you don't think—"

He pulled her to her feet into his arms. "No, I don't," he said firmly. "But we'll go home via the shop to be sure."

She hugged him fiercely, inhaling the familiar, delicious scent of his skin. "It was the way he looked at the cushion, too. It fell to the floor when he stood, and he just picked it up. But suddenly I thought, *Is that what happened with Caterina?* And he *looked* at me... Only then Hat came in and I could laugh at myself again. I suspect he was laughing too."

"Did you tell him we wouldn't be dropping the case?"

"No. I didn't say either way. I suppose we'll have to stop charging him, though. Did you learn anything at the docks?"

"No. One ship sailed for Italy yesterday with passengers, but neither Darrow's nor Caterina's names were on their lists. Nor on anyone else's that I found. I've set further inquiries in motion, but I'm not hopeful. I hope Janey and Lenny had more luck."

"Perhaps she was right and we should just have asked Darrow."

"I don't trust Darrow to tell the truth. We need to know how deep, how committed his relationship with Caterina was. And what Montague found out about it."

"She told him," Constance said.

"And she told him she would end it. According to him. Why would either of them lie unless they are hiding something?"

"Something we're missing," Constance said, drawing back from his arms just a little so that she could look into his face. "Or...are we wasting our time on this, when we have several genuine inquiries waiting for us to begin? We don't even know for sure that Caterina was killed."

Solomon kissed her forehead. "Let's go home. We'll look afresh at everything in the morning."

FROM A DOORWAY across the road from Silver and Grey's discreet office, Carl Darrow saw the couple emerge, looking smug and content. He didn't much care if they saw him. In fact, he was more than happy to harass them the way they had been harassing him. Still, good sense made him crouch down, face mostly averted, while he pretended to be retying his shoelace.

The couple walked arm in arm for a couple of yards to a waiting carriage, and Grey handed her in, the perfect gentleman with his lady wife.

Which was laughable. Carl knew perfectly well that Constance Silver, for all her beauty and manners, was a whore. And Grey, by the look of him, had slave in his ancestry. Who did they think they were, poking their grubby noses into other, more talented people's business?

Darrow squashed the surge of resentment. The carriage drove off without either of them looking in his direction.

Hardly the most observant of detectives, he thought, smirking.

He waited until their carriage was out of sight, then crossed the road to their office. It was tempting to cause a little sabotage—smash a window, or push a burning handkerchief through the letter box. Just as a little payback.

Apart from anything else, they had no right to walk around like the perfect, loving couple, when he had lost his Caterina…

But the street was too busy, and he could not wait until darkness fell. He had an engagement at a private house this evening. He needed to go home and change and collect his violin. But if they came near him again, if they were still asking questions… Well, he had Montague's handkerchief in his pocket, not to burn but to leave at the scene of the sabotage.

If it came to that. And he almost hoped it would. Revenge on Montague and on Silver and Grey at the same time was an appealing proposition.

He walked on past the office. For now.

CHAPTER SEVENTEEN

"DARROW IS WATCHING us from across the road," Solomon murmured. He sat opposite Constance for once, so that he could see out the back window without twisting. "Do you suppose he is working up the courage to confess?"

"I don't think he lacks courage," Constance said thoughtfully as the carriage swung around the corner. She used her umbrella to knock on the carriage roof, and the coachman pulled up the horses.

Solomon leapt out and strode back toward the corner, mingling with other pedestrians. A few moments later, he loped back and ascended smartly, and the carriage moved on.

"Well?" Constance demanded.

"He just strolled past the shop, then sped up and kept walking. He hasn't tried to find the way in at the back."

"Then what the devil is he up to? Trying to intimidate us, like our prim neighbors in Grosvenor Square?"

A couple of months ago, when they had returned from Venice to find two bodies on her establishment doorstep, there had been something of an intimidation campaign conducted against the house of ill repute. That storm had been weathered. But if Darrow truly was a murderer, he had a lot more to lose.

"I don't know," Solomon said. "But I think I shall interrupt his morning practice to ask him."

"What if he comes back during the night?"

"I doubt he'd be that stupid," Solomon said. "But we could

catch up with him easily enough to ask."

Constance hesitated. "No, you're right. And I'd rather make sure my mother is still where she should be."

"I'm not sure Darrow's the confessing type," Solomon mused. "But he might have decided to tell us something new, particularly if it reflects badly on Montague."

"I wonder…" Constance frowned. "If Montague was suspicious of his wife, did he go searching passenger bookings too? Some paper was burned in Caterina's grate, surely around the time she died. It could have been travel tickets." She answered her own question with an irritable hand gesture. "*Could* have been. Always could. There is no *evidence* in this wretched case!"

"Stop thinking about it," Solomon said, shifting across the carriage to sit beside her. "This evening is just for us." His fingertips glided over her wrist and inside her glove.

"I like that idea," she said huskily.

Solomon peeled back her glove and softly kissed her wrist, exactly where he had already made the skin tingle with his caress. "Good. The shop is still open."

Constance blinked, having lost track of where they were. The carriage slowed and she pulled down the window. Gerry was outside the shop with a customer, showing him something from the front display. But in the way of street boys, he saw her at once and grinned.

Constance mouthed, *Where is she?*

Gerry jerked his head toward the inside of the shop. And indeed, Juliet's familiar bright dress swept past her line of vision.

"She's fine," Constance said, refusing to admit the strength of her relief as she raised her hand to Gerry and closed the window again.

"Don't you want to go in?" Solomon asked.

"No. I want to begin this evening that is just for us."

Solomon gave a slow smile, his dark eyes warm with promise. And suddenly it was easy to banish everything but him from her mind.

"I WONDER IF she knew she was dying and came to say goodbye."

"I have several of his notices and reviews..."

"I never heard the man play—always in the wrong place at the wrong time..."

"She wanted to go over old times..."

"We talked mostly of music and musicians."

"Of Carl Darrow, perhaps?"

Solomon opened his eyes with a snap, the remembered words still bouncing around his mind. Most of them had been spoken by George Martin yesterday. The final question had been Constance's.

"...she knew she was dying," Martin had said sadly, *"and came to say goodbye."*

And again, Constance's interpretation: *"...she was saying goodbye because she was leaving the country with Darrow."*

Solomon sat up. "What if she wasn't?" he said aloud. Old words and new ideas still spun around his mind, and his heart raced as though he had been running instead of sleeping.

"Who wasn't what?" Constance mumbled, throwing one arm across his middle and burrowing back into the pillow.

After their luscious night of love, this was not how Solomon had imagined their morning greetings. But the idea was vital and had to be captured—it had to be the center of everything.

"Caterina," he said. "What if she wasn't at Martin's house to say goodbye at all? He was an old friend who shared her love of music, but beyond that we know nothing about him. Except that Caterina hadn't seen him very often since her marriage, before visiting him three times in one week for several hours at a time. Not to say goodbye but to *go over old times* and to talk *mostly of music and musicians*. Why go to Martin and no one else? Who and what is he?"

Constance opened her eyes and hauled herself into a semi-sitting position, leaning against his shoulder. She was frowning with the effort to throw off the mists of sleep and think.

"He listened to her sing at various places across the country," she recalled. "He wasn't really a teacher, but she used his opinions to help her improve because he was so knowledgeable. But somehow, he kept missing Darrow's performances. Which surely implies he heard lots of others in his travels. A keen music lover, known as 'the professor,' who has collected no doubt many program notes, notices, and reviews of performances."

"A source of information, in other words," Solomon said, excitement soaring. "Information about Darrow? We know she talked about him."

"But it doesn't matter what she *talked* about, does it? It matters what she saw, what Martin might have let slip or let her see among his reviews. He could have kept whole newspapers."

"So she could have discovered *anything*," Solomon said intensely, "about her husband, about Darrow, even about Kellar. Both Montague and Kellar are music lovers, after all, an amateur violinist and an amateur singer. Martin could have seen any of them where they had no business to be. Or Caterina could have learned of it by herself. Montague's scandal in India? Sophie Worthington's death… Or where Darrow was when he was *not* at the Royal Academy. God knows what she could have discovered about Kellar. But she was *looking*, Constance, I'm sure of it."

"If one of them threatened her, then she needed to fight back," Constance said. "With information of her own."

"She could have been trying to win her freedom from Montague," Solomon said, "or to counter some threat of Darrow's or Kellar's. She needed to keep one of them away from her… Or all of them?"

Constance's eyes, no longer clouded by sleep, were sparkling. "It's a better theory, but we need to *know*. We need a plan."

She scrambled out of bed, still naked from last night's passion, and found her bag, from which she dragged all her notes before climbing back onto the bed. "When I established the schedule of Caterina's movements, I also noted when Montague left the house for work, alone, and when he returned. If we can find any discrepancy, any time unaccounted for… The trouble is, we can't go there without incurring the wrath of Montague and his police protectors."

"We haven't been forbidden his place of work, though," Solomon pointed out, peering over her shoulder at the notes. Having seen what he needed to, he all but leapt out of the other side of the bed. "And if we're early enough, he need never know we've been. After that, I suggest we return briefly to the office to see if Janey's back and what she has discovered. And then I'll go and shake Darrow while you call again on Martin and find out what information he has in that house. I'll join you there as soon as I can. Agreed?"

"Agreed," Constance said with enthusiasm.

She had that euphoric feeling, perhaps similar to Caterina's on the night she died, that the mystery was almost solved at last.

MONTAGUE'S HOME, SO full of Caterina's presence, still felt heavy with her loss, tugging his spirits downward. But today, as he closed the front door and marched briskly up the path to his waiting carriage, he realized the oppression of his grief lifted in the fresh air. It was a new day, and he had dealt rather neatly with the obstacles of Silver and Grey.

He had been right to go straight to Galsworth at Scotland Yard. By now, surely, the prying pair were well warned off and would not dare come near him again. He had the chance of revival, in every way, and he was going to snatch it with both hands. He would embrace the hard work. It was all that kept the guilt and grief at bay.

His spirits lifted further as his carriage trundled through the morning sunshine toward the offices of Montague and Son. It would soon be a proud firm once more. As soon as he had his hands on Caterina's money, his troubles would be over. In the meantime, he had the promise of it to buy him more credit—and the patience of his current creditors. Money from the next shipment was about to pour in...

He was almost at the door when he caught the distinctive sight of the Greys together, descending the steps from his office door. They made a rather charming picture with their beauty and their closeness, her hand casually in the crook of his arm. Happily trying to destroy what was left of Montague's life.

For a moment, the blood froze in his veins. And then anger flooded in.

How dare *they?*

The carriage had come to a halt. John Coachman was actually opening the door, so God knew how long Montague had been sitting there, staring and fuming, his good spirits vanishing like the sun behind that cloud just drifting over the river toward him.

He got down stiffly, nodding to the coachman before he walked briskly up the steps and swung right toward the clerk who fielded all visitors.

"Good morning, sir," Jennings said nervously. They didn't normally exchange many words.

"Good morning, Jennings. A Mr. and Mrs. Grey just called, did they not?"

"Oh, yes, sir, but they didn't have an appointment. Mr. Grey was afraid he had already missed one last week or the week before. His wife claimed he had forgotten to make it, and she was right. He had." Jennings smiled tentatively. "Perhaps not the sort we wish to be doing business with, sir?"

If only you knew, Jennings, Montague thought savagely. "I suppose you had the appointment book out to look?"

"Yes, sir, of course..."

And they had taken a damned good look. They were still investigating him, still suspicious.

Well, it was time—past time!—that they had a taste of their own medicine. How would *they* like to be followed and harassed?

And since he had already complained to the police about them, it would be very easy to have them arrested the first time they even *looked* as if they might step outside the law. It would be the woman, of course. Grey, he could forgive if he had to, but he was hardly the only rich man in town…

"Cancel all my appointments today, Jennings. I won't be in the office after all."

Montague swung on his heel and walked out of the office in search of the carriage he had just dismissed. He would begin at *their* offices. And follow.

JANEY WAS NOT at the Silver and Grey office. According to Hat, she hadn't come home last night, or first thing this morning. Constance and Solomon stayed on the premises only long enough to drink a quick cup of tea and tell Hat where they were each going.

Darrow had been watching the office last night. Montague could easily discover they had been asking questions at his office—and he had indeed been absent from there without explanation several times in the couple of weeks before his wife's death, once at the same time as Darrow had been with her. Was that when he had discovered Caterina's infidelity? Had he followed her to Marianne Locke's, and seen her with Darrow?

Either way, every sense that Solomon had always relied on warned him not to leave Constance alone for too long. She would be safe enough with George Martin, but he didn't want her anywhere near Montague or Darrow—or even Kellar—until this case was settled.

"Don't go anywhere else without reporting it to Hat," he urged her. "And Hat, if Janey or Knox come back with news, tell them where we are. We need to know everything as soon as possible."

"Yes, sir," Hat said seriously, her anxious eyes darting to Constance. "Take care, ma'am."

"Don't I always?" Constance said.

"No," Solomon said with a hint of grimness, "you don't. Take the carriage to Theobalds Street. I'll use hackneys."

For once she didn't question him, probably due less to any physical fear than to her eagerness to speak to Martin again. Solomon kissed her cheek before he shut her in, but he couldn't control his sudden feeling of dread.

Foolish. If any woman could take care of herself, it was Constance.

He put his hat on and set off for Darrow's rooms.

"I'll be charging you rent soon," Mrs. Philpot said with a cackle as she opened the front door.

The exquisite sounds of Darrow's violin both thrilled and chilled his blood. He did not recognize the piece, but could anyone who played such divine music truly be guilty of such a terrible crime? Darrow certainly had the passion, but it was so finely controlled and channeled.

Solomon made some light reply to Mrs. Philpot and hurried upstairs.

Unlike the previous time Solomon had interrupted his practice, Darrow was clearly playing this piece all the way through. If the man heard his knock, he ignored it. Solomon went in anyway.

Standing by the window in his shirt sleeves, violin beneath his chin, Darrow did not acknowledge his entrance by more than a faint, involuntary spasm. The bow kept moving; haunting notes continued to spill forth for several moments, and then an abrupt, angry discord shattered the melody.

Darrow hurled the bow at his bed and dropped the violin beside it.

"What do you want?" he snarled.

It was the first sign of temper Solomon had seen in him. He smiled, easing his shoulder off the closed door against which he had been leaning to listen, and walked further into the room. He didn't offer to shake hands. In fact, Darrow's tense poise warned him of imminent attack.

"I thought you wanted to see me," Solomon said suavely, "since you came by the office yesterday evening."

A flash of something very like chagrin showed in Darrow's eyes before his lashes came down like a veil. "I am surprised you did not stop to speak to me."

"I had a dinner engagement with my wife. Is there something I can help you with?"

"Yes. I want your reassurance that you'll stop interrupting my life. It's hard enough losing Caterina without your haunting me with insulting questions and suspicions."

"Surely not *haunting*," Solomon said. "But I can assure you that our inquiries are progressing. In fact, you could help speed things to a conclusion for me, if you would. You told us earlier that Mrs. Montague had agreed to leave her husband and run away with you to Italy."

"Yes."

"How were you getting there?"

"I beg your pardon?"

"You said you and she planned to leave together immediately after the performance on Friday. Where to? Did you reserve a hotel room somewhere, or did your ship sail immediately?"

"That," Darrow said stiffly, "is none of your business."

"On the contrary, it is vital. I need to know what ship you had booked passage on."

"It is not relevant. She died before we could leave."

"The implication being she died *because* you were about to leave?"

"I don't know." Genuine anguish suffused his voice. "But I don't put it past that…" He halted and drew a steadying breath. "We didn't book. We didn't mean to leave a trail for Montague to follow. We were going to catch the night train to Dover and take the first packet we could find to France. We didn't even buy our railway tickets in advance."

"I see." Solomon held the younger man's gaze, though he could feel the promising theories in his mind crumbling under the weight of the violinist's sheer pain. "Whom did you tell about your departure? Mrs. Philpot? Mr. Reid?"

Darrow grimaced. "Of course not. I needed every penny I had. If you must know, I intended to flee without paying my rent."

"Then you didn't tell Mr. Martin, either?" It was a shot in the dark, to see if the name meant anything to him.

Darrow frowned. "Who?"

"Caterina's friend, 'the professor,' on Theobalds Street."

"Never heard of him," Darrow said without much interest. "I told no one. And neither did Caterina. Or so I believed." Abruptly, he raised both hands, dragging his fingers through his hair. "Damn it, I hate this. I want it finished. Will you tell me what your suspicions are so that I can allay them, and try to get on with my life?"

Solomon inclined his head, trying not to hope for too much, but he could almost feel the prickles dropping from Darrow's manner. For the first time, surely, the young musician was preparing to be totally honest with a man he didn't much like or trust.

"I want to know why Caterina visited Martin three times in one week," Solomon said.

Darrow exhaled slowly. He seemed…resigned. "I'll get us a cup of tea. The old dragon downstairs might have a pot brewing."

He strode past Solomon to the door, leaving it half open as he called downstairs, "Mrs. P?" Then he clattered the rest of the way down.

And Solomon would never have a better opportunity. He went first to the table, raking amongst the chaotic mix of sheet music, much of it annotated, newspapers, letters, an appointment diary that recorded only professional engagements, including the one Darrow had played at the establishment in the spring. Flicking through to the pages just before and after Caterina's death, he found the orchestra dates and an engagement last night.

He couldn't study it any further just now. He doubted Darrow would be much longer, and there were too many places to look. He wasn't even sure what he was looking for.

He moved to the chest of drawers, discovering a couple of folded shirts, neckties, and underwear, nothing obviously hidden. He went to the wardrobe in the corner, in which hung one good pair of trousers and one mended pair, likewise an old coat and a decent evening coat, plus a heavy wool overcoat that had seen better days.

Hastily, Solomon felt inside the pockets and found nothing more interesting than an omnibus ticket and a miniscule pencil. He looked under the hat on the top wardrobe shelf, swiftly ran one finger around the lining, and abandoned it. All the while, he strained his ears for any sound of Darrow's return. The violinist must have been making his own tea or waiting impatiently for Mrs. Philpot to do it from scratch. Either suited Solomon's purpose, although he was running out of places to look.

He dropped to the floor, peering beneath the wardrobe, and his eye was caught by a half-hidden ball of something on the floor of the cupboard, right at the back among the shadows. He fished it out, discovering it to be a rolled-up coat, very worn and soft to the touch.

What an odd thing to do to a coat. Even one that needed cleaned or mended. His heart racing—surely Darrow could not be much longer now—he uncoiled the garment until he held it by the collar and felt it all over.

There were no holes. It was just a little threadbare. But the back was quite badly roughened, the fabric pulled, as though it had been dragged about stony ground, or…

His fingers encountered something sharp. He pulled it free of the fabric, and a faded red petal fluttered to the floor.

CHAPTER EIGHTEEN

MARTIN WAS CLEARLY surprised to see Constance on his doorstep once more, but he invited her in and asked how he could help her today.

"It's really something we didn't think to ask you yesterday," Constance said, preceding him into the same sitting room. "Do you, by chance, keep any kind of private archive? Commemorating your love of music?"

"Why yes, I do." He beamed at her. "Would you like to see it?"

"I would," Constance said, grateful it had been so easy. "Thank you."

He led her out of the room again and up the narrow staircase to a room at the back of the house. It might once have been a bedroom but it now contained only a narrow table, a chair, and many cabinets, each labeled with a range of letters, A-D, E-H, and so on.

He indicated a large box of cards on top of the first cabinet. "Everything is cross-referenced," he said proudly. "The main files here are under the names of individual composers and musicians. These ones are by the year of each performance. But with the card index, you can easily find concert halls, theatres and music festivals, and you can even search by city too."

"This is a massive undertaking," Constance said in genuine awe. "Are these all concerts and performances you attended personally?"

"Sadly not, though that's how I began. Friends began to send me programs and notices in local newspapers, from here and abroad. I have many papers delivered, too."

"Do you keep the whole newspaper?" Constance asked. "Or just make cuttings of the pieces that relate to music?"

"I try to make cuttings where possible, but where it cuts through interesting articles on the other side of the sheet, I keep the whole thing. And index everything, of course."

"Of course." Constance met his proud gaze. "Is this what you meant when you said Caterina was going over old times?"

He smiled slightly but did not answer.

"Why didn't you say so directly?" Constance asked.

He gave an apologetic shrug. "It was what she wished. She didn't want people knowing what she was looking for."

Constance's heart was beating fast. "And what was she looking for?"

"My dear, I cannot break that confidence. It is all I have left of her."

Constance fought to hide her frustration. After all, she admired his honor. "I understand," she managed. "But will you tell me at least who it was she feared would find out?"

"No one. She just wanted to be the only one who knew. Though we made the connection together."

"What connection?" She knew he wouldn't answer that either, and he didn't, not directly.

He said, "You spoke his name to me already."

Which didn't really narrow it down. She had spoken the names of all three of her suspects to him. Or Solomon had. "Mr. Martin, I believe someone murdered Caterina. Surely you don't want her killer to go unpunished?"

He dropped his gaze, then immediately returned it to hers. "You truly believe that?"

"I do. What name was she looking for?" *Montague? Darrow? Kellar?* She found she was holding her breath.

"Charles Derrick," Martin said in a rush.

Constance blinked. "Who the devil is Charles Derrick?"

Martin turned and went out.

Which Constance took as permission.

DIGBY MONTAGUE WAS annoyed when he observed the couple going separate ways. Now he had to choose which to follow. He picked the woman, because she had already proved she had no scruples about prying. And she would be easier to deal with. Without her, Grey would be broken like him. And useful.

So he got his own carriage to follow Mrs. Grey's. He found it parked on Theobalds Street.

What the devil could she be doing there? He couldn't recall being here in his life before. He knew it was not where Darrow lived, nor Kellar. Nor even Mrs. Locke, who had given her home over to Caterina's adultery.

He signaled the coachman to stop, and climbed down on the other side of the road.

"Excuse me." On impulse, he stopped a messenger boy in an apron who was hurrying up the street in the opposite direction. "Could you tell me who it is who lives at number twenty-one?" It was Montague's best guess. Mrs. Grey could have gone into the houses on either side of twenty-one.

"Twenty-one? That would be old Prof Martin."

Digby smiled. "That's what I thought. Thank you."

The boy hurried on with a grin, and Digby racked his brains for the reason Martin's name sounded familiar. Surely he was a friend of Caterina's? The memory surfaced slowly—an old fellow with wild hair, like Beethoven's. An amateur musician who had spent whatever fortune he had inherited on traveling the world and listening to music he would never be good enough to play himself. Caterina had met him in Italy and introduced him to Digby quite early in their relationship. He had come to the wedding breakfast, though not to Caterina's funeral.

She hadn't mentioned him much in recent months, but she had rarely cut people altogether. Silver and Grey must be clutching at straws, interviewing everyone who had ever known Caterina.

It had to stop. The recovery of Digby's firm depended on confidence and respect. He could not have suspicion hanging over his head. Apart from anything else, prying into his life might well revive old shames, old accusations.

India.

Oh yes, past time to scare them off.

He strolled casually across the road and up the path to number twenty-one. There was no one in the front room, as far as he could see, so he carried on up the path that led around the side of the house to a small garden.

Though it was tiny, someone clearly looked after it. The building was in decent repair too. A movement at the kitchen window caused him to dart back against the wall. Someone, a middle-aged maid, was making tea.

Being careful to avoid her line of vision, Digby looked in the first window, a small dining room. On the upper floor were two windows. And at the smaller, something moved.

A paper folder, almost against the window. A trickle of things spilled from it, printed paper, several smaller pieces, like cuttings from newspapers.

The blood sang in Digby's ears. Suddenly Martin's face sharpened in his mind, as did conversations between the man and Caterina. And what Caterina had told Montague about him. He didn't just travel all over the place to hear music. He kept mementos, reviews, records of everything that touched even vaguely on performances.

All over the world... Digby's one reckless act had been to attend a British concert in India, far away from his own plantations and the center of his trade, a completely different region of the vast country, where no one knew Digby Montague. Or the false name he had chosen. It had been a lucrative visit, though it involved behavior of which he was not proud. It had seemed safe enough to attend the concert under his assumed name, to play his violin for British officials and traders. It had even dulled suspicion at the time…until it had all come out in several papers, his fraud and the connection between his names. And he had never been able to return to India since.

Could that be what Mrs. Grey was looking into? It was certainly her distinctively beautiful face he glimpsed at the window, engrossed and determined.

The back door flew open suddenly and a rough female voice yelled, "That's me away, professor! Your tea's brewing! See you Friday!"

He had time to dart ignominiously behind a large honeysuckle bush. Bees buzzed all around him, but the back door closed, and brisk footsteps clumped away down the path to the front gate.

Digby closed his eyes in momentary relief.

But truly, this was for the best. He took the trouble to look through the kitchen window. The maid had left only two cups and saucers on the tray. Good. There was no one else in the house but Mrs. Grey and Martin. He would never have a better opportunity.

SOLOMON STARED AT the sad little rose petal and the still-sharp thorn on his palm. He saw at once how it was done.

Carl Darrow had picked the roses from Eagle Square's garden and tied them to his back while he climbed up to Caterina's window. The thorns had torn at his coat and trapped a disturbed petal. Solomon even found the length of string in the coat pocket that must have been used to tie the flowers in place.

The riddle of the roses was solved.

Caterina had never agreed to run away with Darrow. He must have tried to threaten her into continuing the relationship, perhaps by making it public and thus humiliating Montague as well as Caterina herself. So Caterina had gone to her old friend Martin in search of information—and she had found it. That accounted for her euphoria. She had triumphed over Darrow and saved her marriage, with whatever she had learned from Martin.

Darrow, still refusing to accept his dismissal, changed his tune, trying instead the romantic gesture of roses, to climb up to her window and get himself admitted into her bedchamber…

Either Caterina had let him in, or he had just climbed through the window and found her asleep.

But from there it was no longer clear-cut. Had he left her to sleep, to wake to his gift of a dozen red roses in a vase? Or had he smothered her with a pillow? Either while she slept or in some struggle when she continued to reject him?

Or did Caterina tell him what she had learned to his discredit? Was that why she'd had to die?

Or…had Montague entered the room with his own key, even found them together, and murdered his wife? Was that why Darrow was so certain in apportioning blame? Keeping quiet about his own presence in order to keep himself as free from suspicion as possible.

No, solving the mystery of the roses did not quite solve the murder. Someone else could still have come into the bedroom *after* Darrow did. Kellar could have made the climb. Montague could have entered with his key.

Only, of course, Montague would surely have known about the arrangement of her pillows. Darrow and Kellar would not.

Did Martin's records give away some terrible secret about one of them?

Or all of them?

Solomon dragged himself back to the present. He dropped the thorn and petal into his handkerchief and pocketed them, before bundling the old coat up and shoving it back in the corner of the wardrobe.

Darrow had some other questions to answer. How best to play this vital scene?

Solomon had to tell Darrow he knew the roses came from him. After that, surely, he would be able to tell whether or not the man was lying?

Where the devil *was* Darrow? How long did it take to make a cup of tea?

Suddenly wary, Solomon strode from the room and into the piano-dominated parlor at the front of the house. He went straight to the windows, already sure what he would find. His hackney had gone.

Perhaps the jarvey had got tired waiting, or…

Darrow was a professional performer. Just like Caterina. An actor.

And I told him about Martin and Theobalds Street. Oh, dear God…

Solomon delayed only long enough to snatch up his hat from Darrow's room, then flew down the stairs, running Mrs. Philpot to earth in her kitchen, where she stood rolling pastry at the table with smudges of flour on her face and powerful arms.

"Where is Darrow?" he demanded before she could speak.

Her mouth dropped open. "He went out the back way. I thought you'd gone."

Solomon bolted from the house.

HAT WAS SURPRISED to open the front door of Silver and Grey's offices and find Mr. Kellar there yet again.

"I'm sorry, sir, they're both out. If you'd care to leave a message, I'll see they get it as soon as they return."

"Very well, I'll do that," the gentleman said amiably.

Hat showed him into the waiting room, where writing materials were provided. "Just hand it to me before you go," she said cheerfully. "I'm in the tiny office at the end of the hall."

Only a couple of minutes later, his shadow fell over her. He didn't half walk quietly. He placed a folded piece of paper on her desk. It was addressed to Mr. and Mrs. Grey.

He smiled at her. "Thank you. I don't suppose you know where I might find them? Just to save time?"

Hat knew not to divulge such information to anyone. Confidentiality depended on such discretion. "I couldn't say, sir."

His gaze remained fixed at a point on her desk. Unease wound through her, but she continued to look at his face, not at the desk.

He smiled again, even touched the brim of his hat. "Of course you couldn't. Thank you, miss."

Hat conducted him to the front door, her heart beating stupidly. Only when she had shut and locked it behind him did she run back to her desk and risk looking for what he might have seen. She found it at once—a carelessly left scrap of paper with the addresses of the morning's visits scribbled in her own hand.

Surely it didn't matter? Mr. Kellar was a client and friend.

Why, then, did she feel so anxious? As if whatever was to unfold was her fault...?

She wished Janey would come home. With Lenny.

CONSTANCE DID NOT hesitate. She went straight to the drawer labelled A-D. She noted files for both di Ripoli and Darrow—which briefly distracted her into searching out Montague and Kellar too. Intriguingly, she found them.

As a young man, Montague had indeed played the violin in amateur concerts in London and in India. And Kellar had apparently sung in private charity concerts in New York and Italy.

She left them for later, since it was apparently Charles Derrick she needed to know about.

Derrick's file was not fat, like Caterina's, so she took the whole folder and spread the contents across the narrow desk at the window.

The heading on his file was *Tenor, Clarinet, Violin, All string and wind instruments.* So, a man of multiple talents. The earliest mention of him was a note by hand, presumably by Martin himself, praising the marvelous new talent at the Reid Festival in Scotland in 1847.

A mere boy with a prodigious talent of voice—outstanding performance in Mendelsohn's Elijah. *The following night played clarinet in the Philharmonic...*

There was a program for a later Scottish Philharmonic concert in early 1849 that named him among the wind instrument players. And a newspaper cutting from York praising his solo performance later the same year. The most recent cutting was from 1850. Although she did come across one dated later that year, it had obviously been misplaced, for it was about a charity concert in York played by an Irish flautist.

She shoved everything back in the folder and stood somewhat impatiently. What was Derrick to do with Caterina or any of their suspects? Was he someone else in Caterina's life that they had never heard of before?

She tutted as the contents slipped through the folder and landed back on the desk. Beginning to pick them up, she saw that one of the cuttings—the piece about the York flautist—had turned itself over. On the other side was part of a news story about a fraudster who had swindled a wealthy lady out of a considerable amount of money before strangling her and fleeing. A hue and cry was out for one Charles Derrick, a talented young musician much lauded in Scotland and the north of England, the fraudster who was suspected of the murder.

Constance sat down again, staring at the cutting, which was clearly not in the wrong place after all, although Martin had obviously made the cutting for the flautist in the first place. He must have seen the reference to Derrick by accident.

A swindler and a murderer. Why would Caterina and Martin have been talking about him unless they knew him? Had he come to London? Why was that discovery so important that it had made her happy rather than frightened?

Because with the information, she could fight back. Win her freedom from either her lover or her husband…or the man constantly in the background of her life. Kellar.

A swindler. Why was the word nagging at her?

Montague in India, according to Solomon's friend Halliwell.

Abruptly, she set the file aside and pushed back her chair. She went to the index cards and carried all the boxes over to the desk. Then, still standing, she rifled through them until she came to Derrick's name.

The card directed her to several Scottish and northern English choirs and orchestras, to the cities of Glasgow, Edinburgh, Manchester, and York, to the years 1847 to 1850. And to the name of another musician.

Got you…

She found herself gazing blindly out of the window. She blinked, trying to force her brain to work. That was when the movement in the garden below caught her eye. In quick alarm, she leaned over the desk, pressing her face to the glass.

A man carrying a tall hat, dressed in a good black suit, striding to the kitchen door. She even heard it open below. Her heart dived dizzyingly, for it was Digby Montague.

Constance seized her bag and flew out of the room.

"Mr. Martin!" she cried. "You have an intruder! Where are you, sir?"

There was no answer, except some faint bump from the stairs—hopefully Martin climbing up to her. Could they barricade themselves in one of the front rooms while they yelled through a window for help? Trapped in the house, there was nowhere to run, and she could not hold off a man of Montague's strength for long.

She rushed along the passage to the stairs and suddenly lost what was left of her breath.

Martin lay on the stairs. She recognized his wild white hair and his baggy trousers, though his face was hidden by one of his own parlor cushions, which a second, younger man was holding firmly over his nose and mouth with both hands.

Martin's legs were twitching, his fingers scrabbling futilely at the cushion that was killing him.

The holder of the cushion glanced up at her with a gleam of hatred but absolutely no fear, let alone remorse. It was not Montague.

CHAPTER NINETEEN

THE HACKNEY THAT Solomon had commandeered from under the nose of an outraged city gentleman galloped into Theobalds Street. Solomon, all but hanging out of the door, saw at once that there were no other hackneys in the street. He hoped that was a good sign, for his own carriage stood like a badge outside number twenty-one.

Solomon flung himself into the street before the horses had even halted and hurled some coins in the direction of the jarvey.

"Is she in the house?" he called to his own coachman.

"Still there, sir."

"Did anyone else go in?"

"One out, one in, from what I saw, but I did walk the horses around…"

Solomon did not wait for more.

"If I shout, come at once," he commanded over his shoulder as he strode up the path and knocked furiously at the door. Hearing a faint bump and rustling inside, he even threw himself at it, shoulder first, though it didn't budge. He bolted around the path to the back of the house and took a run at the kitchen door.

It flew open and he catapulted inside so quickly that he barely had time to register the other presence before a fist hit him in the chest. With the force of his own charge, the blow knocked him to the ground, winded.

His vision swam sickeningly, while all he could think, desperately, was *Constance*.

He had come to save her and was failing.

Kellar's face came into blurry focus, and Solomon forced his limbs to move, kicking out and bringing the older man down on top of him. With a sudden gasp of air, Solomon rolled, pinning Kellar with his weight, and raised his arm, fist clenched.

Kellar bucked, blocking the punch on one arm and shoving hard with the other. Unbalanced, Solomon leapt to his feet. So did Kellar, with impressive agility for a man of his years. No wonder he had been able to climb up to Caterina's window…

Solomon lunged, crashing Kellar into the kitchen door, and again drew back his fist.

Then Constance screamed.

Solomon barely heard her words. It sounded like "Get off, get *off!*" But her voice acted like a switch on both the kitchen combatants. Solomon froze for the slightest instant, which handed the advantage to Kellar.

Kellar didn't take it.

He stared at Solomon, frowning, panting.

Solomon wrenched him aside by the coat and flung open the door. He heard Kellar pounding after him into the hall, but somewhere, he already realized that the diplomat was not the real threat. They had taken each other by surprise, that was all, and lashed out like stupid schoolboys in the playground.

Solomon skidded to a halt on the hall rug, almost crashing into Digby Montague, who stood at the foot of the staircase, clutching his hair in horror.

No wonder. George Martin was lying, twisted, on the stairs, while with one hand, Carl Darrow tried to hold a cushion over the old man's face. The violinist held his other arm up, to protect his head from Constance, who was belaboring him with blows from her bag.

And those blows could be vicious. Solomon had known her to carry heavy stones in that bag for defensive purposes.

"It was you, Charles Derrick!" she was yelling in rhythm with her blows. "You couldn't bear to be rejected, so you blackmailed her to keep her. You drove her to fight back, to find your own secret. And that was why she had to die."

Appalled, clearly physically unable to intervene, Montague only gaped at the scene before him—a man who could be angered and roused to passion, but definitely not a man of violence. Even when he'd tripped Darrow after the funeral, he hadn't waited to see the blood.

Solomon shoved him out of the way, leapt up two stairs, and, grasping Darrow by the arm, dragged him off Martin. Darrow made a last-second attempt to shove the cushion in Solomon's face, but Solomon ripped it from his grasp and threw it over the banister.

Still lying on the stairs, Martin made a horrible, rasping noise in his throat, but at least he was still breathing. Constance had managed to weaken Darrow's hold by forcing him to defend himself.

She sat down abruptly on the top step, her bag slipping from her grip.

"Solomon," she whispered.

For an instant their eyes met. There was time only to touch her cheek, to feel the comfort of her skin, her vitality. And then he swung away, because Darrow, whom he had left to Kellar, was trying to barge past the older man to the front door.

With impressive speed, Kellar shoved him face first into the wall, his arm wrenched too far up his back. Montague scrambled further into the corner.

"Not my bowing arm!" Darrow screamed. "Not my hands!"

"You can always sing," Constance said contemptuously, as Solomon jumped to the foot of the stairs to help hold Darrow. "It might cheer the other prisoners. Before you go to the scaffold."

"It was him?" Kellar said quickly. "Have you proof?"

"There's proof he brought the roses to her room," Solomon said, dragging the useful string he'd found in Darrow's coat from his own pocket and beginning to bind Darrow's wrists. The violinist made an ugly whining noise until Kellar elegantly popped a balled handkerchief into his mouth.

Solomon continued, "I found a red rose petal and a thorn caught in an old coat of his. The back of it is all roughened by thorns. I believe he tied them to his back with this very string, then climbed up to her room, hoping to bribe his way in if he had to. I suppose she was asleep?"

Solomon flung the last question at Darrow, who could only nod. The wild look was vanishing from his eyes.

"He has a past," Constance said from the stairs. She was helping poor Martin into a sitting position against the wall, placing the offending cushion behind his head. "He swindled and murdered an heiress in York. He strangled her. I suppose the smothering was a refinement—he had plenty of time to think about it while he fled from the authorities in York, and changed his name, and concentrated exclusively on the violin, which he hadn't been particularly known for previously. No one made the connection."

"Apart from me," Martin wheezed. "I saw a sketch of Darrow in a London newspaper, couldn't think why he was so familiar, since I'd never heard him play, until Caterina came to talk to me and I realized what—and whom—she was looking for."

"Why didn't you tell us this yesterday?" Solomon demanded.

"The honor of discretion," Constance said. She looked directly at Montague, who was standing perfectly still in the corner, dazed and troubled. "I'm sorry. I thought it was you."

Montague licked his lips. "It *was* me, in a way," he said hoarsely. "She should have been able to come to *me* with this. I was not the right husband for her."

"You were," Constance said. "Don't you see? She did all this, risked all this, for you."

Tears sprang into Montague's eyes.

Kellar said, "Mrs. Grey is right. I can see that now. She didn't come to me either, and I was her oldest friend in this country. I believe I was lashing out at you, Montague, as well as playing my own game. I'm sorry."

Solomon caught his gaze. "Maybe it's time you stopped playing games. If you expect trust, you have to show a little."

Kellar sighed. "I preferred the days when the old were the wise." He jerked his head at Darrow. "What do we do with him? Drop him in the Thames?"

"No," Constance said severely. "We summon a policeman."

"Several policemen," Solomon corrected her. "He's a slippery little brute."

"Pity," Constance said. "He plays like an angel."

"You should have heard him sing," Martin said sadly. "What a waste of so many lives. His own. Caterina's. The poor lady in York…"

"What on earth did you mean to do here?" Solomon asked, staring at Darrow. "Smother Constance after Mr. Martin was dead? And then me? That's a lot of smothered people. Supposing you had succeeded, don't you think the police might have caught on?"

Darrow made a brief noise, and Solomon gingerly removed the handkerchief from the man's mouth, using his thumb and one finger.

"There's more than one way to kill," Darrow said contemptuously. "An old man collapsed on his stairs. A young woman hurrying to his aid falls and breaks her neck. A grieving husband commits suicide." He glanced venomously at Montague. "*Two* grieving husbands. Who'd miss any of them? A third-rate musician with a house full of paper. A whore and her slave. A merchant with nothing to sell and no passion in his soul."

"But we are still alive," Constance said, standing up. "And loved. As was Caterina. Who will grieve for you, Mr. Derrick?"

Somehow, it was painful to see the smug derision drain from Darrow's face. He was a performer and had fooled so many for so long. Now it was as if the performance no longer worked. As if, finally, he saw that even the soul of his music was a pretense, and the rest was emptiness.

Suddenly cold, Solomon tugged the murderer toward the front door. He was anxious to be rid of him.

WHEN CONSTANCE ENTERED the Silver and Grey office, Hat almost fell on her neck, full of apologies for carelessness and neglect.

"I would've come to find you myself, only I didn't want to leave the office unattended, and I thought Mr. Kellar was your friend..."

"Wotcher, ma'am," Janey said cheerfully, ambling along the hall and looking rather pleased with herself. "She means he read some scrap of paper on her desk that said where you and himself was off to."

"Ah, that's why he showed up," Constance said. "I think he and Mr. Grey gave each other black eyes before they discovered they were indeed friends. It's a lesson, Hat, but no harm done. Mr. Kellar was, in fact, quite useful." Apart from the black eyes. "When did you get back, Janey?"

"Just now. Found no trace of you lovebirds."

She almost asked what Janey found to smile about in that, though a moment's reflection kept her tongue still. If Janey had found pleasure in Lenny's company—or their relationship had taken a step beyond friendship—then it was not for Constance to pry.

"No, neither did we," she said, walking into her office. "It was a lie. They had never planned to elope. In fact, Darrow killed her."

Janey followed her in, wide-eyed. "For love?"

"No," Constance said thoughtfully, "I don't think he'd have risked it for love. She threatened his music through what she knew of him. She could have put him in prison for murder. And, in fact," she added sadly, "she did, in the end. He'd killed before, you see, and to avoid the law, he had to start at the beginning again with a new name and a new city and a new favored instrument. I think she probably found out that he had never been to the Royal Academy as he claimed, but didn't care while her obsession was upon her. But when she needed the information to use against him, it was a starting point for her own inquiries."

Janey wrinkled her nose. "Too late."

"Yes. She underestimated him. So did I. I think I let his music blind me. How could a man who plays as he does commit such appalling acts of violence?"

"Pretense," Janey said unexpectedly. "We all play the parts we need to, don't we? Just his needs were selfish and ugly, and he got no line to stop him."

Constance regarded her with some respect.

"I ain't playing a part no more," Janey said, meeting her gaze. "Lenny knows the worst about me, and he still likes me. I can't replace his wife, of course, but he's asked me to step out with him on Saturday night."

Constance smiled with genuine pleasure. "I'm glad for you. And him. You're good for each other."

Janey grinned. "That's what I told him," she said cheekily, and spun away. "Get the tea on, will I? Hat's still too eaten with remorse to be able do anything. Except go and get the pies in, maybe. Hat? Shift your arse!"

Home, Constance thought contentedly, and leaned back in her chair with a sigh.

There would be more tears to mop, of course. Poor Edith would be devastated. And then there was Reid the pianist, and Mrs. Philpot, both of whom had seemed fond of Darrow. One way and another, one crime affected a lot of people.

SOLOMON RETURNED ABOUT an hour later. He walked straight into her office and took her into his arms, which was a lovely place to be.

"I think it was your parting shot that finished him," he said into her hair. "By the time we got to the police station, he was desperate to tell anyone who would listen exactly what he had done. It's a quicker road to fame than music, and I doubt he has long left to enjoy it. He has been charged with the murder of both Caterina and the woman in York. Kellar, Montague, and I all made discreet statements that avoided Caterina's...misjudgments."

"Darrow won't avoid them," Constance said, inhaling the scent of his skin, absorbing his sheer warmth. "He'll shout them to whoever will listen."

"He already has, but since he's admitted the crimes, there will be no public trial. The newspapers will be careful what they print, on account of libel and stepping on the toes of the rich and powerful." His arms tightened around her. "Montague said he had misjudged us."

"I misjudged him, too," Constance said ruefully.

"We both did, but not entirely. He's clearly not a violent man, let alone a killer, but he's not quite the clean potato either. He told me so while we were waiting at the police station. He burned a letter of Darrow's that he found crumpled at the bottom of a drawer—those were the ashes we found in the grate that first day. And in India, as a young man, he really did swindle some people, including a young widow who was in love with him, in order to pay for the transport of his tea, which he couldn't afford without an expensive loan. He used a false name in the fraud, but he was recognized and it all came out. He had to flee back to England. The British, of course, swept it largely under the carpet and pretended it hadn't happened. But rumor persisted and he could never go back there. Understandably, people were reluctant to do business with him. He runs his plantations from a distance now, which is never ideal, and this severely curtails his profits."

"I imagine Caterina was quite expensive, too."

"It's an expense he'd have back in a heartbeat, if he could," Solomon said.

Constance sighed. "I knew I didn't like this case."

"Well, we can begin a new one tomorrow."

Constance was silent for a moment, then she said into his neck, "We misjudged Kellar, too. Juliet was right. He might be dangerous, but not for purely selfish or trivial reasons, not just to obtain a promotion. He would never have hurt Caterina, would he?"

"He brought her here to avoid her being hurt. He says it got him into trouble with his superiors at the time. What does he mean by Juliet?"

"God knows," Constance said fervently. "The even more confusing question is what she means by him. I am keeping well out of it."

"We have invited both of them to the party," Solomon reminded her.

"But Juliet won't come," Constance said. Of that, she was certain.

⌒⁓⌒

CHAPTER TWENTY

THERE WAS LITTLE time on Friday for doubts and nerves. A demanding new case had kept Constance and Solomon busy all day, and although they returned home earlier than usual, a string of questions and trivial problems to be solved took up all their attention.

They barely had a chance to eat, rushing from room to room to quell crises. In fact, the servants had made the place shine, the extra lighting outside and in had been well placed, and apart from a few minor misunderstandings in the kitchen, all was going well. The footmen hired for the evening seemed to be well trained and appeared to Constance to understand what was expected of them.

Only when Constance and Solomon finally bolted upstairs to change, a bare half-hour before their guests were expected, did she find space to breathe, and remember what she had intended to do.

Anne Morris was already waiting for her in the bedchamber. Solomon went into his dressing room. Constance went to the dressing table and took the small leather box from her jewelry case.

"One moment, Anne," she said, and followed Solomon into his room.

He had already flung his coat and necktie onto the bed and was about to pull his shirt off. He paused, letting his hands fall to his sides. "Is something wrong?"

"No." She closed the door and walked up to him, taking his

hand. She placed the little box on his palm and curled his fingers around it. "I thought you might like this. It seems the right occasion to give it to you."

His eyebrows twitched in curiosity, but his distracted face had softened. He opened the box, and his breath caught at the sight of the lapis lazuli ring. He took it out reverently and slipped it onto his finger.

"How handsome," he murmured, moving his hand to catch the light. Then he bent nearer and kissed her lips. "Thank you. I love it. But I'm afraid I never thought of a first-party gift."

"It wasn't really for that. I just had the urge to give you something. I didn't really know why until after I had bought it. Forgive me, Solomon."

He took her in his arms, his brows pulling together. "For what?"

"The fuss I made over this party. I know you're doing it for me. In my selfish temper I forgot how much this costs you. You are not happy at such gatherings, and I was concerned only with how *I* would feel, and how *my* standing would affect yours. I forgot your feelings."

He smiled. "I am always happy with you, Constance."

She took his face between her hands. "And I with you. I love you, and there's nowhere I could be prouder than by your side."

She kissed him and his arms tightened, just as she slipped free. "Twenty minutes, Sol!"

CONSTANCE, WEARING A new ivory silk gown with a deep-red shawl and reticule, and the garnet necklace Solomon had given her as a wedding gift, strolled among her guests, smiling and chatting, making everyone feel welcome.

It was remarkably similar to welcoming men to her establishment, and slowly, she felt that boundary she had tried to draw between notorious courtesan and wife of a respectable man begin to dissolve. This "hostess" role was part of who she was, a talent she had improved on over the years. And there was no time for nerves or worries, although somewhere she was still stunned by the number of people who had accepted her invitation.

She had invited too many in the end, so that the house would not look too empty, and had imagined feeding all of London's poor with the leftovers from the mountain of food she had ordered. Instead, few had refused.

The neighbors had all come, although they might not the next time if they learned her past from other guests. Solomon's closest business and charitable associates were there too, from Sir Nicholas and Lady Swan, whom she had met before, to the Halliwells, whom she had not, and the men who now ran the various branches of his business for him. Griz and Dragan had come early, and were still here. So had Lord and Lady Trench, perhaps at Griz's request. Zenobia Paul had arrived, alone and curious as ever.

Edith was quietly playing her violin in the background. Those nearest her often paused to listen with some appreciation. Later in the evening, she would perform a complete piece by Vivaldi.

Constance gave her an approving smile as she passed, and then, catching sight of a new arrival, went to welcome him.

"Mrs. Grey," said Jason Madly, who had once figured as a suspect in the doorstep case but was a much older acquaintance. He bowed over her hand, his wicked eyes dancing. "You cannot imagine my joy at finally receiving an invitation from you."

"Oh, you must thank my husband for that," Constance said. "He likes you for some reason."

"Poor deluded fool," Madly said, sweeping his gaze around the room, nodding amiably as he encountered Solomon's gaze.

"A glass of wine?" Constance said as the footman hired for the evening approached. "Perhaps I should tell you Mrs. St. John and her daughter Mrs. Cordell are here."

"I already saw them," Madly said.

Constance smiled. "You already knew they were coming."

"We have made our peace, she and I." He leaned closer. "Thank you, Constance."

She smiled as he strolled away toward Solomon. Mrs. St. John, dressed in elegant black, watched him surreptitiously.

"Mrs. Grey, you dazzle as always."

She turned quickly to face another late arrival. Kellar, looking handsome and distinguished in his evening clothes. "So do you! Thank you for coming."

"How could I stay away? Is there any more news on Darrow?"

"He has pleaded guilty to both murders. Beyond that, we have heard nothing. I don't expect to, formally, although I can introduce you to a policeman if you wish. Inspector Harris has become something of a friend and ally."

"I would be delighted," Kellar said politely. "Have I missed your mother?"

Constance glanced at him quickly. "She won't come. She never makes public appearances." She paused, and he halted with her. For the first time since her first guest had arrived, her stomach churned, not with social nerves but with the difficulty of saying what she had to. "My mother lost her pride for many years. Now that she is reclaiming it..." She drew in a breath, "Don't take it from her again."

Kellar regarded her thoughtfully, his face, as usual, giving little away. "You blame me for that loss of pride. With some justification, it must be said."

"No," Constance said. "Juliet made her own decisions. I know that. And she will continue to do so. But she needs truth and peace. Not you chasing your lost youth or whatever it is you meant by searching for her."

Kellar took a sip of his wine. "I understand you," he said at last. "Who is the violinist? She is very good..."

JULIET WAS NOT used to this kind of fear. Like making the decision to dine with him, it had taken a great deal of courage to put on her glad rags and pin up her hair decently. This was worse, though, because it didn't just concern her. It concerned Constance, and she would die before she endangered her daughter's new life.

No wonder her knees grew increasingly wobbly as she approached Constance's house. Many carriages lined the road, and the Greys' house was a blaze of lights. Sweet violin music drifted out among the sounds of civilized chatter and laughter.

Juliet walked by the window, taking in the bright colors, the sparkle of gold and jewels in candlelight. She wasn't convinced her knees would actually carry her to the front door. She wasn't sure she wanted them to.

She knew *he* would be there.

People would know she was Mrs. Grey's mother. She had toned down the vulgarity of her looks, but even so…

Courage, Juliet. You've faced down a hell of a lot worse.

She turned her feet up the path, through the pretty front garden. A liveried footman opened the door. He must have been hired for the evening. She presented her card, and he took her cloak.

She felt naked without it. Naked and common and disgraceful.

Well, if Connie can do it, so can I.

She followed the music toward the big drawing room, where the Venetian portrait of Constance and Solomon hung over the fireplace. She had enjoyed her times in that room, at whatever time of the day.

But the first person she saw was not Constance. It was Sebastian Kellar, strolling past her line of vision, so distinguished and handsome that her heart as well as her knees failed her. She was physically incapable of turning into that room, even though Constance or Solomon, or both of them, would immediately come to greet her.

She walked straight past, along to the servants' hall and down the passage to the back door. She turned the key and went out.

And that was as far as her knees would carry her.

She sat on the little wrought-iron bench, careless of her gown, which would now never be seen by Connie's friends. Nor by Sebastian.

Five minutes to breathe, and then she would go home to her own comfortable little flat, her pride and joy. Her security. Her initial instinct had been right. She should never have come.

But there was no harm done. Connie would see by the card she had handed over that she had dropped in. No one else would ever know. All was well.

She gazed at the setting sun in its glorious pink-and-gold sky and just breathed. She thought of how far she had fallen, but mostly, she thought of how far she had come up again. Scarcely the life she had envisaged at twenty, but it was a good life, an interesting life.

And she had an amazing daughter. Maddening and clever, lovely and loyal and determined. She had long known that if she had done nothing else right in her life, there was Constance. Even when she had worried her the most, Juliet's pride in her had never wavered. Her love had never failed.

And that was enough.

She smiled at the sky. The bench creaked beside her.

She knew who it was, even before he spoke.

"Courage failed you, Juliet?" Sebastian asked softly. No accusation or recrimination.

And yet she knew he understood. "Yes. And good sense rushed at last to my rescue."

"Are you sending me away, Juliet? Again?"

Was she? She considered. "No. As I did thirty years ago, I am staying away. Though from *this*, not necessarily from you. Ours was never a public affair, Sebastian. Whatever it is between us now, it should remain private."

He had always possessed the kind of gaze that burned away the layers of protection. She felt it turned on her now and realized she was not afraid.

"Friendship, you mean?" he asked.

"Yes. If it survives."

"And more than friendship?"

She smiled and turned to meet his gaze. "Seriously, Seb?"

Although she was affectionately amused and inviting him to share the joke, he didn't laugh. His eyes were unexpectedly serious. And steady. She felt her own smile falter.

He lifted his hand to her cheek, startling her by the tenderness of the caress. No one had caressed Juliet for a very long time. Solomon kissed her cheek. Occasionally, Connie hugged her. But they were not *lovers*. She did not think she could bear Sebastian's touch. She did, though it deprived her of breath.

"Juliet," he murmured. "Our years are never wasted."

"What do you mean by that?" she demanded. *Too aggressive*—hiding the unsteadiness of her voice.

"I mean… Your son-in-law taught me a lesson."

Juliet blinked. "He did?"

"He told me to stop playing games. They have become so much my nature over the years that I play them without thought. As soon as I found you, I should have walked into your shop and made myself known. I didn't. I had to do it subtly, giving myself—and you—an easy way out. How can I be an honest man if I have forgotten honesty? A trustworthy man if I have forgotten trust?"

"You were never a bad man. And believe me, I've learned to spot them."

The hand at her cheek slid to her shoulder and gripped. "I know the broad gist of your thirty years, Juliet. I daresay you can guess mine. We need not be ashamed of the details, not with each other. Never despise yourself for surviving. I must live with what

I have done too. But can't we look forward?"

"I am contented. I have a life and an honest business that is working for me. You have an important position in the Foreign Office, where I do not fit."

There, she had said it, without sounding over-humble, too. *I do not fit.* Not *I would ruin you.* Though they meant the same thing.

"And so you offer me a private friendship? That might become something more?"

"In private. If you can ever see past this raddled old body."

"Stop it," he said fiercely. "I *saw* you as soon as you walked into your daughter's dining room. It has always been you, my Juliet."

Quite how it happened she didn't know, but both his arms were around her and his mouth was on hers in the first kiss of thirty years. A sob rose into her mouth and was swallowed in a wash of agonizing sweetness and regret.

"Now," he said unsteadily, "I will tell you *my* terms. No more hiding. I have had enough of that in my life, and I won't do it with you again. If you are my friend, we are friends in public. If I am your lover, we own up to it. If we marry, you are my wife, my hostess, of whom I am proud. Whom I have always loved."

Her jaw dropped. "*Wife?* Are you insane? *Hostess?*"

"You're a natural. You always were. Whom do you think your Constance learned it from? We need do nothing, of course, that makes you uncomfortable. I have enough money to retire tomorrow, if it's what we choose. All that is for future discussion. For tonight, may we just start the way I would like to go on? In honesty?"

He stood up, and for a bewildered moment, she thought he was going to storm off. But he held his hand down to her.

"Shall we return to the party?" he asked softly. "As old friends?"

She stared at him, her heart thundering. But her stomach was quiet, the knot untied and fading.

As though she were stepping off the edge of a cliff, she took his hand and rose.

EDITH HAD BEGUN her Vivaldi piece, and most of the company had stopped to listen, even those clutching a plate in one hand.

Constance, standing by the window beside Solomon, felt her heart swell with pride. To her admittedly untrained ear, Edith was playing beautifully, as well as she ever had. Constance crossed her fingers that there would be many more engagements to come from this evening.

For herself, the party was something of a revelation. It was an unusual mix of people, perhaps, but they all seemed to be curious about each other rather than hostile or condescending. More than that, Solomon's trusted managers, associates and friends, had all brought their wives and seemed disposed not only to tolerate her but to approve of her.

Almost as if they had decided long ago that she was good for Solomon.

I am, she thought. *I make him happy.*

Surreptitiously, hidden by her wide skirts, she slid her hand into his. "Thank you for making me do this."

He didn't speak, merely squeezed her fingers, and she felt one of those reasonlessly happy moments begin to bloom. A movement at the door caught her eye and she froze.

Her mother had just entered the room, on the arm of Sebastian Kellar. They paused just inside the doorway, and he handed her into the nearest vacant chair. He snagged two glasses of wine and gave one to Juliet. Contance could not take her eyes off her mother.

"She came," she blurted.

"Do you mind?"

"Mind?" she said brokenly, "Oh, Sol." Emotion blinded her

and she swung away to face the window rather than her guests.

Solomon held on to her hand. "What is it?" He stood very close, his voice urgent, intense. "This was always up to her. You wanted it to be so."

"But look at her," Constance whispered, tears trickling down her cheeks. "She…sparkles. Solomon, she's *happy*."

And, of course, he understood. How unbearably tragic, and yet how wonderful it was, that this was the first time she had ever seen her mother truly happy.

Solomon's arm wound around her waist, and she knew he was smiling as he rested his cheek against her hair. Life was full of joy and had to be embraced.

ABOUT THE AUTHOR

Mary Lancaster lives in Scotland with her husband, three mostly grown-up kids and a small, crazy dog.

Her first literary love was historical fiction, a genre which she relishes mixing up with romance and adventure in her own writing. Her most recent books are light, fun Regency romances written for Dragonblade Publishing: *The Imperial Season* series set at the Congress of Vienna; and the popular *Blackhaven Brides* series, which is set in a fashionable English spa town frequented by the great and the bad of Regency society.

Connect with Mary on-line – she loves to hear from readers:

Email Mary:
Mary@MaryLancaster.com

Website:
www.MaryLancaster.com

Newsletter sign-up:
http://eepurl.com/b4Xoif

Facebook:
facebook.com/mary.lancaster.1656

Facebook Author Page:
facebook.com/MaryLancasterNovelist

Twitter:
@MaryLancNovels

Amazon Author Page:
amazon.com/Mary-Lancaster/e/B00DJ5IACI

Bookbub:
bookbub.com/profile/mary-lancaster